*Drummer Boy*

A
RED DOOR
NOVEL

# DYAN LAYNE

ISBN: 978-1-7364765-3-6
ASIN: B0B17BMF11

Cover photography: Michelle Lancaster, @lanefotograf
Cover model: Dylan Hocking
Cover designer: Lori Jackson, Lori Jackson Design
Editing: Michelle Morgan, FictionEdit.com
Formatting: Stacey Blake, Champagne Book Design

This book contains subject matter which may be sensitive or triggering to some and is intended for mature audiences.

*Bo Robertson. The drummer. 34. Leo.*
Everybody loves him, yet no one's ever chosen him to love.
He wants to be someone's everything, and for that
someone to be his.

*Ava Liane Harris. The babysitter. 21. Aries.*
The beautiful girl who hides behind her glasses.
She knows better than to look for love, yet love finds her anyway.

*A six-week concert tour. An epic adventure.*
*A summer of possibilities.*
But nothing lasts forever, right? Everything comes to an end.
The memories, though. Those could last a lifetime.

# Playlist

Tool | *Chocolate Chip Trip*
Chase Atlantic | *Into It*
Two Feet | *Go Fuck Yourself*
Cigarettes After Sex | *Dreaming of You*
The Dear Hunter | *Deny It All*
Matt Maeson | *Put It On Me*
Leo Moracchioli | *You Are My Sunshine (metal cover)*
Memphis May Fire | *Bleed Me Dry*
Nirvana | *Heart-Shaped Box*
Lana Del Ray | *13 Beaches*
5 Seconds of Summer | *Complete Mess*
Tommee Profitt (feat. Nicole Serrano) | *One Last Breath*
Ghost | *Enter Sandman*
Guns N' Roses | *Sweet Child O' Mine*
Sub Urban | *Cradles*
Jeris Johnson, Ricky Desktop | *damn!*
Måneskin | *Let's Get It Started*
Van Halen | *Hot For Teacher*
The Rebelles | *The Clapping Song*
AC/DC | *Rock N Roll Train*
Stone Temple Pilots | *Interstate Love Song*
The Cult | *Lil' Devil*
Ghost | *Kiss The Go-Goat*
Deftones | *Cherry Waves*
Nothing But Thieves | *Itch*
The Wanted | *Gold Forever*
Foo Fighters | *My Hero*
Bush | *Flowers On A Grave*
Ghost | *Nocturnal Me*
††† (Crosses) | *Protection*

Hippie Sabotage | *Devil Eyes*
INXS | *Devil Inside*
Red Devil Vortex | *Alive*
Cigarettes After Sex | *Affection*
Drowning Pool | *Sinner*
Drowning Pool | *Feel Like I Do*
Rosenfeld | *Body*
Troye Sivan | *Angel Baby*
Machine Gun Kelly, Travis Barker | *A Girl Like You*
Godsmack | *Moon Baby*
Ghost | *Mary On A Cross*
Golden Earring | *Radar Love (Remastered)*
In This Moment | *Dirty Pretty*
Disturbed | *Hey You*
Taylor Hawkins & The Coattail Riders (feat. LeAnn Rimes) | *C
U In Hell*
Rihanna | *Love On The Brain*
Mark Ronson, Miley Cyrus | *Nothing Breaks Like a Heart*
Spiritbox | *Constance (acoustic)*
Alice In Chains | *Hollow*
†††️ (Crosses) | *Initiation*
The Plot In You | *Too Heavy*
Måneskin | *Beggin'*
The Fray | *Look After You*
5 Seconds of Summer | *Take My Hand*
Rosenfeld | *Till Death Do Us Part*
Cigarettes After Sex | *Sweet*
Ed Sheeran (feat. Taylor Swift) | *The Joker And The Queen*

# Author's Note

This book contains subject matter which may be sensitive or triggering to some readers and is intended for mature audiences.

While it isn't absolutely necessary to read the previous books in the series, as this is a standalone novel featuring a unique romance, it is _highly_ recommended. *Red Door* is a series of interconnected standalone novels. All of the main characters reappear and some storylines entwine throughout each book. For the best experience, the series should be read in order.

If you are following the series, **Drummer Boy** begins prior to, and overlaps with, events in **The Other Brother**.

*Oliver Taylor Hawkins*
*1972–2022*
*It wasn't near long enough, but we were lucky to have*
*you for the time that we did.*
*Rest now, Drummer Boy.*

*The beginning is always today.*
—Mary Shelley

# Drummer Boy

# Prologue

"What's your name?" Bo asked the girl.

She was young, pretty, with long blonde hair and soulful blue eyes. Just his type. Not that he had a particular type—did he? Bo had to admit he was attracted to her, though. There was something about her that set her apart from all the other fans waiting backstage to meet them.

"Shelley."

"Short for Michelle?"

"No. Just Shelley."

"Well, it's nice to meet you Shelley, not short for Michelle."

But she'd already moved down the line.

"I love you, Taylor!" the girl gushed, hugging his bandmate.

Too bad she didn't know the lead guitarist of Venery hated that shit. Bo liked it, though. A lot. He was a hugger. A toucher. A kisser. A lover.

*You put your money on the wrong horse, stupid girl.*

Yeah, there was something about her. Bo couldn't put his finger on it, but as he watched her fangirl all over Taylor, blood rushed to fill his cock. Deliciously fuckable. Soft and warm. Craving some pussy tonight, he licked his lips as if he could already taste her.

If he couldn't have her, then surely another groupie would be more than happy to accommodate him. Bo wanted to fuck *her*, though. Shelley, not short for Michelle.

One of the radio station people put a big plastic cup in his hand. Their logo, the band's logo, and the tour sponsor's branding for a new alcoholic beverage were plastered all over it. A beer and whiskey kind of guy, Bo took a tentative sip of the carbonated Kool-Aid. It wasn't half bad.

"Don't taste like anything's in here. I can get a buzz off this shit?" He downed half the contents in one swallow.

"Yeah, man." The radio station dude bobbed his head, a dopey grin on his face. He reminded Bo of Sean Penn in that old '80s movie his mom liked. Surfer dude. Spicoli. What was the name of it? "Fourteen percent alcohol by volume. Trust me, you'll be feelin' it."

"Well, all right." Bo drained his cup and the Spicoli look-alike put another one in his hand.

These meet and greets grew tedious. He figured he might as well get something out of it. Get drunk. Get laid. Get back on the motherfucking bus. Then tomorrow he'd get to do it all over again.

"Might as well enjoy it," he muttered to himself. Just a few more weeks and they'd be back home in Chicago.

"Enjoy what?" Taylor leaned into him, a plastic tour cup dangling in his hand.

Like the deviant he was, Bo grinned. "Debauchery."

"What's it to be tonight, mate?" His bandmate chuckled. "See a bird or bloke that you fancy?"

He homed in on the girl with long blonde hair. Shelley, not short for Michelle, stood with her nondescript friend at the portable bar drinking carbonated Kool-Aid. Fingers rubbing over his bare chest, his thumb grazed a nipple. Bo's dick twitched in his tight leather pants.

"Yeah." He pointed to her. "I want that one."

# One

A whisper-soft giggle woke him.

Yawning, Bo rubbed the sleep from his eyes and stretched. Light had only just begun to creep in through the stained-glass window above his bed, veiling the room in shadows. Distinctively feminine fingertips skated up the flesh inside his thigh to cup his balls. Gentle squeezes. A thumb tracing along the rugae.

How did she know he liked that?

His bottom lip caught between his teeth. Instinctively, he sought the hands that touched him, and grasped long, luxurious hair in his fingers. Bo opened his eyes.

Locks of caramel honey.

Nutmeg waves.

It was Chloe's soft giggles that had woken him. Linnea, who held him in her palm. Both of them here in his bed with him was a dream come true.

"Mmm…my girlies," he invitingly whispered.

"We're gonna make you feel so good, baby." Linnea smiled, taking his cock inside her mouth.

Chloe licked her lips. "So good."

*Fuck me.*

"Suck that cock." Linnea swallowed him down to the base. "Fuck, baby girl."

Holding Linnea to his dick, he pulled Chloe's mouth to his.

She tasted so fucking good. Sweet as cherry pie. Tongues tangled, they bit at each other's lips.

She pulled away with a giggle, joining her friend between his legs. Together, they languidly ran their tongues up and down his dick, pausing at the pierced head. Linnea flicked at the bead. Chloe licked at her nipple.

*Goddamn.*

Pulling on the strands of caramel in his hand, Bo dragged Linnea to his mouth. He could taste himself on her tongue. Did he die in his sleep? He must have, because he was in heaven.

Nestling her plush bottom against him, Linnea took his hand and pushed his fingers into her hot, wet pussy. Plunging his fingers in and out of her, she glanced back at him from over her shoulder. "I want your cock in me." She bit down on her lip. "Please?"

Did she think he'd say no? There was no way in hell Bo would pass up a chance to fuck her sweet cunt. Hooking her leg in his arm, he spread her wide open and pushed himself inside her. "So fucking tight."

Tugging on her nipples, Linnea rocked into him. "You feel so good, baby."

With his dick cushioned inside her warm, gooey deliciousness, she felt better than good. Better than the jar of marshmallow fluff he fucked when he was fifteen. Even better than Jimmy Tascadero and his girlfriend licking it off of him. Bo ended up fucking her while Jimmy fucked him. What was her name again? He couldn't remember. Good times.

Never mind that.

For however long this lasted, he was going to enjoy it.

Nuzzling her neck, Bo breathed sweet almond into his lungs. Chloe rubbed Linnea's clit as he fucked her. "Look at your big cock in her pretty, little pussy."

He looked, and it was a beautiful thing to see. Chloe fed him her fingers. Bo sucked on them, wetting them for her. "Kiss each other."

Rubbing circles on Linnea's clit with his saliva, Chloe kissed her. He reached across his blonde seraph to finger the auburn-haired goddess. "That's so fucking hot."

Chloe's pussy was molten fire.

"Hard like that for me," Linnea crooned.

He thrust harder.

She rubbed faster.

Linnea thrashed her head back and forth. "Oh, my God."

"I want to taste her when she comes."

Chloe took him inside her mouth, tasting Linnea on his dick. Then facing away from him, she straddled his thighs.

"Your turn." Slim fingers wrapped around his dick, pushing him inside Chloe.

And with her hands on his thighs for leverage, she rode him.

Lapping at Chloe's clit, Linnea gazed up into his eyes. She stopped then, and kissed him. "You're amazing, baby. We love you so much."

*I love you too, baby girl.*

He blinked his eyes open. Daylight poured through the stained-glass window, casting the room in a kaleidoscope of color. And just like he always did, Bo woke up alone.

"Fucking hell," he muttered, rubbing himself as he sat on the edge of the bed.

It seemed so real. Bo wished he could go back to sleep and dream some more, but he had to get into the shower. He was due to meet the boys in the studio at ten. And besides, he had a raging hard-on that needed taking care of.

Squeezing his dick in his hand, he stood under the hot water. It pummeled his skin, easing the tension from his muscles, clearing the fog from his brain. The dream stayed with him, though.

Bo poured a generous amount of organic body wash into his palm. Breathing the botanicals deep into his lungs, he lathered himself. And with visions of Linnea and Chloe, naked and nubile, floating in his head, he leaned his head back against the tiles, rubbing his balls and stroking himself until he came.

He roared with his release, its echo bouncing off the glass to the backbeat of pelting water. Thick ropes of cum dribbled down smooth, taut abs, diluting into rivulets beneath the spray. Pouring more soap onto a sponge, Bo proceeded to meticulously wash himself.

Admittedly, he was OCD when it came to his hygiene—the body is a temple and all that. Bo took great care of his. Working out religiously. Scrubbing. Exfoliating. Moisturizing and manscaping.

He slid soapy fingers down his smooth, hairless chest. The waist-length mane on his head more than made up for the lack of it on his body. On tour, his bandmates busted his ass for taking so long in the shower, so he usually went last. Bo had his bathroom rituals and he did not deviate from them. Ever.

They hadn't been on tour the past couple years. After a wearisome decade being on the road more than they were home, Venery took a much-needed break from touring—and a permanent break from their record label. Nobody owned them anymore. They had their own label, their own studio, and total control of the band they started back in high school.

Taylor was married with a kid, and had another baby—a little girl—on the way. She was due to arrive any day now. He didn't want to be away from his family for long, so they only left home for the occasional weekend gig here and there. But Venery was putting out a new album soon, the second one under their new label, and had committed themselves to a short, six-week tour this summer.

Bo was good with that. He liked being home, loved his house here at the end of Park Place, but lately he'd been craving the adrenaline rush of a fan-packed arena. Backstage. After-parties. Hanging with the boys on the bus.

Okay, maybe not the bus part so much. It's all good the first week and then shit gets real. The monotony of the road sets in. Six bunks, five guys, one bathroom in a tin can on wheels. Bo grimaced at the thought. But if they'd survived six-, hell, nine-month stretches at a time cramped together on that motherfucking bus, then six weeks should be a piece of motherfucking cake.

Maybe after the tour he should seriously consider getting himself a dog. He'd always wanted one. At least then he wouldn't wake up alone.

He pulled on his favorite pair of worn and torn jeans. They weren't the Amiri ones that cost a thousand bucks on sale either, though he had those too. These were an authentic pair of good ol' Levi's his mom purchased for him when he was sixteen, and seventeen years later Bo was still wearing them. It takes years of wear to break in denim just right, to where it feels as good as a second skin. No factory, or fancy-ass designer, could ever duplicate that.

It looked blustery outside his window. The calendar told him it was the first day of March, but the vernal equinox that marked the official start of spring was several weeks away. Fucking winter could drag on forever here. He shrugged on a sweater over his undershirt and went out the door.

"Wait up, man," Sloan called out from his porch across the street.

Dude looked like he'd either just rolled out of bed or never made it there. Knowing Sloan, it was likely the latter. Guilt he shouldn't be carrying, but did anyway, was fucking with his head. He was struggling and Bo wasn't sure how to help him.

"You look like shit."

"We can't all be pretty like you." He sniggered under his breath. "Stud muffin."

"Aww, I think you're pretty."

Girls panted after him, more so than the rest of them, wherever they went. Not that Sloan seemed to notice or care. He'd begrudgingly take a photo with a fan, or sign an autograph now and then—was more likely to if it was a twenty-year-old's breast—but for the most part he put on his untouchable persona and ignored them. To put it bluntly, he was a total dick.

"You just said I look like shit."

"Well, you might want to invest in a good concealer for those dark circles…" Bo side-eyed him. "…or give up the all-night gaming. Take a nap, man."

"I gotta do somethin' when I can't sleep."

"Try warm milk," he advised, slinging his arm around Sloan.

"That's fucking gross."

"Mm, now there's a thought." He smirked. "Hard fucking always does it for me, brother."

With a shake of his head, Sloan snickered. "Club tonight?"

Bo was always up for a little debauchery. His smirk widened to a grin. "Hells, yeah."

The four Byrne cousins were already in the lounge when they walked in, poring over papers spread out on a table between them. Sounds of guitars being tuned drifted up the stairs. Kyan, who was seated next to Jesse, glanced up. "Hey, Bo. Sloan."

"Morning." He made his way to the coffee machine and popped in a pod to brew. "Me and Sloan are going out tonight," Bo announced, shifting his gaze to Dillon. "You?"

He knew better than to ask the other three. With the exception of special events, they rarely went to the Red Door these days. Out of the four, Dillon was the only single dude left. His younger brother, Kyan, was married to the blonde seraph of his nocturnal fantasies, Jesse to his very pregnant auburn-haired goddess, and Brendan, the lucky bastard, to sweet, young, beautiful Katie.

"Club?"

They rarely ventured anywhere else. Being a private, members-only establishment, the Red Door was their only safe haven. No paparazzi. No underage fangirls looking for a meal ticket or a baby daddy. But there was always plenty of liquor, pussy, and cock to be had there when they wanted to indulge in it.

"Yeah."

Dillon winked. "I'm in."

"Well, all right." Bo grinned. "Bring Kodiak."

"Oh, he'll be there."

Jesse and Brendan exchanged a glance. He sipped on his

coffee, then cleared his throat. "Fair warning. Your manager's downstairs."

"CJ's here?"

Sloan rolled his eyes. "What the fuck does he want?"

"You misbehaving again, drummer boy?" Kyan chuckled.

*Sadly not. Does dreaming of it count? Nah.*

"Every chance I get, Ky." Bo winked and grabbed his coffee. "C'mon, Sloan."

They weren't laying tracks today or anything, just working on shit, so Bo found it odd their manager was here. Taylor, Kit, and Matt looked up from their guitars the second they entered the studio. CJ sat in the corner, briefcase on his lap, tapping away on his phone.

Then he glanced up.

And the boys put their guitars down.

Everyone looked at him.

*Uh-oh. What'd I do?*

"Hiya, Bo." CJ tipped his chin. "Sloan."

"Hey, man." He shrugged out of his sweater. "What brings you here?"

"Sit."

Bo pulled up a chair and sat.

"Remember Shelley Tompkins?"

*Shelley, not short for Michelle.*

Of course, he remembered her. And she made sure he'd never forget. Shelley caught his eye at a tour gig in Florida a few years back. Her sights were set on Taylor, though. Somehow, the three of them ended up on the bus together and nine months later she filed a paternity suit against Taylor. As it turned out, DNA tests proved the baby wasn't his.

He swallowed. "Yeah."

CJ handed him a thick manilla envelope.

*Fuck.*

"She's claiming you're the father of her daughter since Taylor isn't." He nodded toward the envelope in his hand. "That's not a lawsuit. Not yet anyway. It's a plea on her behalf from her attorney. Photos of the baby—she just turned two. Shelley is under hospice care. Terminal cancer. They don't expect her to live out the month. She wants you to take Emery and raise her."

"Her name's Emery?"

"Yeah." CJ clasped Bo's shoulder. "You need to do a DNA test."

Bo pulled the photos from the envelope.

He would take the test, but he didn't need one to confirm it.

Just looking at her, he already knew.

She was his.

# Two

*mery.*
Bo silently stared at the photo in his hand. The name fit her. He didn't know the meaning of it, or why Shelley had chosen it, but she looked like an Emery. Sitting on the beach, playing in the sand, blonde hair pulled up out of her face. Pudgy cheeks, and fingers, and toes. Long eyelashes. She looked sad, and he wondered if she was.

"You all right, mate?"

He wasn't sure how to answer that. "It's just…a lot, you know?"

They sat in Taylor's family room. After Bo called his attorney, he'd taken him to the lab to get swabbed. Sloan came along for the ride. Now they were waiting on test results—and for Rossi's to deliver their dinner.

Chasing a toddler around, and Braxton-Hicks contractions on and off all day, had worn Chloe out. Jesse rubbed her feet in his lap. "One step at a time, man."

"Yeah, Bo." Chloe angled her head toward him. "You have to know for sure if she's really yours first."

He lifted his brow. She'd seen the photos.

"Okay, I can see the resemblance…" Chloe pursed her lips to the side. "…but she pulled this once already. I don't trust her."

Jesse squeezed her foot. "She's dying, babe."

"Is she really?" Chloe pulled her feet from her husband's lap and set them on the floor. "How do we know this isn't a ruse?"

"For what purpose, love?" Draping his arm across her shoulders, Taylor combed his fingers through his wife's hair.

Sloan rolled his eyes.

Looking at him, Chloe bit her lip. "I just don't want to see you get hurt, you know?"

"I know, Red." Bo reached over and took her hand. Gently squeezing it in his, he sighed. "But I was with her…so…yeah."

"How long until you know?" Jesse asked.

"I should have the results by Thursday."

"And then what?" Sitting back against the sofa, Chloe let him go.

"Then I get my daughter." He shrugged. God, the words sounded strange coming out of his mouth. "I have a flight booked for Friday."

"*If* she's yours," Sloan added.

Worrying his lip, Bo nodded. "Yeah."

"I can't believe you didn't wrap it, man." Sloan snickered with a shake of his head. He really could be a dick sometimes.

"Dude, don't I always?"

"Yeah, you do. So, you wanna explain to me how your swimmers made it through latex?"

Bo rubbed circles on his temples. "I can't."

*And does it really fucking matter?*

"Something ain't right here." Sloan sat back, fingers laced behind his head. "I'm with Chloe on this one. I don't trust that girl."

Chloe smirked.

"We were both on the piss that night, mate."

*Fucking carbonated Kool-Aid.*

"It's quite possible you forg—"

"I didn't," he insisted, giving Taylor his '*shut the hell up*' face. Bo wasn't about to discuss the minutiae of their night of drunken debauchery in front of Chloe. "I remember."

He remembered everything about that night. Okay, maybe not everything, but most of it. Shelley put his condom on with her mouth, for fuck's sake, and there was no way he could ever forget that.

Bo forgot about *her*, though, for the most part, until she slapped Taylor with the paternity suit that incited baby-mama drama. He, Jesse, and Chloe had just gotten married and were expecting a baby of their own at the time. Salena leaked it to the press and they went through hell—Chloe most of all.

*Why did Shelley wait two years?*

The question took root in his brain. Once it was determined that Taylor wasn't Emery's father, why didn't Shelley pursue him? They both had sex with her that night, so he'd be the next logical candidate, right? But she never did. Bo assumed then, it was because she knew the baby wasn't his, and never gave it another thought. Until now.

The more Bo dwelled on it, the angrier he got.

And didn't he have every right to be?

Dying or not, she had kept his child from him.

But Bo didn't do angry. With a peaceful, fun-loving nature and an easygoing disposition, he was uncomfortable with the burgeoning emotion. He needed to take it and turn it into something else. Something good. Besides, he had to keep his focus on what really mattered here. And that was Emery.

And the music.

Bo pushed himself in the studio, laying down his tracks while he waited for the results of the test. Just in case. They had an album to finish. He didn't want to hold them up. Drums are the heartbeat of a song, its very foundation. They're recorded and edited first, because if he's off, everyone is off, and the song falls apart. The guys come in with their guitars next. Sloan puts down his vocals last.

The engineer flipped the phase switch on a couple mics. "Can I get you to run through that one more time?"

"Yeah, sure."

Brendan stood with Taylor in the booth when he finished. Picking up his discarded T-shirt, Bo wiped the sweat from his chest and went over there. He addressed the recording engineer, "We good?"

"I think so," he said, popping his headphones back on. "Just let me check low end."

Shifting his gaze to Venery's lead guitarist, Bo smirked. "Kit's up."

"Well done, mate."

"Phil's been trying to call you," Brendan informed him.

He was the attorney they kept on retainer. Big downtown firm. Handled anything and everything the Byrne cousins or Venery needed him to.

"The results are in?"

"Didn't say..." Brendan subtly angled his head. "...but that would be my guess."

Bo laid the soft, pink Blabla doll on top of neatly folded clothes. He'd purchased the quirky designer toy on impulse from a shop on First Avenue, where he'd gone walking after he spoke to Phil. A couple feet in length, with arms nearly as long, it would be perfect for Emery to cuddle with on the plane ride home. Or if she was ever afraid of the dark or missed her mama.

"Knit by hand with the softest organic alpaca fleece," the shop attendant convinced him. He didn't know what to buy for a two-year-old girl. Hell, he didn't know anything about them, but he was going to have to figure it out real quick now that he had one.

He heard the front door creak open from his bedroom up on the third floor. Footsteps padded up the stairs. "Bo?"

"In here, Linn."

She poked her head inside his room and offered him a smile. "Hey, Daddy."

"Hey, baby girl." He winked at her with a grin.

"When's your flight?"

"I've got a car coming to take me to Midway at noon." Bo hooked his arm around her shoulders. "Where's my kiss?"

Turning her head, Linnea kissed him on the cheek. "I can't wait to meet her."

"Me too."

She eyed the pink alpaca fleece doll in his bag. "Got everything you need, I see."

"Hardly." With a shake of his head, Bo snickered. "I have no idea what Emery needs."

"You." Sitting on his bed, Linnea glanced up at him. "You're going to be an amazing dad."

"I don't know what I'm doing." He sat down beside her, holding her hand in his lap.

"No one really does. It's kind of a figure-it-out-as-you-go thing, I imagine." She squeezed his hand. "You have the hugest heart, Bo Robertson. You know how to love people, and that's all she needs."

"You make it sound so simple."

"It is so simple." Smiling, Linnea nudged his shoulder with hers. "When do you think you'll be back?"

"Not sure yet. In a few days, I guess. I'll have a better idea once I'm there."

"Well, we'll have everything ready when you get here."

"Thanks for doing her room for me."

"That's what aunties are for." She patted the back of his hand and stood. "You can always count on us to help you with the girly stuff—with anything at all."

The moment Bo confirmed he was going to Florida to bring Emery home, and that was only yesterday, his girlies sprang into action. He had an empty room down the hall and less than twenty-four hours to fill it with even the basic things his daughter would need, not that he had the slightest notion what those were.

Linnea, Chloe, and Katie knew, though. Monica and Danielle weighed in too. They thought of things Bo would have never even thought to think of. Baby gates and child-proofing the house. A crib or a toddler bed? Car seats, strollers, potty-training, and clothes.

Chloe and Danielle agreed that since Emery just turned two, it was unlikely she knew how to use the potty quite yet.

"I have to teach her how to go to the bathroom?"

"Kids don't train themselves, babe." Chloe giggled. "You're lucky girls are easier. We just sit. No aiming required."

Danielle slowly nodded. Her and Monica's son, Elliott, celebrated his second birthday this past November. "Boys are messy creatures."

*I am not messy, thank you very much.*

Diapers and a kiddie step stool, so Emery could reach the grownup toilet and the sink, were added to the ever-growing shopping list.

Along with warm clothes.

Florida and Chicago are a world apart when it comes to climate. She'd known nothing but year-round summer. He'd be carrying his daughter off an airplane to temperatures just above freezing. Maybe even snow. Because in March who the fuck knew? Surely, winter coats and woolies were not wardrobe staples in the Sunshine State, but did he think of that? No, he did not. Fortunately, his girlies thought of it. A weather-appropriate going-home outfit was already packed for Emery in his suitcase.

Not that he was a total dolt, Bo just never had to think of these things before. Having a kid is a huge learning curve that most people have months to prepare for. He would learn.

And his daughter would thrive.

Bo was all in. He was grateful to have been given this precious gift. It didn't come as he'd imagined one day it would, and it wouldn't be easy, but nevertheless, he was thankful. For his baby girl. For his family of friends who loved and supported him. With them, he couldn't fail.

Bo caressed the pink alpaca fleece doll he'd thought to get her and closed the lid.

He *was* going to be the most amazing dad.

For Emery.

She deserved nothing less.

# Three

Five o'clock in the evening, and according to the flight attendant's announcement it was a balmy eighty-four degrees.

"…light winds out of the west at six miles per hour with a ten percent chance of rain. We hope you've enjoyed your flight. Welcome to Orlando."

Bo glanced down at his booted feet. More than forty degrees warmer than when he left Chicago, he was definitely overdressed. He'd be ditching the leather jacket as soon as he could stand up and shrug his way out of it. And the boots. He was pretty sure he packed a pair of flip-flops in his carry-on.

The humidity hit him in the face as soon as he neared the front of the plane. Thick, tropical air leaked inside through the gap between the aircraft door and the jetway to the terminal. Sweating already, Bo pulled his hair back and tied it. He was grateful that at least he didn't have to layer up with clothes here.

Bo wound his way through the throng of Mickey Mouse ears-wearing tourists to baggage claim, then over to the car rental counter. He was trying to remember the last time he'd actually driven one. In the city, having a car was more of a hindrance than a necessity—traffic, parking, and all that shit. He sat in the back of limos, walked, and sometimes, he even took the el.

Imagining the hassle of schlepping a two-year-old, a stroller, and assorted paraphernalia onto a train to go downtown, Bo internally cringed. Nope. Not happening. He added buying a kid-practical car to his to-do list.

"How far is Sanford from here?"

"Not too far. About thirty miles or so northeast." The car rental attendant handed him the keys to a BMW X5. "Trust me, you're going to want to stay off of I-4 and take 417 instead. With the traffic it'll take you an hour to get there if you don't."

"Thanks."

As it turned out, driving a car was a lot like riding a bike. He hadn't forgotten how. And having taken the advice of the car rental dude, Bo made it to the hotel in forty minutes.

After a quick shower, and wearing way less clothing, he glanced at the time on his phone. Just after seven. Was it too late to go over there now? Bo was anxious to see his daughter, but he didn't know her schedule, what her bedtime was, and Shelley was ill. He didn't want to disturb her either.

But now that he was here, Bo didn't want to wait. Shelley was aware, through her lawyer, that he was arriving this evening. She was probably expecting him, and might even worry he was bailing if he didn't show up tonight, right?

Decision made.

He was going to go meet his daughter.

Back in the BMW, he plugged the address into the GPS. His phone pinged with an incoming text.

**Linnea:** Just checking if you got there ok

**Bo:** Yeah, sorry I forgot to text you. Going to see her now

**Linnea:** Send us lots of pictures!!!

**Bo:** I will :-)

**Linnea:** And Jess wanted me to let you know they're at the hospital—Chloe's in labor!!!

**Bo:** Happy birthday, Ireland!!!

**Linnea:** Love you xoxo

**Bo:** Love you too xoxo

He did love her—a lot. Chloe and Katie too.

Sitting on the southern shore of Lake Monroe, Sanford was a cute, historic little town. Older architecture. Live oaks, draped in Spanish moss, shaded tree-lined streets. A brochure in the hotel lobby said there was a zoo and botanical garden nearby. It seemed like a nice enough place to raise a kid.

Following the directions on the navigation system, Bo turned onto a street of older homes. Rundown and in disrepair, they lacked the charm of the downtown area. It reminded him of their neighborhood in the city, before gentrification breathed new life to the old buildings. A renovator's dream, Kyan and the guys would lose their fucking minds here. Maybe he should tell them about it.

With the GPS announcing he'd arrived, Bo stopped in front of a white, two-story frame house. Or was it beige? It was starting to get dark, and with the timeworn paint, it was hard to tell. Four green-painted concrete steps led up to two mismatched front doors, also green, and a covered front porch, the wood planks buckling and warped.

*Uhh, which one?*

No name written on the doorbell—hell, there was no doorbell. Nothing to indicate if he should knock on the right or go to the left. With a fifty-fifty chance, Bo raised his right hand, rapping on the door in front of him.

An older woman answered it. She was robust, with plump apple cheeks, and hair more white than silver, twisted into a pencil bun. Wiping tiny beads of sweat from her brow with the back of her hand, she gave Bo a cursory once-over. "You're not here to fix the air conditioner, are you?"

Glancing down at his feet, Bo rocked on his heels with a subtle shake of his head and softly chuckled. Returning his gaze to the woman, he answered, "No, sorry. I'm here to see Shelley, but I think maybe I'm at the wrong—"

"You're not." Stepping back, she opened the door all the way and waved him inside. "I'm guessing you're Mr. Robertson."

"Yes, ma'am." He followed her inside. "But you can call me Bo."

The front door opened right into the living room of the narrow shotgun-style dwelling. Bo could see the kitchen, and another room behind that from where he stood. The furnishings and decor were outdated. An aged, white leather sofa. Mauves and teals. A throwback to the early 90s, it reminded him of his childhood.

"I'm Connie." The woman patted him on the shoulder. "Shelley's next door. I help her out with Em when she's not feeling up to it, which is pretty much all the time these days." Shaking her head, she clucked her tongue. "Such a shame."

*Em?*

His daughter. Is that what they called her? *Em. Emmy. Emery.* Bo tried out the variations of her name in his head. A name he didn't give her. He'd give her his last name, though.

"Yeah…um…" This was awkward. "…I'll just go next door then. I couldn't tell which door was…"

"Em's here." She took Bo by the crook of his arm and led him over to the old leather sofa. "Have a seat." Connie sat down in a chair across from him. "She's upstairs. Fell asleep right after supper, but I'll bring her down. I'm sure you're anxious to see her. Shelley thought it might be better this way."

"What?"

"For you to meet your daughter without her." Connie lowered her gaze to her hands folded in her lap, then with a bob of her head she raised it back to him. "This isn't going to be easy for Shelley, you know?"

He supposed not, but to be honest, up until now Bo hadn't given much thought to her feelings. Though he was sorry she was so ill, he was angry with her—more than angry—for everything she'd done. Did that make him a shitty person? He'd missed out on the first two years of their daughter's life, but Shelley was the one dying. She'd miss out on all the rest.

*It's a shit situation all the way around.*

"How is Shelley?" he sheepishly asked. "I should go see her."

"She has good days and bad." Connie clucked her tongue again. "But the good ones are few and far between now. I can call over there and see if she's up to having visitors after you see Em." She stood from the chair. "Let me go up and get her."

Bo watched the white-haired woman trudge up the creaky wood stairs. He blew out a nervous breath, taking a closer look at his surroundings. A wicker basket filled with toys sat on the floor in the corner with one of those kiddie xylophones laying on top. He plucked it out of the basket and set it on his lap, absently striking a tune on the keys.

*You are my sunshine…*

She used both fists to rub the sleep from her eyes. Blonde hair in two little pigtails on top of her head. Pink polka-dot pajamas. Connie carried Emery down the stairs.

All the air was knocked out of his lungs. The muscle inside his chest squeezed. Putting the xylophone down on the coffee table, Bo stood.

Emery dropped her little fists and looked at him. He stared back at a face that resembled his own. Bo didn't need a DNA test. There was no denying this darling baby girl was his.

"Look, Em. Daddy's here," Connie crooned to her. "Can you say hi to Daddy?"

"Hi, Daddy."

Her tiny voice was the sweetest sound he'd ever heard.

She reached for him. Opening her arms, Emery wrapped them tightly around his neck, latching herself onto him, and Bo held his daughter for the very first time. A watershed moment. Life, as he'd known it, forever altered.

"Hi, baby."

Holding her in his arms, Bo rubbed the baby's back and kissed the top of her head. He closed his eyes, inhaling sunshine and cotton candy. Sweet baby smells.

*His* baby.

And instantly, he fell in love.

Bo pulled his head back to see her face. He gazed into eyes of the deepest blue, sparkling like a midnight sky, framed with long lashes. Delicately arched brows. Her little pink Cupid's bow lips lifted into the sweetest smile. She was beautiful.

"Hey, Emery." Sitting on the sofa with her, Bo smiled back. "How's my darling?"

She looked up at him from his lap, her smile widening, and touched his cheek.

"Such an affectionate child." Connie took her seat in the chair across from the sofa.

Bo chuckled. "She gets that from me."

"Em's a good baby." The woman smiled with a nod. "She's really a joy to care for. I'm going to miss her."

*Shit.*

See? Bo wasn't sure how to respond to that. While he appreciated the woman's sentiment, and understood her attachment to his child, he didn't know how to deal with the goodbye part. Chrissakes, he was ripping his daughter away from everyone and everything she'd known in her short life.

"I know." He offered up a sympathetic smile. "We'll keep in touch if you'd like. I can send pictures and have Emmy FaceTime you."

Connie brought her hands to her cheeks. "You'd do that?"

"Absolutely."

"Oh, thank you. I'd love that." She dabbed at her eye. "When do you plan on leavin'?"

"Not sure." Emery yawned in his lap, playing with the ends of his hair. "As soon as the legal stuff is all wrapped up. In a few days, I guess." He handed Connie his phone. "Can you take a few pictures for me? I promised to send some back home."

"Of course." She did and handed the phone back to him. "You have family? A wife? Other kids? Shelley only told me you're the drummer in some famous rock band."

"Never been married, so no. No girlfriend either." He sheepishly chuckled. "Emmy's it—just me and her. I have family, though.

An older sister, Allie—she's married. Lives in California. My parents do too."

"They must be so excited to get a granddaughter."

"Yeah." Bo gazed down at Emery. Snuggled against his chest, she'd fallen back to sleep. "My sister has two boys."

"California is a long way from Chicago," she remarked. "Too bad Em won't be close to her cousins. Family is so important."

"Family isn't always blood, you know?" Bo kissed his sleeping daughter's brow. "Some family we choose for ourselves, and I have a big one. The best one." He nodded. "Emmy has plenty of cousins waiting for her in Chicago—aunts and uncles too."

"I'm so glad." Her smile was genuine and warm. "Do you want me to call over to Shelley's?"

"Yeah, that'd be great."

Not that he knew what to say to her. His only thought was for Emery, she was his sole focus. Bo just wanted to have everything wrapped up, get the goodbyes over with, and take his daughter home.

He didn't pay attention to what Connie was saying on the phone. Bo touched the silky hair on Emery's head, rubbing it between his fingers. His heart squeezed just looking at her. In awe, that from a night of drunken debauchery, came such a precious, beautiful child.

"I'm sorry." Connie set her phone down on the table beside her. "Shelley doesn't want to see you."

"That's okay," he responded, rising from the sofa with his daughter in his arms. "Emmy should go back to her bed. I can see Shelley tomorrow."

"No, you can't." Connie worried her lip. "She doesn't want to see you at all."

*The fuck?*

"Say what?"

Seeming as dumbfounded as Bo was, Connie glanced up at him from the chair she sat in, shaking her head. "Let's take Em upstairs and then we'll talk."

What the fuck had he ever done to that girl for her to treat him this way? They had a child together, for chrissakes. There were things they had to talk about. Things he had to know. Shelley had to see him.

Tucking Emery into the portable crib in Connie's spare bedroom, Bo kissed her petal-soft cheek. A light breeze blew in through the open window, ruffling the curtains. He covered her with a blanket.

"Come on," the old woman whispered, taking him by the hand.

Bo followed her to the tiny living room and sat back down on the sofa. He stared at the toy xylophone he'd left on the coffee table, then flicked his eyes to hers. "Does Shelley really think I'm going to leave here and take Emery without a word?"

Maybe he came off as brusque, his tone harsh. Connie just sat there. Bo asked again, "Does she?"

"I don't know." Connie stared at her hands in her lap and swallowed. "Shelley is angry and bitter. I think she's having a difficult time. She doesn't want to say her goodbyes and she doesn't want to face you." Connie lifted her gaze to meet his. "She's ashamed."

"Ashamed?"

She leaned back in her chair and sighed. "Shelley came here and rented the duplex next door from me when she was, oh, three or four months along with Em. Dropped out of college. No family. Her friends abandoned her. She confided in me a lot." Connie smiled and let out a chuckle. "I guess you could say I'm her adopted grandma."

Bo moistened his dry lips and nodded.

"Anyway, she told me all about the concert and meeting you and your friend…Taylor Kerrigan, right?"

"She filed a paternity suit against him."

"I know she did," Connie affirmed, her fingers fidgeting in her lap.

"Why didn't she reach out to me then?" Bo closed his eyes to the anger welling inside him. "I've missed out on two years of my baby's life that I can never get back."

"I can't answer that." She exhaled. "Only Shelley can."

"Why'd she wait until now?"

Connie pursed her lips. "She's dying now. The hospice social worker threatened to involve child services…if Shelley didn't make permanent arrangements for Emery's welfare following her death. They would have put her into foster care, you see, and that's the last thing she wanted for her baby girl." She shook her head with a sigh. "So she asked her attorney to get in touch with you."

"I see."

"Em belongs with you," Connie decreed with a tip of her chin. "You're her family, and…"

"I know." Bo finished her sentence. "Family is important."

But that meant Shelley was family too, right? And regardless, whether she wanted to or not, she was going to talk to him.

"I'll be back for Emmy in the morning." Bo stood up from the sofa. "You can let Shelley know I'm coming, and she *will* see me, even if I have to break the goddamn door down."

# Four

S till angry when he flopped into bed, Bo couldn't sleep. He tossed and turned, punching his pillow to no avail. A shot of whiskey might've done the trick, if only there'd been a damn minibar in his hotel room, but the amenity was lacking. Or a tight, hot hole to sink his dick into would work, but there were none of those to be had here either. So he lay there, hands clasped behind his head, just staring at the popcorn ceiling.

His phone buzzed beside him on the mattress. He answered it. "Hey, baby girl."

Linnea. His untouchable angel. His seraph. Without knowing just how much his life was already entwined with hers, and how enmeshed it would become, Bo was drawn to her from the moment they met. A soul connection is the only way he knew how to put it. His attraction to her wasn't purely sexual, though admittedly, he wouldn't turn down the opportunity to fuck her. Not that Kyan would ever want to share—not with him anyway. Came close once. Kind of.

Three years later, and he could still taste her.

Bo loved her unconditionally, in much the same way he loved her brother, Kodiak. The three of them shared a special bond, that same spiritual connection, and he cherished it. He would do anything for either of them, as they would for him.

"I've been not-so-patiently waiting for pictures here," Linnea teasingly chastised him. "Did you see her?"

"Yeah, I did. Hold on. I'll send them now." Just seeing the photos brought a smile to his face. "Sorry, I meant to earlier, but I got caught up in everything and…"

"Oh, Bo." Linnea gasped on the other end of the line. "She's beautiful and she looks just like you."

He grinned. "I know."

"Ky? Look, honey. Bo and Emery," she said to her husband, who was no doubt right beside her.

"Hey there, Pops." Kyan got on the phone. "Between you and Chloe, Linn's been going out of her mind over here. Congratulations, brother."

"Thanks, man." Bo chuckled. "Chloe didn't have that baby yet?"

"Should be soon, I guess. I'll give you back to Linn. Hurry home, man. We all miss you."

Linn took the phone back from her husband. "I'll text you as soon as Ireland gets here, okay?"

"Yeah, please do." He couldn't mask the weariness in his voice.

"You okay, Bo?"

"I'm fine, baby girl." He let out a breath. "It's just some heavy shit, you know?"

"I know and I'm sorry about that part." Linnea blew him a kiss through the phone. "I wish I could make it better."

"You just did. Night, baby girl."

"Night, drummer boy."

He needed to get some sleep. Bo sat up against the headboard. Since he didn't have a shot of whiskey or someone to fuck, his hand would have to do. An orgasm cured everything, even a self-indulgent one. Gripping the long, flaccid length in his fingers, he gave it a few rough tugs and watched it fill. His head fell back, eyelids closed, finding his groove.

*Fuck you, Shelley, not short for Michelle.*

The anger that flourished within fueled the pump of his fist. Bo could see her in his head. Long blonde hair wound around his hand. Soulful blue eyes staring up at him. Taylor, on his knees, behind her.

*"Get on this dick, pretty girl."*

Bo picked up the pace, quickening his strokes, and mercilessly throttled the hardened flesh in his hand. He remembered being inside her, sheathed within warm, wet walls. Jackhammered into the cramped bunk by the powerful force of Taylor's thrusts in her ass. Sweat. Saliva. The smell of their sex.

*"Feels good, don't it, baby?"*

*"Fuckkk. Yesss. Taylor."*

He pressed his fingers to her clit.

She bit his nipple.

The burn that throbbed at the base of his spine broke free, propelling up his dick. Bo squeezed its pierced head. Muscles contracting, hot cum spurted onto his taut abs. He rubbed it into his skin and opened his eyes.

*It was Tay she wanted, not you.*

"Fuck her." Bo snickered at the popcorn ceiling. He got what he wanted that night, didn't he? And with his fingers in the sticky mess on his stomach, he slumped over on the pillow and fell asleep.

Going to the left this time, Bo knocked on the green door. Connie opened it, letting him inside. "I figured right."

"What?"

"Had a hunch you'd show up here first." She smirked.

The corner of his mouth ticked up. "Where is she?"

"In the sunroom with Em." The old woman tipped her head, hitching her thumb over her shoulder. "Straight back."

Shelley lay on a hospital bed, a book in her hand, reading to Emery in the crook of her arm. Jalousie windows cranked open to let in the morning breeze. A fan oscillated on a table in the corner, another circled overhead, and yet, the sickly-sweet stench of impending death pervaded the room. Bo wrinkled his nose at it. Musky, medicinal, and metallic, the fetid miasma seeped inside his pores.

"From the midst of this darkness, a sudden light broke in upon me..."

"...a light so brilliant and wondrous." Bo knew the passage.

Shelley glared up at him.

"*Frankenstein*. It's one of my favorite books."

Odd choice for story time. Dr. Seuss would have been better suited to read to a two-year-old.

"Daddy!" Emery scooted from her mother, and raising her arms in the air, she flung herself at him.

He scooped her up. Holding his daughter close, Bo kissed her hair. "Hey there, darling. How's my baby girl this morning?"

Sweet baby giggles. Midnight eyes locking on his, Emery beamed. She grabbed a handful of his hair and nestled her head into the curve of his shoulder.

"You read?" Shelley scoffed, then mumbled under her breath. "Never would have guessed that. Thought you just liked to pound things."

"I read." Bo smirked. "A lot, actually. And I *love* to pound things. Sometimes I even use wooden sticks."

"Jesus." Rolling her eyes, Shelley tossed the book onto the bedside table. "Em loves it when you read to her. I've been reading to her since before she was born, so..." She paused to swipe her dry tongue over cracked lips.

"I'll read to her," he said, putting a bottle of water in Shelley's hand. "Every day."

Glassy-eyed, Shelley gazed at their daughter in his arms. "She's like a little koala bear. Loves to cuddle and snuggle."

*Like her daddy.*

But he didn't say it. "Emery is a pretty name."

"I read it in a book once and I liked it." She shrugged. "Changed the spelling, though."

"Which book?"

"I don't remember. Some romance novel, maybe. Why?"

"When she asks, I want to be able to tell her the story of how she got her name." He smiled.

"Sage green is my favorite color." Shelley stared at nothing out the window.

*Random.*

"Oh. Uh…"

"Emery Sage Tompkins. There's your story."

*Emery Sage Robertson.*

But he didn't say that either. "I like it—the name and the color."

"You can change it if you want," she said, still staring through the slats of glass.

Bo shifted into her line of vision so she'd have to look at him. "I'm not going to change it. That's the name you gave her."

Taking a long pull of water, Shelley didn't respond.

"I'm giving her my last name, though."

She was silent for a long moment, then soulful blue eyes, now sullen, snapped up to his. "It wasn't supposed to be you. I didn't want you to be Emery's father."

*Fuck you.*

He already knew that.

Still, the words stung.

"But I am."

"You can leave now," Shelley spat the words like poison. "Take her. Go."

Her gaze fixed on nothing out the window, she wouldn't look at him. Unshed tears swam in her once-vibrant eyes. Shifting Emery in his arms, Bo sat in a chair by the bed. "Stop it."

She turned her head in his direction, chin jutting, lip curling, and sneered in a low tone, "The only reason I let you fuck me was so I could be with Taylor."

"You think I don't know that?" His temper sparked. "The only reason Tay was even there was because I…" Licking his lips, Bo paused and took a calming breath. "…I wanted you."

Wasn't he good enough for Shelley to have wanted him too? With the exception of the band, it seemed like nobody ever picked him for anything. When Bo was a kid, he sucked at sports—didn't have much interest in them really—so he was usually the one sitting on the bleachers waiting for his name to be called. And it was always last.

Maybe he wasn't good enough. No one had ever chosen him to love. Linnea picked Kyan. Chloe didn't have to choose between Jesse and Taylor, she loved them both. Katie had Brendan. In the end, even Kodiak didn't choose him. They were all in his family of friends, and he knew they loved him, but still.

He could fuck almost anyone he wanted to, and male or female, he had. God knows, he loved fucking. But sex was merely a physical connection. Give him the emotional, the spiritual connection with it.

Bo wanted a someone of his very own. Someone who wanted *him*—mind, heart, body, and soul. A lover. A partner. A friend. For once, he wanted to be someone's everything and for that someone to be his.

"You wanted me?" Shelley gazed at him curiously, as if she didn't believe him.

Pursing his lips to the side, Bo nodded. "Yeah, there was something about you…I don't know…but yeah."

Color rose to her cheeks, reminding him she was young—way too young to be dying. She reached out to their daughter, who sat on his lap, brushing her fingertips on Emery's skin. "I never planned to tell you about her."

His brow raised along with his hackles. "Why not?"

"Because I didn't want to share her. Em was just mine, you know?"

"But…"

"Taylor?" Wringing her hands, Shelley glanced away. "That was a mistake and I don't want to talk about it. If I hadn't gotten sick, you wouldn't be in her life…but I am sick, so here you are. I couldn't let them put her in foster care, like I was…or put her up for adoption. Not when she has a father who's capable and has means. I'm sorry…"

The tears swimming in her eyes finally spilled. Saturating her long lashes, they silently dripped down her face. She inhaled, shakily. "It looks like she loves you already. Just give her a good life."

"I will." He kissed the baby's head. "I promise."

"I'm tired and I need to rest now." Shelley returned her gaze to the window. Her voice cracked. "When are you taking Em to Chicago?"

*Christ.*

This was tearing him in two. Cancer was taking his baby away from her mother, not him. Bo exhaled. "I'm not sure yet."

Shelley closed her eyes, dismissing him.

He carried Emery into the kitchen where Connie sat working a crossword puzzle. Tapping her pencil, she glanced up at the ceiling. "Strips in a club. Five letters."

Bo snickered.

She smirked at him. "You should know this one."

"And whatever gave you that impression?" He feigned offense.

Her brow arched and she clucked her tongue. "Just a hunch."

"You've got a dirty mind, Miss Connie. I think I like it." Bo nodded with a grin. "Bacon."

"Bacon?"

"Strips in a club…" He winked. "…sandwich."

"Well, aren't you just the devil?" Shaking her head, she scribbled the answer on the paper.

"Heh, I've been called worse."

Connie put her puzzle aside. "How'd it go in there?"

"I'm not sure." He put down a squirming Emery and she crawled into the old woman's lap. "She's resting now."

"Well, I gave her a pain pill right before you came," Connie informed him, combing his daughter's hair with her fingers. "Hopefully, she'll sleep until the hospice nurse gets here. Shelley didn't get much last night."

"Cici, cookie." Emery pointed to a painted ceramic jar on the counter.

'*Life is short, eat the cookie.*'

*Damn. Ain't that the fucking truth?*

"You've got to have some breakfast first, okay, Em?" Connie smiled over at him. "Cici is easier for her to say. Can I get you a cup of coffee while I fix Em some cereal?"

"No, thanks." Handing his daughter a cookie from the jar, Bo smiled back at the woman. "Actually, I was thinking of taking Emmy out for breakfast and to the park—or maybe the beach. Is it far?"

"You can get to Cocoa, Daytona, or New Smyrna Beach in about an hour. Em loves the beach. Shelley takes her all the time…" Biting her lip, Connie glanced toward the sunroom. "Well, she used to."

Not sure how to respond to that, Bo shifted his gaze to his daughter, happily gnawing on an Oreo. He held his arms out to her. "Want to go get pancakes with Daddy, baby?"

Displaying a chocolatey grin, Emery scrambled down from the old woman's lap. He scooped her up, her little legs straddling his waist, and kissed her button nose.

"Do you have a car seat?"

"Yeah, they gave me one with the car," he answered, wiping cookie from Emery's face.

"Do you know how to use it?"

"Can't be that hard." Bo chuckled. "It's not rocket science. I'll figure it out."

"Okay then." Connie picked up her crossword with a smirk. "Em's bag is by the door. You two have fun now."

Bo plucked the pencil from her fingers. "This is my number," he said as he wrote it down. "Call or text if you need anything— like help with your puzzle." He handed the pencil back and winked. "Five across is butterscotch."

She swatted him. "Smartass."

# *Five*

"This *is* fucking rocket science," Bo muttered under his breath as he played tug-of-war with the car seat's buckle. He pushed the red button and yanked to no avail. "What kind of genius designed this thing?"

Emery patted him on the head and giggled. Her fingers, sticky with pancake syrup, caught in his hair. Beads of sweat erupted on the surface of his skin. Bo glanced up at her and grinned. "Hold on, baby. Daddy'll get the hang of it."

"Daddy." She giggled again.

Sweetest sound in the world.

With one thumb on top of the other, he pressed down hard on the button and the latch released. *Thank fuck.* Bo peeled off his T-shirt and wiping sweat from his brow, lifted Emery out of the seat. He set her down, and holding onto her sticky, little hand, they walked over to the swings.

Squeals of delight bubbled up from Emery's throat with each gentle push, her pudgy fingers gripping the hanging ropes. Bo roasted in the late-morning sun. It had to be ninety degrees in the shade—if there was any. And humid. God, it was stifling. It sure as hell explained why the park was empty on a Saturday.

*How do people live in this shit?*

Three months of summer is one thing, but all year long? No, thanks. Bo loved all four seasons. He couldn't imagine living in a world where there wasn't snow to build a snowman and where Christmas lights were strung on palm trees. Rainy days and tulips in spring. Bonfires, hayrides, and the glorious colors of fall.

"You're gonna love Chicago, Emmy." She looked up at him as he gave her another push. "There's a big park right next to our house, a zoo—American Girl Place is downtown. We'll go there and get you a doll. Would you like that?"

She just giggled.

"Aunt Chloe says you will. She knows all about this stuff. You're going to love her too." He smiled. "You got a new cousin today. Her name is Ireland. Actually, you have a bunch of cousins waiting for you. Declan's just a baby, but Chandan and Elliott are close to your age—and he lives right across the street. Ryan and Logan are all the way in California with Aunt Allie, Uncle Ry, and Grandma and Grandpa."

Bo slowed the swing to a stop and knelt on the ground in front of her.

Emery tugged on his hair.

"We'll go on an airplane and visit them. We're going to do all the things and I promise to always try to be a good dad. I'm going to make some mistakes, though."

Like he did at IHOP. Who knew a tiny two-year-old could make such a big mess with pancakes? Bo ordered Emery a big chocolate chip pancake—the one they make into a face with whipped cream and maraschino cherry eyes. Mistake. Maybe he should have gotten her the sprinkles instead, because before he could swallow a bite of hash browns, she'd finger-painted a Picasso confection on the table.

Bo cleaned up the mess, and Emery, as best he could with napkins and wipes he found in her bag, but she was still sticky. He didn't want to take her in the men's room and he couldn't take her to the ladies' room, where there was a sink, and water, and soap. Maybe it was the OCD in him. Grubby hands didn't seem to bother his daughter much at all.

"Up." Emery raised her arms.

"I got you, darling." Bo lifted her out of the swing. "Wanna go down the slide next?"

She clung to him as he carried her up the steps. Bo held her tightly on his lap. "Ready? One…two…three…" And they took off, Emery squealing all the way down.

"Up." She pointed to the top of the slide.

They went down again. And again, and again, and again. Sitting at the bottom of the slide, laughing between breaths, Bo held Emery to his chest, kissing her sweaty head. His daughter looked up at him and he melted. She was his everything. And he was hers.

"I love you, Emery." He hugged her tight. "Daddy loves you."

Connie, looking frazzled, was coming out of the sunroom as Bo, carrying a worn-out Emery, came inside the house. "Is everything okay?"

"Yeah." With a shrug, she glanced behind her shoulder. "It hasn't been one of Shelley's better days, but the nurse is here now." Smiling at Emery, she combed through her sweat-dampened hair with her fingers. "Did you have fun with Daddy? It sure looks like you did."

He chuckled. "She needs a bath."

"And a nap," Connie added, reaching for the baby. "Here, I'll take her. She's plumb tuckered out." She headed toward the stairs. "There's cold drinks in the fridge if you want one."

*Cool. Guess that means I'm staying.*

He took a bottle of water from the fridge. Being here, this situation, everything about it was still rather awkward. *Just a few more days.* Phil along with Shelley's attorney would have all the legal stuff taken care of by Monday. As soon as that was done, Bo could take Emery home.

"No more." The agonizing cry came from the sunroom. "Just get the fuck out and leave me alone."

Two women were in the room with her. One, obviously a nurse, in brightly colored scrubs, eyes cast downward, chewed on her fingernail in the corner. The other stood at the side of Shelley's bed, patting her shoulder. Older, she reminded him of a hippie chick from the '60s. Maybe she was, once upon a time. Birkenstock sandals. Flowing flowered skirt. Long, wiry, salt-and-pepper hair.

Setting his water on the table, Bo sat down on the edge of the bed and took Shelley's hand in his. Tears rolling down her cheeks, she looked away from him. "Hey," he said, wiping her face. "What's the matter?"

Turning her head toward him, Shelley closed her eyes, and more tears seeped from beneath her lashes.

"Who are you?" hippie lady inquired.

Glancing up at her, he answered, "Bo."

"Told you I was telling the truth." Shelley's eyes remained closed.

The woman extended her hand. "I'm Beatrice—Bea, Shelley's social worker."

*Ohh.*

"I'm her friend." Bo smirked. "And Emery's dad. Nice to meet you."

"She didn't believe me." Shelley snickered through her tears. "Not that I blame her."

"Are you taking custody of the child?"

"She's my daughter." Bo wasn't sure if he cared for this woman. Weren't social workers supposed to be bleeding hearts? She spoke as if she didn't have one. "Of course, I'm taking her."

And with her hands covering her face, Shelley sobbed.

"Sh, sh, sh." Bo held her head to his chest as she cried, glaring at the heartless hippie lady. "Take a breath."

"Make her go," Shelley begged. "Please."

"You have to understand, my job is to see to the welfare of the child."

"Then your job is finished." He rocked Shelley, brushing her long blonde hair with his fingers. "I've got it from here."

The woman bit her lip with a nod and went over to talk with

the nurse in the corner. Gently, Bo dried Shelley's tears with some tissues.

"*Em loves the beach. Shelley takes her all the time…*"

"Why don't we get you out of here and take Emmy to the beach tomorrow? Would you like that?"

"I wish I could. It's my favorite place on Earth." Peering up at Bo, she sniffled. "Why are you being so nice to me? Because I'm dying, right?"

Hippie bitch, Bea, took a step forward. "Shelley is far too ill for that."

"Is that so?" Bo looked to the nurse.

"I think it'd be—"

"I said Shelley's too ill," Bea cut in, her mouth tightening. "There's transport. A nurse would have to accompany her." She shook her head. "The beach is out of our jurisdiction."

"I'll hire one then." Bo flicked his gaze back to the nurse. "Want a side gig?"

"Stop…" Shelley squeezed his arm. "…being so *fucking* nice to me. I don't deserve it."

Connie walked into the room, a freshly bathed Emery in her arms. "Mommy. Daddy."

"Hush now." Rubbing Shelley's fingers that gripped his flesh, Bo smiled at their daughter. He got up, and taking Emery from Connie, announced, "I'm stepping out for a minute to make a call."

He took out his phone on the way to the kitchen.

Linnea answered on the first ring.

Her head cradled against his chest, Bo breathed in the floral, fruity scent of baby shampoo—the happiest smell imaginable. Maybe Shelley didn't think she deserved it, but Emery sure did.

"Hey, baby girl. I need you to help me with something."

*Yeah, guess I'm staying.*

# Six

He owed her one. Big time.

By some miracle, Linnea had been able to help Bo find a little vacation cottage to rent right on the beach at the height of tourist season. It wasn't fancy, but it was comfortable and homey, with a small swimming pool and a big covered porch where Shelley could take in the fresh salt air and watch the waves. For however many days she had left, the ocean would be her backyard.

Connie opted not to go with them, even though Bo invited her. It seemed goodbyes were difficult for her too. She and Shelley said theirs in private. The nurse, whose name he learned was Tammy, decided to take him up on his side-gig offer. And hippie bitch, Bea? She could go pound sand. He was now listed as the baby's father on her birth certificate. She was officially Emery Sage Robertson.

Tying his hair back, Bo glanced over at the house. Tammy had Shelley settled in the special chair they'd been able to get for her on the porch. It was like having a La-Z-Boy recliner on wheels. Easily maneuverable, she could relax in any room of the house or enjoy the outdoors. Shelley found it much more comfortable than being in bed, and they didn't have to transfer her as much, which had become increasingly painful for her.

"Wave to Mommy, baby."

Emery sat between his legs, digging in the sand. She let go of her pink plastic shovel to wave to her mother. With a book on her lap, and a smile on her face, Shelley waved back.

And this is exactly why they were here instead of boarding an airplane to Chicago. More time. For Emery to be with her mother and both of her parents together. For Bo to discover all the stories he'd share with her when she got older, to learn how to be her dad with the guidance of her mom. Because for Shelley, there was precious little time left.

She seemed to be less surly, now that they were here. Shelley had her favorite place on Earth and her daughter with her. She wasn't quite ready to deal with letting go. Bo understood that, and so he decided to stay until the end came.

Taking Emery by the hand, Bo walked her to the shoreline. She giggled as the waves splashed her feet. "C'mon, darling." He lifted her up, wading into the water. "Quick dip to get all the sand off, then I'll make us some dinner, yeah?"

Laughing, her head quickly bobbed up and down. Bo couldn't know for sure if Emery understood what he was saying, but it seemed as if she did. Holding her in the ocean, buoyant in the water, the breeze cooling under a blazing Florida sun, he happened to glance back at the house.

Shelley watched them from the porch.

And the inside of his chest squeezed.

She looked so incredibly sad.

Holding Emery in one arm, Bo gathered their things and carried her back to the house. Shelley was engrossed in her book—she pretended to be anyway. Tammy read a book of her own, stretched out in a chair beside her. He wrapped his daughter in a fresh towel and deposited her at her mother's feet.

"I'm gonna throw some burgers on the grill." He pointed his chin toward Shelley. "Hungry?"

"I suppose I should eat something." She didn't have much of an appetite.

Bo raised his brow.

"I'll try, okay?"

Emery fell asleep, curled up in her mother's lap, while he sautéed mushrooms and onions to top the burgers with on the side burner. Bo felt eyes on his back. He half turned to find Shelley staring at him. "What?"

"You've gotten tan." She pursed her lips with a half shrug of her shoulder.

"I've been using sunscreen."

She laughed at him.

He turned around all the way. "Too much sun can damage your skin. I don't want wrinkles and shit."

"Put a shirt on then, but a little bit of color won't kill you." Shelley rolled her eyes and muttered, "You looked like a pasty-ass winter ghosty when you got here."

Tammy giggled. "Sorry."

"It *is* winter." He flipped the burgers. "And I don't like wearing shirts."

"We noticed." With a shake of her head, Shelley snorted. "Why? I thought it was just an image thing for the band."

"Drumming is very physical, you know. I sweat my ass off up there," he said. "But it's a sensory thing. That's why I don't like wearing them."

"Oh." She pressed her lips together, stifling a grin. "Okay."

"I don't like the way most fabrics feel on my skin. They're annoying." He shrugged. "Constricting."

She cocked her head. "But tight leather pants are okay?"

"That *is* an image thing, but they feel good, actually. I like leather." He winked. "Besides, I have to wear pants. Can't have everyone seeing my junk, now can I?"

"I think everyone's already seen it."

Tipping his chin, he raised his brow. "Well, you've more than seen it."

Tammy's head shot up. "You have?"

*How did this woman get a college degree?*

He slowly nodded. "We did make a baby, Tammy."

"You can see his junk too, if you want." Shelley giggled. It was nice to see her laugh, even if it was at his expense. "It's all over the internet. Turn off safe search on Google."

Bo locked eyes with the middle-aged nurse. "Don't."

She didn't listen. Plating the food, he heard her exclaim behind him, "Oh my God! His penis is pierced!"

"Yeah." Shelley snickered. "And that's how Emery got here."

"What?"

"Your piercing tore the condom." She rubbed a finger back and forth across her bottom lip. "Though it could have been my teeth when I put it on, I suppose."

"You're shitting me."

"Nope," she replied, matter-of-factly. "Don't you remember?"

"Not that part."

Chewing on the inside corner of his lip, Bo set the platter of burgers on the table with a swift shake of his head. He snickered to himself. *She fucking played me.*

Florida was a nice place to visit, but Bo would never want to live here. High humidity made the air feel like pea soup, between the prickly grass, sand spurs, and fire ants, walking barefoot was hazardous to his feet, and he had yet to see the glow of a single firefly. Why was that? How could a kid grow up without experiencing the wonder of catching one? Here, little lizards squirmed in flower beds and the cockroaches—Shelley called them Palmetto bugs—could fly.

*And don't get me started on the fucking mosquitoes.*

Bo had their favorite blood type, it seemed, because they didn't bother the girls very much. He found it odd at first, but now he understood why so many swimming pools, patios, and porches were screened in.

Emery was tucked in her crib for the night in the master suite. Tammy had the evening off and went to catch a movie. Shelley was in her chair on the back porch. Listening to the ocean. Reading a book. She'd only picked at her dinner again, so Bo thought he'd try making her a smoothie. Maybe she'd be able to get that down. She was getting thinner, and more gaunt, by the day.

"Here." Taking a seat in the chair beside her, Bo handed Shelley his concoction. "Try this."

"What is it?" One nostril flared, she side-eyed him.

With a smirk, he popped the tab on his beer. "A smoothie."

"I see that," she said, sniffing the contents. "What's in it?"

"Strawberries, bananas, pineapple…" Bo took a pull of his beer. "…Greek yogurt, orange juice, and spinach."

Shelley set the glass down. "Spinach? Gross."

"You can't even taste it," he countered. "Besides, it's good for you."

"I don't think it matters anymore." She sighed with a tilt of her head. "I'd rather have what you're having."

"Beer wouldn't mix well with your meds."

"What's it gonna do, kill me?" There was a burst of sardonic laughter. "I'm already dying."

"Yeah, well, I'm not gonna help you there." Bo put the smoothie back in her hand. "Drink."

"You're no fun." She sucked on the straw and smacked her lips. "Not bad."

"I'm lotsa fun." Turning his head in her direction, Bo winked. "And you know it."

Shelley just rolled her eyes.

"How'd you end up with cancer?"

"I don't know." She shrugged. "How does anyone get cancer? Don't worry, it's not genetic."

That thought had crossed his mind.

"What I meant was, how come they didn't give you chemo or something?"

"Oh." Taking the beer from his hand, she took a sip. "It was way too late for that. Wouldn't have made a difference in the end anyway."

"Why not?"

"Osteosarcoma grows super fast—it had already spread by the time I got diagnosed." Shelley tipped more ale down her throat and swallowed. "Surgery wasn't an option. They offered chemo—said it might buy me a little bit more time. I declined." She chuckled with a shrug. "At least I get to keep my hair."

Bo reached for a long blonde lock and rubbed it between his fingers. "I'm sorry."

"It's my own fault. I ignored all the signs. It started with pain in my hip. First, I blamed it on being pregnant. Then I thought it was from carrying Em around all the time." She stared out at the whitecapped waves rolling onto the dark beach. "But it kept getting worse and…" Shelley turned her head toward him. "…then it was too late. Doesn't matter, I guess."

*Fuck.*

"Course it matters." Bo let go of her hair to squeeze her bony fingers.

"I'd still end up dead."

Not knowing what to say to that, he looked out toward the water and whispered, "Shelley, not short for Michelle."

"My mom named me after Mary Shelley," she offered.

*"Frankenstein…"*

"Was her favorite book." Shelley wistfully smiled. "She read it to me all the time, and now I read it to Em. There's another story for you."

"I'll read it to her too." Even though he still thought it an odd choice for a little girl. "I promise."

"You don't have to."

"I want to."

They were silent for a time. Holding hands. Just listening to the roar of the ocean.

"I've always known it was you," Shelley admitted. "There was never any other possibility."

"I know."

"You do?"

"Yeah." Bo didn't look at her. He couldn't. "So, why?"

"Taylor?"

"Yeah."

"I don't know what I was thinking." He heard her sigh. "It was, um, right after Christmas. This lady calls me and says she knows I'm pregnant with Taylor's baby—that she can help me."

Bo turned toward her then. "Help you with what?"

"Money, I guess." Shelley looked down at her lap and shrugged. "She said he'd want to do the right thing and I was a bit desperate by then."

"And he had a baby of his own on the way then," he seethed, smoldering with resentment. "Do you have any idea how the stunt you pulled affected his wife?"

"I didn't know he'd gotten married—or whatever it is they call it." She waved a hand through the air. "Salena said it wouldn't go that far, that—"

"Salena?"

"That's the lady who called and got me the lawyer. She took care of everything." Her eyes flicked over to his. "Why? You know her?"

*Fucking hell. You were right, B.*

"I did. We all did."

"Did?"

With a quick nod, he told her, "Did. Past tense. She was killed just over a year ago."

"Sorry. How?"

"Murdered. Cops were never able to determine with certainty who did it at the time, but since then a close friend of hers was arrested somewhere on the East Coast—Oceanview Beach, I think. Turns out he's a psycho-ass serial killer. The MO fits, and it was hella gruesome." Bo shook his head. "They'll never be able to prove it was him, though."

"Oh, that's terrible."

*Yeah. Thanks for taking out the trash, Milo.*

"No comment." His gaze returned to the water. "I would have taken care of you."

"I know."

"Things could have been so different."

*If only you had chosen me.*

Closing her eyes, she murmured, "I know."

# Seven

B o opened his eyes to bright sunlight pouring in through the plantation shutters and Emery staring at him from the portable crib across the room. Seeing he was awake, her cherubic face broke into a wide, happy grin. As much as he loved his daughter now, he couldn't imagine his life without her.

"Good morning, darling." She stood, arms raised, as he lifted her out of the crib. "Shall I fix us some breakfast?"

"Cookie." Emery bounced in his arms, fingers tangling in his hair.

He smacked a kiss to her button nose. "How about pancakes?"

Tammy sat at the island, thumbing through a magazine, when Bo carried Emery into the kitchen. Not seeing Shelley, he glanced around, noting her empty chair parked in the living room. "Isn't she getting up?"

"Don't think so." Putting the magazine down, Tammy flicked her eyes up to him. "Not now anyway. She's sleeping."

"She have a rough night?" Bo secured Emery in her high chair and went to the fridge to get her some juice.

"No."

He turned toward Tammy, carton of orange juice in hand.

She glanced at his daughter, then gave him a beseeching look. "Shelley's comfortable. Slept right through."

Spidey senses tingling, a chill flashed through him. Goosebumps rose on his skin along with the hair on his arms. And why did he have this strange feeling in his gut? Raising his brow, he asked the question without speaking.

"Sit down. I'll make breakfast." She stood, patting Emery's silky hair. "And we'll talk."

"It's the end, isn't it?" Bo poured some orange juice into a sippy cup for his daughter and sat.

Measuring pancake mix into a bowl, Tammy nodded. "I take it you haven't been through this before."

He slowly shook his head. "No."

"The process varies from person to person, but you can expect Shelley to sleep more now. She'll become less responsive as she gradually withdraws from us and her surroundings." Tammy patted his hand. "Don't be surprised if she rallies again before the end. Some patients do."

"What are we supposed to do?"

"Keep her comfortable." She offered him a sympathetic smile. "Just focus on Em, but…" She paused for a beat. "…if there's anything you want to say, any peace you need to make with her, do it now. You might not get another chance."

And with the plantation shutters closed, soft music playing in the room, Shelley slept.

Tammy sat, reading a book at her bedside.

Holding Emery, Bo leaned over the bed. "Give Mommy a kiss bye-bye." She did, and he followed, kissing Shelley's forehead. "We're going out to get some ice cream, but we'll be back in a little bit, okay?"

No response. Nothing.

With her lips pressed together, Tammy glanced up at him.

Bo asked her, "You want anything?"

"Where you going?"

"Twistee Treat," he replied, rubbing circles on his daughter's back. "Shelley told me she always gets Emmy a baby cone with sprinkles."

"Ohhh, I love the pistachio soft-serve they have." She licked her lips. "Bring back a pint, then when Shelley wakes up, maybe I'll be nice and split it with her."

"You got it."

As he drove down the highway, late-afternoon sun pelted through the windshield, blinding him. He squinted behind his sunglasses. It was too bright here. Bo glanced at Emery in the rearview mirror. The world shouldn't be so vibrant while a young mother, his daughter's mother, lay dying.

Three weeks ago he woke up and contemplated getting a dog. Today he was the single father of a soon-to-be motherless two-year-old. Bo hadn't given much thought to the actual event that was on the horizon. Death and dying had been such an abstract concept. Until now.

How should he be feeling? Bo wasn't sure. Stuck on autopilot, vacillating between his calm exterior, while inside he was a complete mess. Between wanting to take Emery home, yet not wanting her mother to die. Even though he knew the inevitable was coming, it was happening so fast. And right this minute, he couldn't think beyond a pint of pistachio ice cream.

Shelley was still sleeping when they got back.

Bo put the ice cream in the freezer.

He was getting Emery into her pajamas after giving her a bath, when Tammy poked her head inside the door. "Shelley's awake."

She sat up, propped against the headboard with mounds of pillows. Alert and aware. Blue eyes shining. Color in her cheeks. Beaming, Shelley opened her arms for Emery. Bo gently placed her with her mother.

"Hey, sunshine." Shelley hugged their daughter, peppering her face with kisses. "Did you go to the beach with Daddy today?"

"Daddy." She looked up at her mother with a grin.

"We went for ice cream." Bo blinked at the tears that were building. "Got you some."

"Oh, yeah?" She coyly smiled. "What kind?"

"Pistachio."

Her gaze darted to Tammy. "That's her favorite." Then those

soulful eyes were looking up at him. "Mine's cherry vanilla—the kind with chunks of dark chocolate and nuts in it."

"I'll get you some tomorrow." He sat down on the bed beside her.

"Okay, but I'll take some of that pistachio for now."

Tammy shook her head with a chuckle.

"What?" Shelley grinned. "I'm hungry."

Bo winked at the nurse. "Get the girl some ice cream, Tammy."

"I feel so much better," Shelley said, reaching for the book she always kept on her bedside table. "Guess I just needed some sleep."

*Yeah. Maybe so.*

"I'm glad." He squeezed her shoulders, drawing her and Emery closer.

Shelley opened the book. An old, worn copy of *Frankenstein,* and turned to page one.

Bo read the opening line.

*"You will rejoice to hear that no disaster has accompanied the commencement of an enterprise which you have regarded with such evil forebodings."*

He didn't sleep well, if he'd actually slept at all.

Afraid Shelley could slip away during the night, Bo tossed and turned. He texted Sloan, who he could count on to still be awake, at three in the morning. Everything was good at home—cold as fuck, but good. They'd finished the guitar tracks last week. He'd start recording vocals tomorrow.

As the sun came up over the ocean outside his window, Bo gave up and got out of bed. Emery still slept, hands folded beneath her cheek, blanket at her feet. He covered her and tiptoed into the en suite to shower.

Tammy stood at the island whisking eggs when Bo made it into the kitchen with Emery. He didn't see Shelley, nor her chair parked in the living room.

"Good morning." Her gaze never leaving the bowl of eggs, she smirked. "Shelley's out on the porch. She wants French toast, so that's what y'all are having for breakfast."

"Yeah?" The corners of his mouth lifted.

She glanced up at him. "Yeah."

"Well, I'm good with that." Bo kissed his daughter. "How 'bout you, Emmy?"

"Go on." Tammy chuckled. "We can eat outside. It's a beautiful morning."

He spied Shelley through the glass, blonde hair floating in the breeze. "Yeah, it is."

They breakfasted al fresco. Sitting between his legs, Emery played with her toy xylophone, striking random keys. Bo wrapped his hand around hers, teaching her a tune.

*You are my sunshine…*

And Shelley hummed along.

Claiming she was still full after such a big breakfast, Shelley passed on lunch. "I might have one of those smoothies of yours later, if you'll make me one."

"Sure thing." Bo winked.

She made a face. "No spinach, though."

"Deal." He chuckled.

With a yawn, Emery laid her head in his lap.

Tammy got up from her chair. "Here." Extending her arms, she reached for the baby. "Let me take her in for a nap. I could use one myself."

Bo kissed Emery on the forehead, waving as the nurse carried her inside. Only he and Shelley remained, looking out at the ocean. Neither one of them spoke for a time, instead listening to the rhythmic crash of waves upon the sand, accompanied by the squawking melody of seagulls overhead.

Her head lolled to the side, soulful blue eyes appraising him. "You're not at all like I thought you were."

"Oh?" He met her gaze. "And how's that?"

"You know…" Shelley pressed her lips together.

Bo angled his head, waiting for her to continue, but she didn't.

"Tell me about your life," she said instead.

"What do you wanna know?"

"Where you live. What your house is like…"

"Chicago, but you already know that." Smirking, Bo swept his tongue across his bottom lip. "A couple years ago, me, the boys in the band, and our friends—our brothers, we all grew up together, so we're close, you know? Anyway, we went in on a deal together and bought ten three-flat apartment buildings on Park Place. Converted them. Now we each have a big-ass house and own the whole damn block." He chuckled with a nod of his head. "Gated it too. Keeps the paps out."

A corner of her mouth quirked up. "Except when they send drones in."

"Heard about that, huh?"

"It was all over social media. You can still watch Taylor's speech on YouTube." Biting her lip, Shelley glanced down at her lap. "I caused a lot of trouble, didn't I? Please tell him…everyone…how sorry I am for that."

"I will." Bo reached over to take her hand. "Everything turned out okay. Besides, Salena was the one behind it all, so…"

"Not just that…" A tear rolled down Shelley's cheek. "…I'm so sorry I kept Em from you. You have every right to be angry with me. If I could go back and make it right, I would."

*But you can't.*

"I'm not angry."

Wasn't he, though?

"Yes, you are." Blue eyes met his in challenge. "And I bet you'd be letting me know what a horrible person I am if I wasn't dying. Like dying gives me a free pass or something. It doesn't. Why is it we turn dead people into revered saints, even when they don't deserve it?"

"To hold onto them," he said, giving her hand a gentle squeeze. "It's the good parts we remember."

"You should hate me."

"I don't hate you."

"I'm glad." She squeezed back. "Now, I need you to admit you're angry and then forgive me."

"Will you feel better if I do?"

"No." Her fingertips skimmed his cheek. "But you will."

Not understanding her logic, his brows pulled together.

"Tell me how you feel, Bo Robertson." Shelley poked his chest with her finger.

*Jesus.*

"Fine. I'm mad at you." He expelled the air from his lungs. "There, I said it. Happy now?"

"C'mon, you can do better than that."

"I'm fucking mad at you. And I'm sad." Bo peered up at the covered porch ceiling. "I'm sad I wasn't there when Emmy was born, that I missed her first birthday…and her second. Her first steps. First word." His gaze returned to Shelley's face. Tears slid down her cheeks. "I'm just sad, okay?"

"I know," she said, nodding. "And I'm sorry."

"Not just for all the things I missed with Emery." He wiped her eyes with his thumbs. "For what I maybe could've shared with you."

*And now we'll never know, because now it's too late.*

But Bo couldn't say it out loud.

She smiled at him with watery eyes. "Now say you forgive me."

"I forgive you."

Letting go of his hand, Shelley turned her head toward the beach and sighed. "Do you have someone special in your life, Bo?"

"No."

She smiled. "The beginning is always today." Looking out at the ocean, Shelley reached for him again.

Bo laced their fingers together.

"I wish I could be out there, floating in the water."

He stood, and without any hesitation at all, Bo carefully lifted Shelley out of her chair and into his arms.

"*Bo*," she shrieked, clasping his neck. "What are you doing?"

Carrying Shelley across the sand, he waded with her into the cool water of the ocean. He stared into the shining eyes looking up at him and he kissed her. Soft and gentle and sweet. Her head cradled in his palm, she threaded her fingers in his hair, and kissed him back.

"That night in Tampa…" She lowered her lashes.

His forehead dipped to hers. "Yeah?"

"I'm sorry I didn't pick you. I should have." Her voice quaked. "But I'm so glad it's you. Emery got the best daddy in the entire world." Softly, Shelley touched her lips to his. "You're a good guy, Bo Robertson, and you're gonna meet someone, a helluva lot smarter than I was, who sees that."

He just held her. Suspended in the water, and safe in his arms, she floated.

Smiling, Shelley closed her eyes and shivered.

"Are you cold?"

"A little."

"I'll take you back."

She shook her head. "Just give me five more minutes."

*Shelley, not short for Michelle, I'd give you forever if I could.*

# Eight

Cherry vanilla ice cream.

Blurry-eyed, Bo stared at the container in the freezer. He'd barely slept these past two days—or was it three? They all blended together and somehow he'd lost track.

Tammy was watching from the porch when he carried Shelley out of the ocean. "Decided to go for a swim, did you?" She laughed, and armed with a towel, she took over. "Let's get you bathed and comfy now, hmm?"

"Need any help?" Dripping on the porch, Bo wrung the salt-water from his hair.

"Nah." She tossed him the towel. "I got her."

"Okay." Bo kissed Shelley's brow. "I'm gonna go on an ice cream run."

She smiled up at him. "Cherry vanilla?"

"With chunks of dark chocolate and nuts." He winked.

But she never got to have any. By the time he got back from Twistee Treat, Shelley was already asleep. And she hadn't woken up again since.

He slammed the freezer door closed. Raking his fingers through his hair, Bo sank against the counter and closed his eyes. He couldn't even remember what he came into the kitchen for.

"You should go lie down," Tammy said, patting his shoulder. "Get a little shut-eye while Em is napping."

"I can't." Grasping her hand, he opened his eyes. "I should be there when she wakes up."

"Bo." She spoke so softly, tilting her head to gaze up at him. "She's not going to."

"What?"

Tammy sat him at the kitchen table and took a seat beside him. She gathered his hands in hers. "Remember when I said she might rally before the end?"

"Yeah."

"She did. That was it." Squeezing his hands, tears pooled in her eyes. "Shelley gifted you and Em with one last good day. Hold onto that."

Bo swallowed past the lump in his throat. "I didn't think it would happen like this. I thought we'd at least get to say goodbye."

"Just because she doesn't respond, doesn't mean she can't hear you." Tammy squeezed his hand once more. "Say your goodbyes, and anything else you want to tell her."

"How do you do this?" Chin trembling, Bo looked at the nurse who'd become a friend. "How can you stomach watching someone die over and over again?"

"Death can be beautiful."

His brow shot up. *What the fuck?*

"Yes, it's sad, because we won't get to see that person anymore, and we'll miss them." Tammy bit her lip with a nod. "But for them..." She lowered her lashes, a wistful smile on her face. "...it's a transition to whatever comes next.

"I used to be a labor nurse, helping moms bring their babies into this world. Now I help people ease out of it. Death is like birth— only in reverse. Not everyone is fortunate enough to get one, but we all deserve a good death. To be surrounded by the people we love, comfortable, and at peace."

"What do you think comes next? After we die."

Heaven? Hell? Bo had always considered himself a spiritual person, though not a particularly religious one.

"I'm not sure." Still holding onto his hands, she stood. "But I know something does. I've witnessed too many people make their transition to believe otherwise. Get some rest now."

So as not to wake her, Bo gingerly lifted his daughter from her crib. He lay on his bed, propped against the headboard, with Emery asleep in the crook of his arm. Inhaling sweet sunshine, he kissed the top of her pretty head and closed his eyes.

He heard a giggle. Little fingers tugged on his hair. "Daddy, up."

Bo rubbed the kink from his neck. Scooping her up, he held Emery in the air over his head. Giggles turned into belly laughs. He brought her in for a kiss on the nose. "I guess we needed that nap, didn't we, darling?"

They must've slept for a while. With the sunlight fading, shadows lengthened in the room. As much as Bo didn't want to, after dinner and her bath, he was going to bring Emery in to see her mother. It wasn't for her so much. She wouldn't even remember it, or understand this was goodbye. It was for Shelley.

The woman on the bed no longer resembled the vibrant young girl he met three years ago. Hell, Shelley didn't look anything like the woman she was just three weeks ago.

She was a ghastly color, if you could call gray a color. Skeletal. Her lips were bluish. Her once-pretty hair stringy and lackluster.

He sat with Emery on the bed beside her mother. Clinging to him, his daughter seemed to sense something wasn't right. "It's okay, Emmy. Mommy knows you're here."

Leaning from his lap, the baby patted Shelley's cheek. No response. Nothing. Not a flutter or twitch to indicate she was aware they were with her.

Tammy stood off to the side, chewing on her fingernail, just like the first time he'd met her. Maybe it was something she did when she was anxious. Bo could tell she was fighting to hold back her tears.

Emery tugged on her mother's hair. "Mommy, up."

"She can't, baby." God, he was going to lose it. Maybe this wasn't such a good idea. His voice cracked. "But you can give Mommy kisses, okay?"

Her little arms wrapped around Shelley's neck. Emery kissed her mother's cheek.

Tammy muffled a sob in her hand.

"Come to Daddy now, darling." She climbed back into his lap and he held her tight. "Tammy, can you take Emmy to the living room and play with her until bedtime?"

"Of course."

"I'll stay with Shelley."

Bo held her cold, dry hand. He waited for her next breath. It took longer and longer for them to come. They rattled in her chest. It pained him to watch Shelley suffer, but he couldn't leave her. No one deserved to die alone. She was only twenty-two.

Tammy came back in and took a set of vitals. She smiled at him. "You okay?"

"Um, I'm not sure." Bo anxiously wet his lips. He could use some water, but he didn't say anything. "Are you sure she's comfortable? It doesn't sound like it to me."

"I can give her some morphine."

An hour later, as tears poured down his face, Bo watched her take one last breath.

He kissed her forehead. *I love you, Shelley, not short for Michelle.*

And pulling the door closed behind him, he didn't have the slightest clue what the fuck he was supposed to do now.

Beyond the glass, the sun had yet to peek on the horizon, but the sky was beginning to lighten. Tammy was on the phone in the kitchen. Going through the motions, Bo poured himself a cup of coffee, but he didn't drink it. Elbows on the island, he clutched the mug in hands, methodically rubbing the warm ceramic with his thumb, staring at nothing out the window.

"They're on their way." Tammy put her phone down.

"Who's they?"

"The mortuary." Her arm came around his shoulders. "They're coming to take her."

He blinked. Streaks of pink and violet began to appear on a backdrop of dark, desaturated blue.

"I'll get some breakfast ready for Emmy." Tammy patted his back and turned for the pantry. "Lord knows, she rises with the sun."

Without another word, Bo left the kitchen. He went to the room he shared with his daughter and scooping her out of the crib, blanket and all, held her tightly to his chest.

"Where are you going?" Tammy called out, as he whisked past her.

"I need air."

His bare feet hit the cool sand. Throat constricting, lungs burning, Bo ran until he neared the water's edge. He sat where the waves could lap at his toes, with his daughter, rubbing the sleep from her eyes, cradled in his arms.

Kissing her silky hair, Bo settled Emery in his lap, and they watched the sun, majestic and bright, burst onto the horizon. They listened to the roar of the ocean while plumes of orange and gold changed the color of the sky.

Emery tilted her head to smile up at him. Her eyes sparkled like sapphires in the light of the rising sun, unaware that her life had just changed forever. She would never see her mother again, or remember her hugs and kisses. The only memories she'd ever have of Shelley would be the ones he passed on to her.

*"The beginning is always today."*

"I love you, Emmy." Little fingertips grazed his wet cheek. "We're gonna be okay."

Bo zipped up the last of their bags and dropped it in the hallway with the others. Emery was sitting with some toys on the living room floor, watching cartoons. That wouldn't keep her occupied very much longer, but he was about done here.

The box sat on the counter.

He picked it up.

There was one last thing he needed to do.

"C'mon, darling."

It didn't seem right that all that was left of her was five pounds of ash in a cardboard box. Bo stood with his daughter in the wet sand and opened the lid. He scattered Shelley's ashes at her favorite place on Earth. The wind carried them away, briefly floating in the air before dispersing into the ocean.

He thought he should say something, but there was nobody there except his daughter to hear him, and he didn't have the words anyway. "Throw your flower now, baby."

With a giggle, Emery tossed the white rose she held into the water.

"Blow kisses." He blew one with her. "Say bye-bye."

"Bye-bye." She waved to the flower as it washed away in the surf.

*Bye, Shelley.*

He was never very good at goodbyes. Bo kissed his daughter. "Let's go home."

She was waving 'bye-bye' to the beach house as he buckled her into the car seat. Pulling the SUV out of the driveway, he didn't glance back.

They had a couple stops to make before they got on an airplane to Chicago. First, he placed an order at the drive-thru window. "A vanilla baby cone with sprinkles, please."

"Anything else?"

"Yeah. I want a cherry vanilla cone." He smiled. "Can you dip it in chocolate?"

"Yes, sir."

"Awesome, thanks."

No doubt Emery would make a mess with that ice cream, but there wasn't a Twistee Treat where they were going. It was one of the few things he would miss here. Bo gave her the cone. He had to change her into warmer clothes for the trip home when they got to Connie's place anyway.

She was waiting for them on the buckling front porch when he pulled up to the curb. Hair up in a pencil bun, wayward strands of white haphazardly framed her face. He'd miss her too. So would Emery. Bo set her down and she ran to the old woman.

"Cici!"

"Look at you." Connie scooped her up. Hugging Emery to her buxom chest, she glanced over at him and smirked. "Covered in sprinkles."

Hands in his pockets, Bo shrugged with a grin and followed them inside. Shelley's place was just as they'd left it, but it felt empty without her.

Connie set Emery down and she made a beeline for the toy box. "How is she?"

"She seems okay." Watching her play, Bo gnawed on his lip. "But it's hard to tell. I don't think she understands Shelley is gone yet, you know?"

"A two-year-old can't be expected to, though."

Bo flicked his gaze from Emery to Connie. He spoke in a hushed tone. "I mean, she hasn't asked for Mommy or anything."

"Oh, I see," she said, nodding. "She will."

"I know."

And he was dreading it. He never wanted to see his daughter sad.

"I shipped Em's things to Chicago like Shelley asked, but she left something here for me to give you." Connie squeezed his hand.

Bo opened the large padded envelope. There were two books inside. He read the title, "*Mama, Do You Love Me?* by Barbara M. Joosse."

"For you to read to Em." She smiled, swiping tears from her eyes.

He hugged the old woman. "You know I will."

It wasn't until they were on the plane, Emery buckled into the seat by the window beside him, hugging her Blabla doll of pink alpaca fleece, that Bo pulled out the other.

A volume of short stories written by Mary Shelley.

With a shake of his head, he read the author's dedication out loud, "The beginning is always today."

He glanced down at his daughter.

She looked up at him.

And she smiled.

# Nine

It was a whopping thirty-four degrees when the plane touched down at Midway. Rain drizzled onto the tarmac. Emery might not have to wait until next winter to catch her first glimpse of snow. While they waited to disembark the aircraft, Bo got her into her coat and tucked his hair inside a wool beanie. Just in case. Without the boys and the leather pants, folks usually passed right by him, but for the welfare of his daughter, tonight he wasn't going to take any chances.

Emery glanced around, wide-eyed, as he carried her through the busy terminal, rolling the carry-on behind him. It had to seem so strange to her. Foreign. This wasn't the land of Twistee Treat and Mickey Mouse. There were no palm trees here. No beaches. Well, that wasn't exactly true. Chicago had Lake Michigan, and it looked like an ocean. Bo chuckled. When they were little, Jesse believed it was.

She was in awe of the moving sidewalk, fascinated by the escalator taking them down to baggage claim. Brendan and Sloan stood waving at the bottom. Catching sight of them, Emery enthusiastically waved back.

Bo kissed her cheek. "Welcome home, darling."

It was a relief to be back. City sounds and smells seeped inside through the glass doors that opened for passengers scurrying to catch shuttle buses and waiting taxis. Breathing easier here, he inhaled deep.

"Hey, man." Sloan bro-hugged him. "I missed you."

"Same, brother. It's so good to be home. You have no idea." He smiled at his daughter, still clutching her Blabla doll. "Emmy, this is your Uncle Sloan and that's your Uncle B."

Emery tipped her head back, sizing up Brendan, then her gaze settled on Sloan. She grinned. "Unkey."

Sloan held her while he and Brendan retrieved their bags. By the time they got to the Mercedes SUV in the parking garage, the voice of Venery was singing "Baby Shark" with his two-year-old.

"Are you recording that, Robert?" Brendan chuckled, loading their luggage into the back. "Would go viral, for sure."

"No, man." Bo laughed too. "And don't call me that."

"I know. Your dad is Robert." With a smirk, Brendan closed the hatch. "C'mon, let's get you and Emery home. Just wait 'til you see what the girls did."

Later that evening, Bo tucked his daughter in her 'big-girl' play-house bed, in her room down the hall from his own. Walls of soft gray. Linens of blush and cream. Chloe, Katie, and Linnea had transformed the space into a comfortable, cozy, and dreamy wonderland while he was gone.

He covered her with a downy-soft comforter, kissed her brow, and lay with her until she fell asleep. Bo tiptoed to the open doorway and watched her for a moment. New room. New home. New city. New people. Shelley died three days ago. They scattered her ashes just this morning. And still, Emery hadn't asked for her mother.

It worried him.

He left the nightlight on.

"She seems to be adjusting well." Monica squeezed his shoulder. They watched Emery, Elliott, and Chandan playing with the dogs in the Kerrigan Nolan family room. The Cubs played on the big-screen TV, but Jesse, with baby Ireland napping on his chest, and his father were the only ones paying any attention to the game. "Emery has a big, beautiful family here, and being with children her own age makes it easier too. She has a loving father who adores her, a nurturing environment, and stability. She's going to be just fine."

"You think so?"

"I do." Monica smiled up at him and tipped her chin in the direction of the kitchen. "And your mom is over the moon with her granddaughter."

"Yeah, she is."

Cynthia and Robert Robertson, Sr. flew in to visit, which surprised him. His father hated to travel, detested flying. In the years since they'd left Chicago to follow his perfectionist of a sister and her brainiac husband to California, Bo almost always went to them. But they were here now to see Emery, so he wasn't complaining.

His mom and Chloe's grandmother, Betsy, had taken the reins in the kitchen. Smelled like Italian. It was one of their typical weekend gatherings, where they all hung around having dinner and maybe a few beers, while the little ones chased each other around the house.

"Robert?"

Bo glanced over to his father, but he was so into the Cubs, either he hadn't heard his wife or he was ignoring her.

"Dad."

"No, honey." His mom held up a tray of food. "I was calling you. Can you take this to the dining room for me?"

"Your husband is Robert," he told her jokingly, but it really did annoy him.

"And so are you." She pushed the tray into his hands. "That's the name we gave you. Says so on your birth certificate."

Why his parents had a thing against nicknames, he'd never understand. His mom went by Cynthia, not Cindy. His sister was Alicia, not Allie, like everyone else called her. But he got saddled with Robert. Robert Robertson—who does that to a kid? His dad, having grown up with the same double moniker, should have known better.

Chloe was passing out slices of spumoni cheesecake for dessert. Bo had just put a heavenly forkful in his mouth, cherries and pistachio reminding him of ice cream runs to Twistee Treat, when his mother tapped him on the shoulder.

"Emery is coming to stay with us in California while you're on tour, isn't she?"

He choked down his cheesecake. "No. I'm not leaving her. I just got her."

"What do you plan to do then, son?"

Taylor's eyes ping-ponged between them.

Bo quietly set his fork down and turned to his father. "I'm taking her with me."

"Honey, you can't bring a baby on a tour bus." His mom shook her head, giving Emery a spoonful of cheesecake.

He lowered his voice. "And she just lost her mother. I can't leave her."

"Your mum has a point, mate." Taylor leaned back in his chair. "Sharing a tour bus with the likes of us is no place for a child."

"See?"

"I'm aware, Tay." Bo rolled his eyes. Did Taylor actually think he was an idiot? "I thought I'd rent a motorhome and hire a driver."

"A caravan, I dig it." Sloan's mouth was full, but that didn't stop him from talking. "Can I ride with you, man?"

"That's actually not a bad idea," Monica said, with a purse of her lips and a nod. "Emery needs the security of her father's presence, especially now."

"Who's going to watch her during sound checks and shows?" Taylor wanted to know.

He failed to mention the obligatory meet and greets, after-parties, and media interviews.

Bo wasn't about to either. "Mom, wanna go on a road trip?"

"For six weeks?" She wiped crumbs of graham cracker crust

off Emery's face. "I can't leave your dad that long…or your sister. She needs me to help her with Ryan and Logan."

*Well, I need you too.*

"Yeah, right. Never mind."

"Robert…" She sighed.

"It's okay, Mom." Bo got up from the table, retrieving his daughter from her grandmother's lap. "And for the love of Christ… never mind."

"Can't you get like a traveling babysitter or something?" Sloan offered. At least his mouth wasn't full of cheesecake this time.

Katie and Chloe exchanged a glance, the kind that makes a man think '*uh-oh*'. Conspiring. Brendan's wife smirked. Rolling her teeth over her bottom lip, Chloe nodded her head and winked.

"What?"

In that innocent way of hers, Katie smiled at him. "Nothing."

Later that evening, after Emery was in bed and his dad went upstairs, Bo and his mom sat in front of the TV. With so much on his mind, he wasn't really watching it. The tour was only three months away, so he had to figure something out soon. He could call an agency, he supposed, but the thought of being in such close quarters with a stranger for six weeks didn't appeal to him. Maybe he'd ask Connie. She was cool.

If it weren't for his needy-ass sister, he could probably convince his mom to come—and Cynthia Robertson was way cooler. But, of course, she picked Allie over him. Bo sensed a reoccurring theme here. Story of his life, right?

"What's that face for?"

"What face?" His gaze was fixed on the TV screen, even though he couldn't say for sure what was on it. *Ozark*, maybe?

She sighed. "I'm your mother and I can tell when something's on your mind, so spill it."

Turning toward her, Bo shook his head. He was too old, and it was too late, to have this conversation. "It's nothing, Ma. Just thinking."

"About?"

"I wish you could come on tour with me and Emmy." He shrugged. "That's all."

"Honey, I wish I could too." His mother held onto his arm with both hands and laid her head on his shoulder. "It'd be a lot of fun hanging with you and the boys. Just like when you were all in high school, practicing in our basement."

"You used to make us grilled cheese sandwiches and tomato soup." He smiled at the memory.

"Well, it got cold down there." She chuckled. "I'd really love to spend more time with you and my beautiful granddaughter."

"You should come then."

"Honey, you know why I can't."

*Not really.*

"Yeah, you said." He audibly exhaled. "Allie needs you."

She lifted her head. "And your father."

*What the hell for? To do his laundry? He's a grown-ass man.* Pursing his lips, Bo held his tongue.

"Don't be like that."

"Be like what?"

"You're making me feel guilty."

"You feel guilty?" Bo snickered. "Whatever for? Putting Allie before me."

"Sweetie, you know that isn't true," she said, combing her fingers through his hair.

"No?" His long-buried resentment roused, Bo couldn't stop himself. "You just packed up and left *me* to move to California for *her*."

"Your sister needed me." Her hand slipped to rest on his shoulder. "You didn't."

"How do you know I didn't?"

"Because you're just like me." She smiled. "Alicia not so much. Ryan and Logan were born. You were on the road with the boys more than you were home. You didn't need me."

"I need you now."

His mother took his hand in both of hers and squeezed. "Let Emery come to California."

"I love you, Mom." Bo kissed her cheek. "You understand why I can't."

Biting her lip, she nodded.

"I'm her dad. She needs *me*."

*And I need her.*

# Ten

Sitting beneath the shade of the big maple tree on the campus common, its brand-new leaves rustling in the mild breeze, she decided of all the months in the year, May had to be her favorite. That's when the peonies and tulips bloomed, the city's festival season started, and this dreadful semester would finally end. The program's required fieldwork hours, on top of a heavy load of classes, were kicking her ass.

Ava flipped the pages of her Child Development textbook to chapter twenty-one, scanning the passages she'd highlighted in yellow, while she sipped on her bottled water and dipped apple slices into organic peanut butter. It certainly wasn't the most appealing lunch option, but it was healthy. She wasn't vegan, or vegetarian, or anything like that, but she tried to eat clean whenever she could.

After reading the same paragraph fifteen times, the words began blurring together. Ava scraped up the remaining peanut butter with her last slice of apple and closed the book. Finals were next week and her brain had officially turned into mush. She was done with this semester and needed it to be over.

"I've been looking for you."

Licking peanut butter from her thumb, Ava glanced up. "Hey, Katie."

Dropping her backpack, the pretty blonde sat herself on the ground beside her. They'd met in algebra class her sophomore year.

Katie, a freshman, was dating Cameron Mayhew at the time. Ava briefly dated Cameron's teammate, and that's when they really became friends.

Not the super close BFF kind. They didn't know each other's secrets or hang out and go to parties together or anything like that. Besides, Katie was married and had a baby now. Ava babysat for her sometimes.

"Thought I'd find you in the food court or the library."

"It's too nice out to stay inside today." She leaned back against the maple tree. "What's up? Need me to watch Declan?"

"Nope." Smiling, Katie stretched out on her side with her elbow planted in the grass, holding her head up with her hand.

"Chloe?" She'd sat for her, too, on occasion.

"No." Katie giggled. "But I was wondering what your plans are for summer break. You didn't register for any classes, did you?"

"Hell, no." Ava stretched her arms up over her head. "I am free of this place until September."

"Good." She grinned. "That's good."

"Why are you asking?"

"I don't have time to explain now." Katie sat up, reaching for her backpack. "I've got class in ten minutes. Meet me at Beanie's later? Say three o'clock?"

"Uhh…okay."

"Great! I'll tell you everything then." Katie pulled her backpack on, glancing over her shoulder. "Trust me. You're going to be so excited."

Her curiosity piqued, and a class of her own to get to, Ava gathered up her things. She listened to the professor's final lecture on early literacy in the classroom while doodling on her notepad. An education major, she was one year, seven courses, and six hundred thirty student-teaching hours away from obtaining her degree. After graduation, she'd teach at an elementary school. First grade. Children are so eager to learn at that age. Unlike so many of her peers, at twenty-one years old, she had her future all figured out.

Okay, maybe not all of it, but Ava knew what her purpose

was, what she was capable of, and what she wasn't. And she'd always wanted to be a teacher. Growing up, people classified her as nerdy. Nose always buried in a book. Straight As. Honor roll in high school. Dean's list in college. Uncoordinated, she sucked at every sport she tried to play. She wasn't artistic or creatively gifted, unless finger-painting with a six-year-old counted, but she excelled academically and thrived in a classroom.

Her older brother played Minor League baseball.

Her sister danced.

*God, I'm boring.*

She wasn't, though. Not really. It was just the current state of her life was lacking anything that resembled fun. Ava blamed her demanding course load, but the truth of the matter was she could've made the time for extracurricular activities. She just didn't.

"Your final exam will be in two parts," the professor droned from the lectern. "One hundred questions—multiple choice—and a minimum five-hundred-word essay…"

*Welcome to hell week.*

Tossing the pen in her bag, she closed her notebook. Sunlight poured into the vestibule, warm spring air bathed her skin as she stepped outside. Ava headed toward the old, off-campus row house she shared with four other students. And then she remembered she was supposed to meet Katie at Beanie's.

She turned around and walked in the direction of First Avenue.

Fifteen minutes early, Katie wasn't there yet when Ava arrived. Leo, rocking bleach-blonde dreads today, played barista behind the counter. More than familiar with Beanie's Coffee Roasters, being she infused herself with caffeine here often enough, she and the baker were well-acquainted. He made these buttery and delicious banana-nut muffins that were to die for.

"Ava, *ma chérie.*" He leaned across the counter, speaking in that flamboyant way of his, and kissed her right on the lips. Shame he was gay, because he was hella gorgeous, even if he did look better in pink lip gloss than she did. And shredded. And judging by his skintight jeans, pretty impressive beneath that zipper. "What can Leo make for you, *bébé?*"

"Caffè misto, please."

He smirked. "Almond milk and one pump of lavender?"

*Isn't that what I always get?*

"You know it."

"And a muffin?" Leo waggled his perfectly arched brows. "They're fresh and warm in the back."

"Oh, God, yes." *Good fucking thing I only ate an apple for lunch.* "When I get fat, Leo, it's gonna be all your fault."

"*Bébé*, you're perfect any way you are." He kissed both of her cheeks. "For here?"

"Yeah, I'm meeting Katie."

She'd already scarfed down four hundred and fifty calories of warm deliciousness when Katie slid into the seat across from her with a large iced latte. Couldn't tell by looking at her, she had an eight-month-old baby. "Where's Dec?"

"Bren had a meeting out of the office. They're trying to buy a warehouse so they can turn it into a mall or something. My aunt's watching him today." She spooned whipped cream into her mouth with her straw. "He's upstairs."

"Oh, I see." She didn't really. "So…"

"So." Katie grinned. "First off, I've got to say I thought of you right away."

"Thought of me for what?"

"I think I have the perfect opportunity for you. An adventure." She added a nod to go with her grin. "Would you like to travel? See the country?"

"Uh, maybe."

Katie grabbed her hand from across the table. "With Venery."

"Huh?"

"With their drummer, actually." She bit her lip. "He needs a babysitter."

Ava giggled. "Isn't he old enough to take care of himself?"

"For his daughter, Emery. She's two." Katie snorted,

play-swatting her on the hand. "They're going on tour for six weeks this summer. Bo needs someone to stay with her during shows."

She was trying to remember who the drummer was. Ava knew Venery, of course. Knew they all lived on Katie's street. She'd met Taylor once when she babysat for Chloe. But she didn't know their music. They were a metal band and she was more of a Harry Styles kind of girl. She made a mental note to google as soon she got home.

*God, Ava, you're boring and lame.*

"So, the adventure is babysitting?"

"On tour with a rock band."

She'd have to be out of her mind to even consider it. "Uh, I don't know."

And even crazier not to.

"I have a marvelous idea!" Katie clapped her hands together. "Come over next weekend after finals. We'll have a barbecue—Bren knows how to grill a steak, let me tell you. Meet Bo, Emery, and the boys. See how you vibe. No pressure. Then you can make a decision. Sound good?"

*It sounds like a potentially bad decision in the making.*

"Yeah, okay, I guess."

"Yay!" Katie leaned across the table and hugged her.

"Okay to the barbecue," she clarified. "I didn't say yes yet."

"You will."

*Maybe.*

A quick search on Google told Ava everything she needed to know. More than she ever wanted to know. *TMZ* had been quite thorough in their reporting of Venery's exploits throughout their career. Hanging around with them would be an adventure, all right, if their account was indeed accurate. She had her doubts about that, but then photos don't lie, do they?

*C'mon, Ava. That rag in the grocery store had a photo of a human-pig hybrid baby on the front page. Of course they can.*

Sex parties.

A paternity suit.

Taylor's scandalous wedding.

Models, groupies, and drugged-out starlets.

More sex parties.

Bo Robertson was packing a helluva lot more than Leo inside his tight leather pants. Except in the photo the only thing he wore was his birthday suit—and a piercing on the end of his dick. Damn, he was beautiful too. Angelic face. Body, sinewy and lean. And, God, that hair. Ava didn't realize how sexy long hair was on a man until she saw it on him.

This was so not a good idea.

She should turn her ass back around right now.

*Chill, it's a backyard barbecue. That's all.*

Ava punched in the code to the Park Place gate, wondering which house belonged to him. Then she took a deep breath and knocked on Katie's front door.

But it wasn't Katie who opened it.

The man had dark hair that went just past his shoulders, a pair of crystal-blue eyes, and a wedding ring. She didn't know who he was. He wasn't one of the dudes from Venery, but he sure was pretty.

"Are you Ava?" He extended his hand.

She shook it. "Yeah, I'm a friend of Katie's."

"I know." He chuckled. "I'm Brendan's cousin, Kyan. Well, Katie's too. C'mon in."

Kyan stepped back to let her pass and she stepped inside.

"We've been waiting on you."

Ava glanced up at him. He was tall. Not as tall as Katie's husband, but still. "Am I late?"

She was never late.

"No. Relax." He chuckled again, patting her shoulder. "Katie's upstairs with the baby, but she'll be down in a minute. C'mon, we're all out back. I'll introduce you to everyone."

"Okay."

"Katie told us you're an ed major. What are you going to teach?"

"I am." This man was genuinely kind. Ava could tell Kyan was trying to make her feel comfortable. She cleared her throat. "Elementary school."

"That's awesome. Teaching is a noble profession." Kyan paused at the family room. Through the French doors to the backyard, Ava could see what looked to be a lot of people. "You don't look like a teacher."

"Oh, well, trust me, when my hair is up and my glasses are on, I do."

"Doubt that'd make a difference." He winked. "I never had a teacher as pretty as you."

Ava just knew she was blushing like an idiot. Her cheeks were burning.

"You nervous?"

"Maybe a little bit."

"Don't be." Kyan's arm came around her shoulders. "I've known them my entire life. They're just people. You ready?"

Pursing her lips, she nodded. "Yeah, I'm good."

"Okay."

Cursing herself for wearing it down, Ava smoothed her long, blonde hair over her shoulder.

Kyan opened the door. "Ava's here."

Even more beautiful than his photo, he smiled at her from across the patio. The little girl scrambled from his lap and ran toward her.

Ava bent down to catch her.

And the little girl flew into her arms.

"Mommy."

# Eleven

B o held Emery up to the glass, and they waved at the plane making its ascent into the clouds until it disappeared and was gone. "Bye, Grandma. Bye, Grandpa. See you again soon."

"Bye-bye."

Seemed like they were always saying goodbye. It was depressing. Where were all the hellos?

"C'mon, darling." He carried her away from the window. "Want to go play?"

"Pay."

Bo chuckled. *Close enough.*

After almost two months of practice, he had this car seat thing down to a science now. Bo buckled Emery in, gave her a sippy cup of water and some Cheerios for the ride home, and drove out of the parking garage. He liked the X5 he'd rented down in Florida, so he bought one here. M Series. Shiny. Black. Leather.

Traffic was light on the expressway for a Saturday. The drive back home was quick, but by the time Bo pulled into his detached garage, Emery was fast asleep. He carried her into the house, carefully laying her down on the sofa. She could finish her nap right here while he threw something together for dinner.

As he peered inside the refrigerator, thinking he just might order a pizza instead, there was a soft knock at the door. "Bo?"

"In here, Katie." The corner of his mouth instantly rose. Bo pulled his head out of the fridge to see her tiptoe past his sleeping daughter into the kitchen. She leaned over the island, plunking her elbows down on the polished wood top, pert breasts peeking out of her shirt. "How's my favorite coffee girl?"

"Peachy." Katie smirked.

"Oh, yeah?" Bo leaned onto the island across from her. "Can I feel your fuzz?"

Moving in closer, she smacked a kiss to his lips and giggled. "Your parents get off okay?"

"Yeah," he answered with a sigh.

"I take it your mom didn't change her mind."

"Nope."

Bo's mother would not be going on tour with him. He even tried guilt-tripping her, but there was no convincing her otherwise. The band had a date at the Hollywood Bowl, so he and Emery would get to see her there at least.

"I think I have the perfect solution for you." She winked, straightening.

"Do you now?" He couldn't help but notice the outline of her nipples through the fabric of her shirt. "And what's that?"

"A babysitter, and I happen to know someone." Katie caught him looking at her chest and rolled her eyes with a grin. "A friend of mine from school. She watches Dec for me sometimes. Chloe uses her too."

Bo snickered. "Do you really think that's a good idea?"

"What do you mean? I think it's brilliant, actually."

"You want to put your friend in an itty-bitty motorhome with me for six weeks?" Bo tilted his head to the side with a wink.

She giggled. "Can't behave yourself that long?"

"Do I ever?" He waggled his brows. "Don't answer that."

Katie shrugged with a smirk. "I'm sure you'll have plenty of fangirls and boys to misbehave with."

"And thank fuck for that." His dick twitched at the thought. "I'm getting mighty tired of my hand. This parenting thing has put a damper on my sex life, you know?"

"Babe, if you ever need a night out with the boys, to go to the club or something, just come to me." Katie squeezed his shoulder. "I'd be more than happy to have Emmy."

"Leaving her just doesn't feel right to me."

"Because it's so new." Her neck craned to gaze up at him. "But trust me, every parent needs time for themselves now and then—even if it's only a few hours. And you'll be a better dad for it."

"Maybe."

Katie pulled out her phone. "So, Ava is perfect. She's going into her senior year, studying to become a teacher. I already talked to her."

"And she's willing to go on tour with me?"

"She's willing to consider it." Handing him the phone, she smiled. "That's Ava."

Bo looked at the Facebook profile of Ava Liane Harris. Twenty-one. Aries. College student. Book lover. She had an older brother and a younger sister. Light blonde hair and big blue eyes behind a pair of tortoise shell frames.

*Fucking gorgeous.*

"Definitely a bad idea." He gave Katie her phone back. "But then I am very good at being very bad—not to mention making bad decisions."

She swatted his arm. "Oh, shut up. You'll meet her then?"

*I shouldn't.* "Yeah, I'll meet her."

"Yay!" Katie clapped her hands together. She seemed to do that whenever she got excited, which made him wonder. "You, Emmy, and the boys can meet her next Saturday. I invited her over for a barbecue."

"Sounds like a plan, coffee girl." He peered down Katie's shirt. She didn't have a bra on.

"Try and behave, will you?" She pinched his nipple. "I'd hate for you to scare her off before she has the chance to really know you."

*Let's hope she's not skittish then.*

"Can't promise you that, Katie-Kate." He winked. "But I'll try."

"Ava's here."

She appeared like an angel. Standing there with Kyan, framed by the French doors, she looked even more beautiful than she did in her photos on Facebook. Long blonde hair swept over her shoulder, down past her breast. Average height, he supposed. Slender, but not too skinny. Ava glanced at him with her blue Bambi eyes. He could drown in those eyes of hers. Bo knew right then and there he was fucked.

Emery slid off his lap. With her hands waving in the air, pigtails flying, she scampered to Ava as quickly as her little legs would take her.

"Mommy."

Bo knew this moment would come.

"No, baby. This is Ava." Stroking her cheek, he softly said, "Mommy died."

Emery didn't know what that word meant, or what death was, but Monica advised him to always tell her the truth regardless. To use the real words, even if they were difficult for him. Children as young as his daughter were easily confused, so he had to be clear. Shelley was dead and she wasn't coming back.

"I'm Bo." Ava stood up with his baby in her arms. "Sorry about that."

"I know." She extended her hand. "Ava."

Her grip was firm, her skin soft and warm. Holding onto her hand longer than was customary for a simple greeting, Bo brought it his lips. He kissed the back of her hand and smiled. "I know."

She let go, pink infusing her cheeks. Bo decided he liked seeing her that way. He made a mental note to make her blush, and to do it often.

Katie came out of the house with Brendan carrying their son right behind her. "Well, I see you two have met. Hey, sunshine. Come with Auntie Katie." She took Emery from her friend and winked at him. "We've got some fun stuff to keep the little ones occupied while Brendan and Ky do their thing on the grill. Can you introduce Ava to everyone for me?"

"I can." Bo linked her arm with his. "Pay attention now. There's a lot of us and it can get confusing." He tipped his chin to the man beside her. "This pretty boy is Kyan Byrne."

"I've already had the pleasure, drummer boy." Kyan smirked.

*Charming little shit.*

"Ky's the baby of the bunch, cousin of that Neanderthal over there—you know Brendan, right?"

He could tell Ava was biting her lip to contain a grin. "I do."

"And Jesse?"

"Yes."

"He's his other cousin. Ky has a brother too." Bo asked, "Where's Dillon, man?"

"Milwaukee. Cubs are playing the Brewers. He and Kodiak had tickets for the game."

"Well, all right." Leading her away from the French doors, Bo leaned into her ear and explained, "Kodiak is Ky's brother-in-law and one of my closest friends."

Her intoxicating scent invaded his senses. Ava smelled like a decadent dessert just waiting to be devoured. Blackcurrants and raspberries mingled with jasmine petals, moss, and sandalwood. God, he'd love to eat her up.

*Cannot play with the babysitter.*

*TMZ* would have a fucking field day with that.

Bo was attracted to her, and that was rather inconvenient. Not one to hold back, he was an openly affectionate and physically demonstrative person. How the fuck was he going manage six weeks in a rolling sardine can with this girl? He breathed her in deep.

This was a bad idea.

A very bad idea.

*She might not say yes.*

He prayed she wouldn't say no.

"You into baseball?"

"Not really." Ava tilted her head to look at him. "I should be, I guess. My brother, Perry, pitches for the Clearwater Threshers."

"You don't have to love baseball." Bo squeezed on her arm. "But I bet you're still his biggest fan, am I right?"

"Of course."

Peals of laughter rang out from toddlers romping on the grass with the girls. Jesse and his four bandmates eyed him from their spot on the other side of the patio, Taylor's smirk telling him he was enjoying this. The bastard knew him far too well.

"C'mon, I'll introduce you to the rest of the boys." He held onto her as they walked across the bricks. "Ava, this is Matt—he's rhythm guitar, Kit plays bass, and Sloan is the voice. You know Tay and Jess."

"Hello."

The boys were on their best behavior, fussing over her, making conversation. Jesse jumped up and got her a drink. Taylor leaned into him. "Good luck, mate."

"With what?"

Taylor sat back, the smirk never leaving his face, and he winked.

"So, are you coming on tour with us, Ava?" Sloan all but batted his eyelashes at her.

Bo shot him a look.

"Maybe." She took a sip of her drink and turned toward him. "Bo and I still have to talk about it."

"I hope you do." His lips quirked up into a devious grin. "You should know Bo snores and he hogs the bathroom…"

"Shut it, Sloan."

"…but he is potty-trained. Never misses the bowl and he always puts the seat back down after he's finished."

Taylor sniggered.

Ava let out a cute, little giggle.

"Fucker."

"And he swears a lot," Kit added.

"We all swear a lot, asshole." Matt elbowed Kit in the ribs and threw Ava one of his boyish grins. "Hope you're not easily offended."

"Just watch your mouth around the baby or I get the soap out."

Holding his hand over his heart, Matt nodded. "Yes, ma'am."

"I think they like you." Bo draped his arm around her shoulders.

*I like you.*

"So, what do you think, Avie?"

Her tongue swept across her full, pouty lip.

*Say yes.*

"I think we can talk about it and see."

Bo was okay with that.

She didn't say no.

# Twelve

Ava carefully applied a second coat of mascara. What the fuck was she doing? This wasn't a date. It was just dinner. A business dinner. Nothing more and nothing less. She wasn't delusional.

Bo insisted on taking her out so they could talk about the tour. Ava could list a plethora of reasons why she should politely decline. Not that she'd ever say them out loud.

They were the very reasons she was dying to say yes.

She left her hair down, pulling some of it back loosely at the crown, flaxen strands framing her heart-shaped face. It was flattering enough. Ava didn't want to look like she was trying too hard. Actually, she wanted it to seem as though she hadn't tried at all.

"Ugh, you're being ridiculous." She tossed the brush down and swiped on some lip gloss just as the doorbell rang.

Ava hurried down the stairs, grabbing her purse and a sweater on the way. It was almost June, but it could still get chilly at night. He looked up and smiled, her stomach doing this crazy somersault thing, the second she opened it.

Bo Robertson was beautiful. There was no better word to describe him.

He stood there looking like an angel out of a Renaissance painting. Expressive eyes of the deepest indigo. Straight nose. A jawline so chiseled it could cut cake. Luscious, full lips that Ava imagined were capable of all sorts of delicious things. But it was that wicked smile of his making her knees weak.

"Hi."

"Hi." Pulling her in for a hug, Bo kissed her on the cheek. "You're so pretty."

She wasn't expecting that and she didn't know what to make of it. Ava glanced away from him, smoothing the simple navy-blue dress she wore down her thighs. "Thank you."

"C'mon." He took her hand, leading her to a black BMW parked at the curb. "We've got reservations at Geja's. Do you like fondue?"

"I don't know." They stood together at the passenger door. "I've never had fondue."

Bo opened the door for her. "You're going to love it."

"And here I was thinking we'd go for a burger and a beer," Ava mumbled to herself, buckling her seatbelt.

"Where's the fun in that?" He slid into the seat beside her. "We can get a burger anytime." Bo turned his head, looking at her intently with those eyes of his, a mischievous gleam to them, and that devilish smirk.

Returning his gaze, Ava breathed in a lungful of new car, leather, and him. Unable to formulate a witty response, she just smiled instead.

The place was on the fancy side. Dark, with red uplighting, it had a romantic, intimate vibe. They were brought to a candlelit booth set inside a draped alcove. An orange pot sat on a stand at the end of the table. Bottles of wine lined the walls.

"Translated from French, fondue means to melt. It's an experience." He settled into his seat across from her. "It's the last form of communal cooking, you know."

"I didn't know that." Ava unfolded the linen napkin, placing it on her lap. "Isn't it Swiss?"

"The cheese is, yes." Bo chuckled, leaning inward. "We're going to be sharing a very small space for six weeks. That's a lot of togetherness. We have to be comfortable with each other, you know? So, you and I are going to create and share a delicious meal here together."

"*If* I agree to do it," she reminded him.

"Yeah, well, that's the other reason we're here." He laid that endearing smile on her again. "So I can convince you. I don't want an outsider, some stranger from an agency. I want someone I know and trust. Katie and Chloe trust you, so I trust you."

The waiter stood beside their table.

"Please tell me you eat meat."

Ava held a finger to her lips and chuckled. "Yes."

"Seafood?"

"Uh-huh."

"Cool." Bo grinned.

He was really very sweet. And smart. Much smarter than she'd initially given him credit for. Ava had the feeling there was a lot more to this man than what she'd gleaned from Google.

"Will you be having the wine pairings with your dinner, Mr. Robertson?"

"Absolutely," Bo said to the waiter.

She was reminded she was sitting here with the drummer of a famous rock band. "He knows who you are."

"Nah, I don't think so." Bo shook his head. "I could be wrong, but he looks more like a Michael Bublé fan, than one of ours."

"But he knew your name."

"Ava, baby." He reached for her hand from across the table. "My name's on the reservation."

*Duh.*

Bo made her laugh. "You're funny too."

"I'm good for that." He squeezed her hand. It felt rather nice. "I try to keep a low profile at home. We all do. But you can count on the paps getting photos of you, me, and Emmy together at some point. They'll draw their own conclusions and write their own headlines. Are you prepared for that?"

"I hadn't really thought about it."

"Comes with the gig, beautiful." He sat back and let go. "We have security, of course, and I'll protect you from that as much as I can, but they're relentless vultures."

The waiter brought them a basket of assorted breads, vegetables, and fruits, all of it cut into chunks. He lit the flame beneath the orange pot and poured them each a glass of prosecco, leaving behind the bottle.

Bo picked up his glass. "To six weeks of togetherness."

"Maybe." Ava clinked her glass with his. "Cheers."

"Cheers." He winked.

Clearing her throat, she picked up a long fondue fork. "How together?"

"What do you mean?"

"I've never even seen the inside of a motorhome." She pursed her lips. "Where would we all sleep?"

"Oh." He chuckled, spearing a chunk of pretzel bread with his fork. "You'll have your own bedroom—there's two."

"What about the driver?"

"There's a bunk in the overhead cab for him."

"You've got it all figured out, don't you?"

"Class A all the way, baby." Bo nodded, dipping his bread into melted Swiss Gruyere cheese. "Nothing but the best for my girls. Full kitchen, LED TVs, washer and dryer. Helluva lot better than the bus."

*My girls.*

"What's it like?" Ava stabbed at a piece of apple.

"What? Being on the road? Touring?"

"Yeah, I guess. All of it."

He popped the dripping cheesy morsel in his mouth and chewed. "I'm not gonna lie. It isn't as glamorous or exciting as you might think. It's grueling. Thirty gigs in forty-two days. Drive, set-up, sound check, show, backstage meet and greet, after-party, tear it down. Drive. Do it again."

"You're doing a fantastic job of convincing me." She dipped her apple and took a bite. "Oh, God, this is good."

"We'll have some downtime for fun stuff." Bo wrapped his hand around hers, tipping her remaining apple into his mouth. "That is good."

"And you're bad." Ava sniggered.

"You've googled me, haven't you?" He winked. "Look, my daughter just lost her mother. I need to be there for her, and I need you to be there when I can't."

"I'm sorry about your wife."

The smile slipped from his face. "Shelley and I weren't married. She wasn't even my girlfriend. Our relationship was, um…complicated. I'll tell you about it sometime."

"I just assumed." She bit her lip. "I shouldn't have."

"It's okay." His smile returned. "I've never been married. I've never had a serious girlfriend—or boyfriend. My favorite food is *not* sushi. How about you?"

Her face broke into a grin. "I've never been married. I've had a few boyfriends. And I detest sushi."

"Do you have one now?"

"A boyfriend?" Shaking her head, Ava skewered a piece of bread and dunked it in the cheese. "No."

"C'mere." Bo patted the space beside him.

The waiter stood there with a platter.

Ava got up and sat next to Bo. He leaned into her ear. "We're gonna do this together."

Fresh glasses. The bottle of prosecco was replaced with a bottle of cabernet. They cooked Australian lobster tails, white shrimp, scallops, and beef tenderloin together in their orange communal pot. Feeding each other bites. Laughing. Sampling the variety of dipping sauces.

Ava liked him. He was easy to be with. Easy to look at. Six weeks on the road with him wouldn't be a terrible thing. And Emery was the sweetest little girl. She even called her Mommy. So why was she hesitating?

Because she liked him. A lot could happen in six weeks.

*Like what? You could fall in love and live happily ever after with a rock star? Now you're being delusional, Ava.*

Shit like that only happened in romance novels.

This was real life. Her life. She was just the babysitter, nothing more. If she remembered that, and kept her head on straight, she'd be okay. This experience could be an epic adventure, though.

They roasted marshmallows together for dessert. Bo held his hand over hers, turning the skewer over the open flame until the confection turned a golden brown. He dipped it in the chocolate fondue. She rolled it in finely crushed graham crackers.

"Have I convinced you yet, Avie?"

"I don't know." She couldn't help but smile.

He fed her a s'more. "Say yes."

"Do you really snore?"

"Is that a dealbreaker?"

She swiped her tongue across her lip. "No."

"I snore like a motherfucking freight train."

She grinned. "And you hog the bathroom."

"I'll let you go first." He wiped chocolate from her lip with his finger. Licking it from his skin, he dropped his forehead to hers and whispered, "Say yes."

How could she say no?

"Yes."

# Thirteen

Today was going to be a fanfuckingtastic day.

His blood pumping, sweat pouring down his bare chest, Bo ran through his warm-up on the kit. He was always super-charged with energy before a show—even more so when Venery was playing the hometown crowd. And their annual gig at the summer street festival in Coventry Park was tonight.

He and Taylor pared down the setlist to some of their most popular songs, a couple covers, and a few of the new tunes off their soon-to-be-released album. It would be the first time they were performed live, and the first time anyone heard them. So, in effect, tonight's show was a preview of their new music, as well as a kick-off to the start of next month's tour. Ava would get a glimpse into his world and everything she'd signed up for.

She was upstairs with Emery, getting her ready to take her out to the festival with Katie and the girls. Bo suggested they spend some time together before the tour. Ava agreed it was a good idea. They would make a day of it, while he and the boys got ready for the show.

White flashed by in his peripheral vision. Without missing a beat, Bo glanced up from his kit, the corners of his mouth ticking up into a grin. Lovely Ava stood in the corner holding Emery, who was bouncing in her arms. Blonde hair in a messy pile on top of her head. White tank dress. Purple Chucks.

"Shouldn't you be saving all that..." She twirled her hand in the air. "...for later."

Setting the sticks down, he picked up a towel to wipe the sweat from his skin. "Gotta warm up, Avie."

"That was warming up?"

"Yeah." Bo got out from behind the kit and went over to them.

"Daddy."

"Hey, sunshine. Aren't you pretty?" Emery threw her arms around his neck. He kissed the top of her head. "Daddy's all sweaty, baby."

Ava tittered. "I don't think she minds."

"Hmm, and what about you, beautiful?" Bo leaned in closer, kissing her cheek. "Do you mind?"

He smiled, hearing her breath catch, watching her skin flush.

"I, uh, just came down to let you know we're going to meet up with Katie and everybody now." She hiked Emery higher on her hip.

"You two have fun." Bo ruffled his daughter's hair. "I'll see you at the show."

Wiping more sweat from his chest, he watched Ava retreat up the stairs. The things he imagined doing with this girl. Why did she affect him so much? How the hell was he going to survive six weeks with her? Licking his lips, Bo reminded himself he had to behave. And the tour hadn't even started yet.

The bus was parked behind the commissary tent. It's not like they really needed it here, Coventry Park was in their backyard after all. Taylor insisted they needed a place to escape to, and while over-zealous fans and the stealthy paparazzi followed the bus after the gig was over, they'd sneak into the town car that waited to take them back to their houses behind the locked gate on Park Place.

Bo tipped the bottle back, emptying the beer down his throat. The rigger had been eyeing him all afternoon and he needed to take the edge off. He canted his chin in the direction of the bus. Dude followed him.

Without saying a word, the rigger unzipped Bo's jeans and pulled his cock out. Already hard, he hissed at the contact of someone besides himself touching his flesh. He needed this. He needed the cum sucked out of his dick and he needed to get the girl out of his head.

"Want your mouth fucked?"

"I wanna drink your cum."

"Yeah?" He shoved his fingers in the man's mouth. "Get 'em nice and wet for me."

If the dude sucked cock like he was sucking on his fingers, this wouldn't take long at all.

Bo lowered his pants to his thighs as the rigger lowered his face to his dick. A groan escaped at the first pull of the man's mouth. Ava came to his mind. He could picture her on her knees for him, long blonde hair fisted in his hand. He could hear her gasping, choking on his length. He could smell her. Raspberries and jasmine petals.

*Fuck.*

Pushing two fingers inside his ass, Bo fucked the rigger's face. He opened his eyes, but it was still Ava that he saw. Drinking him in with her big Bambi eyes. Mascara staining her cheeks. So fucking beautiful.

This wasn't working.

He squeezed his eyes shut, frantically rubbing at the sweet spot inside him. *Just. Feels. So. Fucking. Good.* Bo railed the man's mouth until he erupted inside it. Then after, relieved it was finished, he fell back against the sofa. His dick, coated with cum and saliva, bobbed between his thighs. And the door to the bus squeaked open.

"Fucking Christ, man." Sloan leaned against the banquette. "You know there's no fucking on the bus."

The rigger wiped his mouth off with the back of his hand.

"Wasn't fucking." Bo snickered, looking for a towel. "Got my dick sucked."

"Whatever."

Bo tipped his chin toward the dude, dismissing him. "Thanks, man."

Sloan watched the rigger get off the bus without a backward glance and tossed him a towel. "Clean yourself up, asshole. The girls are here."

"Give me ten minutes."

Ava was in the commissary tent, cutting up fruit for Emery, when Bo walked in after a quick shower on the bus. Katie, Chloe, and Linnea sat at the round table with her, baby strollers at their sides, forming a circle. It struck him how out of place a kiddie table seemed here.

CJ and Taylor immediately flanked him, their manager draping his arm around his neck. "Glad you got it all worked out," he said, flicking his chin toward Ava and his daughter. "Now, don't fuck it up."

"What are you saying, man?"

"Do I have to spell it out for you?"

*Not really.*

"Introduce me to the babysitter."

"Why?"

Taylor leaned into his ear. "He's been bloody eye-fucking her for the past twenty minutes."

"Relax, I just want to meet her." CJ smirked.

"Yeah, well, you just keep that skinny, little dick in your pants, Curtis." Bo shrugged out of his arm. "She's mine...she's my babysitter."

"Uh-huh." Taylor snickered.

"Shut up, Tay." Bo warned him, "Don't even start."

Emery looked up from her banana. He scooped her out of her seat in the stroller, peppering her face with kisses, and glanced down to catch Ava staring at his crotch. "What?"

She swallowed. "Nothing."

"Ava, baby." He tipped his head behind him. "I wanted you to meet CJ. He's our manager, but don't worry, he won't be touring with us."

"I just might this time." CJ took her hand and kissed it. "Pleasure to meet you, Ava."

"Asshole," Bo muttered to himself. He returned Emery to the stroller and walked over to Chloe, kissing her on the lips. "Hey, Red. How's my girl?"

"She's my girl." Taylor winked.

Chloe giggled, Ireland suckling at her breast. "I'm good, babe. Tired, but good."

Bo patted the baby's downy-soft hair. "Good."

"Ready for tonight?"

"You know me. I'm always ready." He grinned, and turning to Katie, Bo kissed her cheek. "You're killing me, coffee girl."

"What'd I do?"

He raised his brow and whispered in her ear, "Sent me an angel."

"Ohh." She nodded with a wink. "Behave, Bo-Bo."

"But it's so hard, Katie-Kate." He winked back.

"Goofball." She snickered with a shake of her head.

No one ever took him too seriously, but this time he meant it. Ava was going to be the death of him. He glanced over at CJ, making small talk with *his* angel. Undressing her with his eyes. Touching her arm. Bo knew his moves. It was taking every ounce of restraint he possessed to keep from turning around and punching him in the face.

*You just got a blowjob, man. Ava's not your angel. She's here for Emmy.*

"Baby girl." Wrapping his arms around Linnea, Bo held her tight. They rocked from side to side. "Where's my kiss?"

She pecked his cheek and laid her head on his shoulder.

"You okay?"

Linnea glanced up at him and smiled. She looked pale. "Yeah, just tired."

"Ky needs to take better care of you." He tucked a strand of hair behind her ear and kissed the tip of her nose. "I don't wanna have to kick his ass. Where is he?"

"He was with Bren and Jesse a few minutes ago."

Bo surveyed the tent. Matt, Kit, and Sloan were grabbing plates at the buffet. The crew milled about. And the Byrne cousins stood sentry at the entrance like they owned the place, which they kind of did, considering their company sponsored Venery's appearance at the festival.

Dillon and Kodiak arrived. High-fives and bro-hugs all around, then they headed inside the tent. "Looks like the gang's all here. Must be chow time."

"Kelly's not here yet," Katie chimed in. "She's bringing my brother."

*Yippee.*

Kyan kissed his wife and stood behind her chair.

Jesse and Taylor took their place with Chloe.

Brendan sat Katie on his lap.

Nudging CJ out of his way, Bo rested one hand on Ava's shoulder, stroking his daughter's hair with the other. She craned her head to look up at him with those beguiling Bambi eyes and smiled. And for one brief moment he forgot she didn't really belong to him. He liked how that felt.

"I'm starving." Dillon rubbed his hands together. Dude was always fucking hungry. "Let's eat."

Bo leaned over, his bare chest brushing up against Ava's shoulder. "I'll fix you and Emmy a plate. Be right back."

"Oh, okay. Thanks."

He stood behind Dillon in the buffet line. Kodiak stood behind him. Brendan, who led the pack, took his sweet-ass time filling plates for himself and Katie, holding the rest of them up.

"C'mon, Bren." Dillon tapped a finger on his Rolex. "I got places to go."

"You're not staying for the show?"

"Yeah, I'll be here for some of it." He winked. "I gotta bounce early, though. Hot date with a legal secretary downtown. Or is she a paralegal? I don't remember. Doesn't matter."

Bo rolled his eyes. "Sounds exciting."

"You've got a hot babysitter." Kodiak tugged on the ends of his hair. "We should go to the club after the show."

"Suck my dick, man."

Kodiak smirked. "I already have."

"Yeah, and that blowjob almost had me writing my vows."

"Aww, I love you, stud muffin. Where's my kiss?" He puckered his lips.

Bo turned around, and grabbing Kodiak by the hair, pulled his mouth to meet his. He slipped his tongue inside, pulling hard on the long chocolate waves in his fingers. Kodiak asked for it, didn't he?

"There's your kiss. Now, fuck you."

"Are they always like that?" Ava asked Katie from the table beside them.

Chloe giggled.

"You've got so much to learn." Linnea leaned past her husband. "Let me explain."

Bo looked at Kodiak, and Kodiak looked at him. He slung his arm around his shoulder, both of them laughing their asses off.

*Who has more fun than us?*

They chuckled all the way through dinner.

Bo sat behind his kit on the darkened stage, straining to find Ava and Emery in the crowd. She said she'd watch. They should be right up front, but he didn't see them. Where was she?

Then he noticed Brendan, a head taller than everyone else, move into the front row. Katie holding Declan coming in beside him. And there she was.

Ava and Emery had changed into Venery T-shirts. She pointed to him, and holding his daughter's hand, she waved. Then she turned around. The back of her shirt read, '*I'm here for the drummer.*' Emery's shirt said, '*My daddy rocks.*'

Bo smiled so big his cheeks hurt. Today was a fanfuckingtastic day.

*Let's get this show started.*

He counted off.

"One, two."

"One, two, three, four."

# Fourteen

Bo had the tunes cranking, the sunroof wide open, and Ava beside him in the front seat. Her head was tipped back, eyes closed, breathing in the fresh, vanilla-like fragrance of sweetgrass that grew alongside the highway. Emery's head bopped to the beat, using her sippy cup as a makeshift drumstick, like the little rocker she was.

*Yeah, my baby girl's got the rhythm.*

He smiled to himself.

It was almost like the three of them were a little family taking a nice Sunday drive. He could get used to this. He shouldn't. This was temporary. But he could. And it wasn't Sunday, even though it felt like it. Holidays falling on a weekday always messed him up. The Fourth was on a Monday this year.

They had another forty miles on the highway before he reached the exit to the Byrne family lake house. He'd been coming up here with Brendan and his cousins since they were little kids, when their parents drank highballs together on the deck, while they paddled boats on the water. Seemed like another lifetime ago. Good times.

Ava lowered her arm, her hand resting on the center console. Without thinking, he moved his hand next to hers, their pinkies almost, but not quite touching. Bo resisted the urge to lace their fingers together and hold her hand on his thigh. That was something couples do, and a couple they were not. He couldn't afford to cross that line, though that line was getting blurrier by the day.

Admittedly, he was attracted to her. He couldn't seem to get her out of his head, for fuck's sake. After the festival, Bo thought maybe, just maybe, the feeling was mutual. He could probably get Ava into his bed, but is that what he really wanted?

*Absofuckinglutely.*

That wasn't all he wanted, though. And as much as Bo wanted to fuck Ava six ways from Sunday, at this point, having sex with her would only muddy up the water. He had a kid to think about now. Risking his own heart was one thing, but he couldn't take that risk with his daughter. Emery'd lost too much already.

Removing his hand from the center console, he took the exit off the highway.

The amount of stuff they brought with them for just a day at the lake was mind-boggling. As Bo unloaded, Matt, Kit, and Sloan pulled in and parked behind him. From the back of the SUV, he stood there, watching Ava get Emery out of her car seat.

"You got it bad, man." Sloan pressed into him from behind.

"What are you talking about?"

He chuckled in Bo's ear and crooned, "Hot for teacher."

"Dick."

Matt slung his arm around his shoulders. "Yeah, I predict you'll be tapping that before the bus pulls out of Chicago."

Kit snickered. "He wishes."

Jostling Emery and a big canvas tote bag, Ava came around to the back. The warm July breeze blew her hair across her face, some of it clinging to her lip. Bo reached for it, tucking the silky strands behind her ear.

"Where can I find a bathroom?" Her gaze lingered on him. "Emmy has to go potty."

"Pee-pee, Daddy."

"I'll show her," Kit offered with a chuckle. "C'mon." And he led Ava inside the house.

"Goddamn, she's got some pretty tits." Squeezing the air with his hands, Matt licked his lips. "Round like cantaloupes. Are they real, man?"

"I don't know." Bo gritted his teeth. "And don't you be looking at Ava's tits."

"She's got a nice ass too."

"They ain't for you, asshole."

Sloan began singing, "He's got it bad, sooo bad…"

"What, you think you're David Lee Roth now?"

"Course not. You know I'm better than him, Bo." Sloan grinned. "Prettier too."

"That's not saying much." Matt shook his head with a smirk. "Dude's gotta be close to seventy now."

"Will the two of you just shut up and help me bring all this shit in the house?"

Matt planted a kiss on his cheek. "Sure thing, stud muffin."

By the time they hauled everything inside, Ava and Emery were out on the lawn with the girls. They sat on a blanket, criss-cross applesauce, each of them playing with a child on their lap. Kyan and Brendan were firing up the grill. Dillon filled a cooler with bottles of beer on ice. Sprawled on the outdoor sofa, Jesse napped, using Taylor's thighs as a pillow.

"What's wrong with him?" Matt pointed his chin at Taylor. "He sick or something? It's barely noon."

"He's knackered." Taylor leaned over and kissed Jesse's brow. "The baby was fussing all night. She wouldn't settle for me or Chloe. Only Jesse could soothe her. Grab me a beer, will you, mate?"

Glancing from his bandmate to his daughter on the lawn, Bo was reminded of the babyhood he'd missed out on, though he tried really hard not to dwell on that. Linnea held four-month-old Ireland, while Chloe played Patty Cake with her and Chandan. Ava glanced up at him and waved. Emery waved too. Waving back, he reached into the cooler for Taylor's beer.

"*Revolver* would like an exclusive interview, feature us on the cover," Taylor informed them as he popped the cap off his beer. "CJ will make the arrangements if you're all okay with that."

After all the drama that started with Shelley's paternity suit and ended with drones in Brendan's backyard, they were wary of the press, and rightfully so. But since *Revolver* was a leading publication in the music industry, and they had a new album to promote, it was already a foregone conclusion they'd do it. Not to mention, CJ was a personal friend of its editor-in-chief.

Bo peeled off his T-shirt, and opening a beer of his own, sat next to Sloan. "Yeah, I'm cool with it."

"Showing off that baby-smooth chest for your girl?" Sloan teased, rubbing the skin between his pecs.

"Knock it off, man."

He got up and stood at the deck railing, drinking his beer. Katie and Ava sang a rhyme down on the lawn, clapping along to it in a pattern, like the girls used to do at recess back in elementary school. It looked like Chloe was attempting to show Linnea how the game was played.

"Someone's touchy."

"Must be on his period."

Behind his back, Bo gave Sloan the finger and went down the deck stairs to the lawn.

"I'm going to take Emmy for a swim." He reached for his daughter. "You can come if you want."

"Okay, sure." Ava smiled, shielding her eyes from the sun. "Let me grab the floaties."

*Huh?*

"Floaties?"

"Yeah." She reached inside her big canvas tote and pulled out a pair of inflatable armbands.

"Oh." Bo chuckled. "Water wings."

"Whatever."

"C'mon." He extended his hand, helping her up from the blanket. "Emmy loves the water."

He should let go, but he didn't. Bo held onto Ava until

they reached the shore. She dropped a towel onto the sand and reached for the hem of her cover-up, a short, sexy thing with a graphic of the American flag on it. He watched her lift the fabric, pulling it over her head, and he gulped.

*Happy Fourth of July to me.*

It's not like he'd never seen a beautiful girl in a bikini before, but this was Ava, and she was different. Delicious curves in all the right places. Her tits weren't just pretty. Hell, they were perfect. Ripe and ready for him to suck on and bite. A plush bottom. Wide hips he could just imagine sinking his fingers into as he drove himself inside her over and over again. The imprints he'd leave behind.

*Fuck.*

What the hell was wrong with him? Thinking about Ava like that with his kid here, not that either one of them had the slightest inkling of the debauched visions in his head, but still. Looking down at his daughter, he glanced away from the voluptuous temptation mere inches in front of him, and tapped her cute button nose. "Ready, sunshine?"

Then they each took one of Emery's hands and waded into the lake.

Maybe she should have given this a lot more thought.

But then Ava hadn't realized how difficult keeping her head on straight was going to be.

Sometimes, it was so easy to forget she was only the babysitter. Katie's friend from school. Bo made her feel…things. And she didn't mean the zing she felt in her lady bits whenever he was close to her. It was this feeling of belonging, that she was right where she was supposed to be. With him and Emery.

*God, I am delusional.*

Was she, though?

Ava saw him looking, and she knew that look. Maybe he just

wanted to get in her pants, not that he'd even tried, but then why would he? Surely, Bo Robertson could be with anyone he wanted. Not to mention, she wasn't even sure which team he batted for. He'd been with girls, obviously. Emery was proof of that. But according to *TMZ*, he was known to swing the other way too. And she did see him make out with that Kodiak guy.

Bo was sweet, thoughtful, and affectionate toward her. Kind of goofy. Kind of flirty. Okay, a lot flirty, but then he seemed to be like that with everyone. Maybe it was just his way.

Probably.

*Stop it, Ava.*

Nope. She hadn't given this enough thought, but it was too late to change her mind now. She'd made a commitment. Bo needed her and Emery adored her. Everything was all arranged. They were leaving three weeks from today.

He sat beside her on the deck now, hunched over his plate, biting into a burger, while she helped Emery with her macaroni and cheese. It was her favorite thing to eat besides ice cream with rainbow sprinkles and Apple Jacks cereal. Firecrackers went off from across the lake, the sound startling her, and she dropped her spoon.

"It's okay, sweetie," Ava consoled her. "We'll get you a new one."

Linnea grabbed a clean spoon, handing it to her. "Here you go."

"Thanks."

Linnea sat down across from them with her husband, wide grins on their faces. They looked at each other and Linnea nodded. Clearing his throat, Kyan stood back up, a bottle of beer in his hand. "Linn and I have something to tell you all…"

Chloe grabbed Jesse's hand and bounced in her seat.

"…we're expecting a baby in January."

"I knew it. I knew it. I knew it," jumping up and down, Chloe shrieked.

"Aww, man, Dill," Bo whispered to himself.

Ava glanced to the man introduced to her as Kyan's brother. He smiled, surrounded by everyone congratulating the expectant couple, but his eyes told a different story. She just couldn't say what it was.

Bo leaned into her ear, his hand on her thigh. "Linn was told she might not ever have one, so this is extra happy news."

"Oh. Oh, really?"

"Yeah."

He got up and went over to them then, bro-hugging Kyan and slapping him on the back. Ava watched Bo pull Linnea into a tight embrace. He stroked her hair and kissed her right on the lips. It made her wonder if there'd ever been something between them, but then no one else seemed to think anything of it.

Everyone dispersed down to the lawn or the lake after dinner. Emery had fallen asleep on her lap, so she and Bo stayed up on the deck with her. Ava could see dark clouds far off in the distance. The wind picked up, blowing her hair. He caught a lock of it, twirling it around his finger, then let it go.

"I'm thinking there won't be any fireworks tonight."

"Why do you think that?" He patted her hair back into place.

Ava tipped her chin toward the lake. "Look."

"It could blow over." Bo leaned against her, stroking Emery's cheek. "Storms often do."

This. It was the tender touches, the familiarity, that was messing with her head.

"You and Linnea seem very close. You all seem that way, actually."

"We are." He laid his head on her shoulder. "Linnea is very special to me."

"Did you date or something before she was married?"

"No." He chuckled. "I had a thing with her brother once, though."

"Mmhm, yeah." Ava giggled. "That was pretty darn hot."

"Yeah?"

Pursing her lips, she nodded. "Oh, yeah."

"Good to know." Bo began twirling her hair again. "Why?"

"Why was it hot?" *Because it was you.* She shrugged. "I don't know. It just was."

Ava could hear thunder rumbling.

Maybe it was her heart pounding.

Matt clambered up onto the deck. "Storm's rolling in. We're gonna bounce. There's not going to be any fireworks now anyway."

Kit walked past them with Sloan, humming an old Van Halen song.

Her breath caught in her throat.

"No?" Bo lifted his head, looking at her with that devilish smirk on his angelic face. "I wouldn't be so sure about that."

# Fifteen

S he changed her mind.

Walking down First Avenue, Ava took in the summer air, bedazzled by all the sights, the sounds, and the smells. A fireball of orange blazed onto high-rises of glass and steel, reflecting the colors of sunset to the pavement below. Street vendors manned their carts, hawking everything from flower bouquets to Italian ices. The world around her just seemed so much more vibrant and vivid. Alive. And she was about to embark on the grandest of adventures.

So, yeah, she'd changed her mind. July just might be her favorite month of all.

Kevin was stocking the coffee bar at Beanie's when she arrived. Ava and Katie were going to walk over to Coventry Park together, where Brendan and Bo were waiting for them with the kids. Tonight was movie night in the park. *Forrest Gump* on the outdoor screen. Sitting on a blanket under the stars. Popcorn and snacks. Emery and Bo.

"Hey, Kev." She propped her hip against the counter. "Where's your sister?"

Glancing up from his task, Kevin wiped off his hands on his apron, taming his grin into a smirk. "Hi, Ava. She's changing in the back." He leaned across the counter and wiggled his eyebrows. "Want something while you wait?"

She bit her lip, containing a giggle. Was he flirting with her? "Uh, sure. Almond milk iced latte. One pump of…"

"Lavender. I know." He winked.

*Oh, yeah. Definitely flirting.*

Katie's younger brother hadn't been here for very long, and Ava didn't know him all that well. Kevin was going to be a freshman at the university in the fall on a football scholarship. He was probably some hot-shit jock in high school, used to being top dog and all that. Getting whatever he wanted by flashing his aqua eyes. But he was in the big city now. And being the new kid in a new school, he'd get knocked down a peg or two.

Ava took a seat on one of the plush sofas that lined the brick wall. Legs crossed, her sandal-clad foot swung up and down to the Stone Temple Pilots playing softly on the sound system, as she aimlessly scrolled through her phone. She looked up and Kevin stood before her, drink in hand.

"Thanks, Kev."

Instead of going back behind the counter, like she presumed he would, Kevin sat down on the sofa beside her. Arm casually draped across the back of it, he turned toward her. "Wanna hang out with me sometime?"

*Oh, dear.*

"Hang out?"

"Yeah, you know, catch a movie…maybe a Cubs game or something."

This was Katie's brother, so she had to tread lightly. "I, um… I'm leaving in the morning and I won't be back until Labor Day, but you're sweet to ask. Thank you."

"When you get back then." He stood up and winked. "Cubs'll still be playing in September."

"Yes, they will."

Katie's timely appearance saved her from having to respond further. She came out from the back, pretty and perfect as always with her hair swept up in a high ponytail, a large Beanie's tote on her arm.

"Kev, can you grab some bottled water and that organic juice

Dec likes for me, please?" Katie turned to her then, raising the bag on her arm. "I packed us some goodies. Leo baked a batch of muffins before he left."

"I fucking love those muffins."

"How'd I already know that?" Katie giggled, doing a double take. "Girl, you look gorgeous!"

"She's always gorgeous." Kevin winked at Ava, adding the bottles to his sister's bag.

"I'm going away for six weeks." Warmth crept into her cheeks. "Had to get my hair done."

Long layers. Fresh highlights. On impulse, she got a mani-pedi too, which she regretted now. Her nails would look like shit in a few weeks and she had the feeling an afternoon at a salon would be impossible on a concert tour. She had to admit they looked nice, especially with the suntan she'd been working on. Normally, Ava was not so high maintenance, but if she was going to be surrounded by beautiful people, then she had to be beautiful too, right?

"I love it." Katie ran her fingers through her new layers. "And I love the outfit."

Okay, she went shopping too. Ava might have gone just a teensy bit overboard on the amount of new clothes she bought for the trip, but the salesgirl at Akira was really convincing. She smoothed the yoga pants down her thighs. They weren't yoga pants exactly, but she didn't know what else to call the wide-legged, casual Ramona LaRues. Her ass sure looked good in them, though.

"Thanks."

"Someone else we know is gonna love it too." She nodded with a smirk.

*I hope so.*

More blood rushed to her face and she snickered. "Oh, stop."

Katie hooked her arm through hers. "Let's go."

Bo and Emery waited on a big white blanket. Em noticed Ava first, a smile lighting her eyes the second she saw her. The toddler tugged on her father's hair to let him know she'd arrived. He turned his head in her direction, indigo eyes slowly traveling her curves, and a wide grin split his face.

"Hi, Avie." Bo patted the space beside him and she took it. He kissed her cheek, whispering against her skin, "You're beautiful."

For some reason, when he said it, she actually believed it.

"You hungry?" He reached inside a soft-sided cooler. "I made barbecue chicken salad for us."

"You made it?"

"Yeah." Bo chuckled. "How do you think I feed Emmy?"

"Uber Eats?" Sheepishly, Ava smiled. "You keep on surprising me."

"Oh, I'm just full of surprises, Avie."

*Yeah, I just bet you are.*

She spread some of his chicken salad on a cracker. "Oh, my God, this is really good. Barbecue. Who'd have thought it?"

"My mom," he said, fixing some for Emery. "She used to make it all the time. You'll get to meet her when we're in LA."

Meet his mother? Ava didn't even want to think about that.

He must've seen the panic written on her face. Bo chuckled. "Mom's cool. You'll like her."

As the sun continued its descent, the six of them picnicked together, waiting for the sky to darken and the movie to begin. Emery settled herself in Ava's lap. Reflexively, she began stroking the child's hair. A sweet, affectionate little girl, she couldn't stop herself from falling in love with her.

Bo leaned back, resting on his elbows beside her. Ava watched him tip his head back, taking a deep breath. "I love that smell."

"What smell?"

He lifted his head. "The grass."

"Oxygenated hydrocarbons." With a little smirk, she glanced over at him. "That lovely smell is actually the grass crying."

"What?" He was looking at her like she had ten heads.

"Serious," Ava responded, nodding. "When grass is cut it releases chemicals to signal it's in distress. The smell calls beneficial bugs to come to the rescue."

"To rescue it from what?"

"In this instance, the blades of a lawn mower," she answered, laughing. "But usually from being eaten by other bugs."

"Damn, you're really smart." Getting off of his elbow, Bo ran his fingers through her hair. "I like that."

*I like you.*

Her belly did a flip-flop. She strained to breathe. Holding Emery on her lap, Ava sat up straighter. "I know some things."

Bo leaned back again. The sun had disappeared and the summer sky dimmed. "*Forrest Gump* is one of my favorite movies of all time."

"Yeah?"

"Yeah." He chuckled. "First movie I ever saw in a theater. My mom took me and my sister. I was six."

*And I wasn't even born yet.*

Not that she was going to remind him of that. "It's a good movie."

The opening credits began to roll. Ava leaned back on her elbows beside him. Her hand rested next to his, their pinkies almost, but not quite touching. Bo lifted his little finger and linked it with hers.

An unspoken pinky promise.

He smiled at her.

She just wasn't sure what it was he was saying.

"Yeah, she's gonna like it."

Ava should be here any minute now. Bo sent a car over to pick her up. He stepped out of the motorhome, Emery in his arms, and looked at it from the outside. Long and sleek, it was almost as big as Venery's tour bus parked directly in front of it.

"Christ, man." Sloan came up from behind him, slinging an arm over his shoulder. "Can I ride with you? I'll suck your dick and shit."

"No." Bo snickered. "And watch your mouth in front of the kid."

"Sorry." He pouted, sticking his bottom lip out. "I keep forgetting."

"Which is exactly why you're staying on the bus."

"C'mere, my little ray of sunshine." He extended his arms to Emery. "Uncle Sloan needs a hug. Your daddy made him sad."

"You're always sad, man."

The gate to Park Place swung open and the town car pulled in. Ava was here.

"Am not." Bouncing the baby in his arms, Sloan winked. "Seeing a pretty blonde makes me happy, doesn't it, Em?"

Bo took his daughter back. "Get one of your own."

Laughter bellowed from his throat. He walked backwards across the street. Singing. That. Fucking. Song.

She stepped out of the car. Sloan waved to her. "Hi, Ava. Your chariot, and your prince, awaits." Then he turned around and went inside his house.

*Asshole.*

If he didn't know the inner demons his brother wrestled with, he'd kick the living shit out of him.

"Hey, Avie." He leaned forward to kiss her cheek, Emery falling into her arms. "Ready to see our new digs?"

From the number of bags the driver pulled out of the car, Bo thought Ava might have packed for six years instead of six weeks.

"Ready."

She was wearing glasses, her hair up in a pile once again. Sweatpants, sneakers, and a tank top. And she looked sexy as all fuck. Bo helped Ava up the steps. For a moment she stood there, speechless, her jaw hanging open.

"Holyyy shit."

*She likes it.*

"Told you." He put his arm around her waist. "Only the best for my girls."

"This is *not* a motorhome. It's a palace on wheels."

"When we're parked, this can slide out to make the living area bigger." Then he pointed to the ladder up to the over-cab bunk. "That's where Ed sleeps."

"Ed?"

"Our driver. He's over on the bus with Lon at the moment." Bo chuckled. Moving her along, he pointed out all the amenities. "My room—Emmy's with me—and this one's all yours. Once you've unpacked we can store your bags down below."

"This is…" Ava ran her fingertips along the edge of the bed. "… wow, I don't have the words."

"And you don't have to think about cleaning or anything," he rambled to distract himself from imagining her naked in that bed. "We have a service that comes to every gig for that. They'll clean, do all our laundry, restock the provisions. If there's anything special you want, text it to CJ."

"Okay." She nodded. "When are we leaving?"

"In about an hour. We usually give the crew a head start—they left at six. And the boys are still loading up the bus." Ava looked a bit overwhelmed. "You okay?"

"Yeah."

"I know it's a lot to get used to." Bo took her hand and squeezed it. "But trust me, you'll be bored in a week."

Her eyebrow arched, she said, "Ohh, somehow I doubt that."

Letting her hand go, he smiled. "Maybe not."

*I hope not.*

There was a knock up front. Matt poked his head inside. "Bo? CJ's here. C'mon, everyone's outside to see us off."

"You said an hour."

He wrapped an arm around her shoulders. "That's about how long goodbye can take around here."

A row of bags sat in front of the bus, its storage compartments open. Sloan came out of his house hauling two more, Ed and Lon taking them from him. Matt and Kit disappeared inside, carrying on backpacks and duffel bags. CJ was barking orders at someone on his phone.

"You're looking at organized chaos," Bo explained, glancing down at Ava. If she wasn't overwhelmed before, she surely was now.

"It's not so bad." Lifting one shoulder, she sighed. "You haven't been in a classroom with thirty six-year-olds."

"Not since I was six."

Still barking, CJ waved them over. Ava hiked Emery higher on her hip while they waited for him to get off the phone and whispered, "He always like that?"

Bo leaned into her ear. "Only when he doesn't get his way."

"Sorry 'bout that." CJ pocketed his phone. "You all set, Bo? Need anything?"

"I'm good, man."

"Ava." He took her hand and kissed it. "How about you, lovely?" Not waiting for an answer, CJ reached into his pocket and handed her a card. "Anything you need, you call me, you hear? My cell's on it. And keep an eye on this Bozo for me, will you? He's probably going to need more looking after than this little cutie-pie here."

*Dick.*

"Uh, yeah, sure." Angling herself away from their manager, Ava looked up at him, rolling her eyes. "If you don't need any looking after, me and Emmy will be right over there with Katie, okay?"

"Okay." Bo squeezed her shoulder with a chuckle. "I'll be there in a minute."

"Damn, she is—"

"Enough." He flicked CJ on the chest.

Hearing his daughter's giggles, Bo turned around to watch them. Emery held Ava's cheeks with both hands, bestowing kisses upon her. He walked over to the open bus door as Matt jumped down the steps, whooping, "Time to get this show on the road."

Looping an arm around his shoulder, Taylor chuckled, nudging him toward their people waiting to see them off. Already, Chloe was blinking back tears. They weren't for him, but Bo hugged her tight anyway. "You gonna miss me, Red?"

"Next to Tay, I'll miss you most of all." She sniffled, pecking his cheek. "Be good, okay? I love you."

"I'm always good." Bo caught her tear with his finger. "I love you too." Then he hugged Jesse beside her. "Love you, man. Take extra good care of her while we're gone, okay?"

Jesse patted him on the back. "Extra, extra good. I promise."

Dillon and Kodiak stood off to the side, on their own. Bo went to them next. "See ya in six weeks, brother."

"It's not gonna be the same around here." Dillon bro-hugged him. "Boys' night at the club when you guys get back."

"Absofuckinglutely." Chuckling, Bo grabbed Kodiak. "C'mere, lover."

"I'm so *not* gonna kiss you again." He sniggered.

"Just a little one?"

"Dick." Kodiak smacked a kiss to his lips. "You're lucky you're cute." He flicked his chin toward Ava. "She seems like a good one, you know?"

"Yeah, I do."

He winked. "Love ya."

Linnea waited with Kyan. Bo opened his arms. "Baby girl."

"Drummer boy." She stepped into them.

"You too, pretty boy," he said, waving her husband over. "Group hug."

"I'll look after everything while you're away." Biting her lip, Linnea patted him on the chest.

"Just look after you and your little munchkin in there," Bo replied, rubbing her tummy. He hooked his arm around Kyan. "Love you, brother."

"You got this."

"Got what?"

"You know." Kyan hugged him once more. "Love you."

One by one, the boys waved and got on the bus. Only Taylor remained. Holding Chandan in one arm and Ireland in the other, he kissed Chloe and Jesse goodbye.

Katie kissed him on the cheek. "Make sure you behave."

"I don't think he knows how, sweet girl." Brendan snickered, leaning in to hug him. "Love you, man."

Ava moved in beside him.

His arm went around her waist.

"Ready?"

She nodded. "Ready."

They sat together at the window with Emery, her face pressed to the glass.

Ed started the engine. "Here we go."

The bus ahead of them pulled forward. Everyone began waving. Bo looked at each of their faces as they slowly rolled past. This family he'd chosen for himself. Jesse and Chloe held up their babies. Dillon. Kodiak. Brendan. Katie, holding Declan, and Linnea alternately waved and blew kisses. Kyan caught his gaze and grinned, giving him a salute. He waved back, returning the gesture.

They turned out of the gate. Bo couldn't see them anymore.

"We got this, Avie." Gazing into big blue eyes, he hooked his pinky with hers. "Together."

# Sixteen

Lying on a sumptuous bed, she opened her eyes to pitch darkness. Not a sliver of light could be seen. Ava had set her alarm to wake up early, long before the sunrise, or anyone stirred. She wanted to be showered, dressed, and ready for the day when Bo and Emery got up.

She caressed the sheets that covered her. Soft and luxurious, they felt like silk. Maybe they were. It was so heavenly, she could lay here all day. However, that was not on the laminated itinerary Bo had left in a three-ring binder on the dresser.

They made it to the Kansas City venue last night. After a quick meal of their famous barbecue, the three of them passed out in their beds. Today was set-up, sound checks, and rehearsals. The gig itself wasn't until tomorrow.

And tomorrow was Bo's birthday.

Slipping out of bed, Ava flipped on the soft LED lighting, and tiptoed into the bathroom. If it could be called that. She'd never seen anything quite like this before, even in an actual house. There was a huge glass-surround shower that could easily hold four people, with a gazillion jets coming out of the walls and ceiling, and mood lighting that changed colors. A soaker tub, sauna—for real, a fucking sauna—and even a bidet. She was going to have to give that thing a go.

Her stuff was neatly arranged on the left side of the double vanity, Bo's on the right. He had a bigger collection of cleansers, serums, and moisturizers than she did. He had more bottles than she had lined up in the shower too. Rows of them.

She really wanted to wash her hair, but it hadn't been a full seventy-two hours yet, and her stylist had instructed her to wait. Ava was going to be around music people today, she imagined, and she wanted to look put-together. She wanted to fit in. And she wanted Bo.

*Girl, don't you even think about going there.*

It's not like Ava intended to pursue him or anything—she hadn't completely lost all sense yet—but thinking about the man couldn't hurt, right? She punched a dozen buttons in the shower until the nozzles she wanted began to spout water. Then she picked up the bottle of shampoo and washed her hair.

By the time she made it to the kitchen, after blow-drying, dressing, and applying a little makeup, the sun was creeping up. Everything was still quiet. Ava peeked out the window. Venery's bus remained dark, but a couple of vans were pulling into the lot. She figured there wasn't much time left before things got busy and started on breakfast.

The smell of bacon frying must have woken him. Bo ambled out of his room dressed in a pair of gray knit boxers that didn't leave much to the imagination. He came up behind her, peering over her shoulder, and all Ava could smell was the sinfully delicious scent of him. Earthy and herbal. Spicy and sweet. Notes of black pepper, patchouli, and vanilla. It definitely suited him.

"Good morning." With his hands on her shoulders, Bo leaned down and kissed her cheek. "This is unexpected. Thank you, Ava."

She sucked in a breath. God, he felt good. Smooth, firm flesh pressed into her back. The warmth of his body belied the goosebumps sheeting her skin. Ava turned to face him, and that was a mistake. Bo smirked down at her with half-lidded indigo eyes. Messy hair. She could feel the heat from his bare skin seep right through her U-neck tank and the lace bralette top beneath it.

"Are you always so..."

He picked up a lock of her hair, rubbing it between his fingers. "So…what?"

"So naked."

"I could be more naked." Hooking an arm around her neck, Bo winked. "But I put on underwear just for you."

"You might as well be naked."

"Can't have you ogling my junk, now can I?"

Looking away from the mischief in his blue eyes, her gaze dropped to the bare skin of his smooth chest, past the ridges of his abs, down the V that led to a sizable, semi-hard bulge inside those gray boxers. Heat blooming in her cheeks, Ava involuntarily wet her lips and muttered, "How do you like your eggs?"

"Any way you make 'em." He threaded his fingers in her hair and kissed her on the forehead. "I'm gonna go take a shower before Emmy wakes up."

Then she ogled his fine backside as he left the kitchen.

Bo and the boys would be inside the venue all morning. Ed and Lon took advantage of being parked for two days, which apparently wouldn't happen often, and took off to explore Kansas City, leaving Ava and Emery on their own. And that was fine by her. She'd come on this adventure prepared.

"Emmy, want to help me bake a cake?"

"Patty cake." The tiny tot grinned, clapping her hands together.

"No, sweetie." Ava giggled, swooping Emery up into her arms. "A birthday cake for Daddy."

She didn't know what kind of cake Bo liked, but Ava figured she couldn't go wrong with vanilla. Emery helped her pour the buttermilk batter into round cake pans. Tomorrow they'd fill the layers with raspberries and frost it in a delicious orange buttercream. She'd just wrapped the cakes, putting them away in the fridge, when Bo returned.

"What are my girls up to, huh?" He picked Emery up, kissing her on the nose.

"Uh, nothing much." Ava closed the refrigerator door, turning her back to it. "I was just going to fix us some lunch."

"Come with me." Bo extended his hand and she took it. "They feed us. You and Emmy can stay for soundcheck."

She held onto his hand, meandering through a maze of hallways and wires to a nondescript room with the same oblong tables you'd find in any school cafeteria. He escorted her to where the spread was laid out, handing her a plate. "We can eat right here or go to the dressing room with the boys."

"Is it safe?"

"Maybe not." Bo snickered. "But the seating's a helluva lot better."

He wasn't wrong.

They sat together on a comfortable couch while they ate their lunch. Sloan lay on another sofa across from them, popping grapes into his mouth. Matt tuned a guitar in between bites of fried chicken.

"See?" He was staring at her.

"What?"

"Not so glamorous."

Emery scooted off her lap to pounce on Sloan. He laughed, choking on a grape, and lifted her over his head like an airplane.

"Sing," Emery ordered.

"What shall we sing, precious?"

"Baby Shark."

Sloan grinned. "Again?"

Pigtails bouncing, she nodded.

Then Kit strolled in, Taylor right behind him. "They're ready for us."

A concert venue with all the lights on and no people filling it is a strange sight to behold. Eerie almost. Sloan carried Emery on stage with him. "Gonna sing with me?"

Her little hands shackled his neck. So darn cute. "Yesss."

He brought Emery up to the microphone and they sang a chorus of "Baby Shark" together, before he handed her over to Ava. Sitting with the little girl on the side of the stage, she watched as they played to empty seats, crewmen ducking all around them, but her gaze was fixed on the bare-chested drummer.

Bo winked at her.

She was so fucked.

He glanced at the clock on the wall backstage. It was almost ten.

*C'mon. Let's go.*

Bo stood in a receiving line with his bandmates, shaking hands, signing autographs, taking countless photos. The rigger sat on a crate in the corner, sucking on his beer while giving him the eye. Discreet, he was not.

Sloan smacked his ass. "I think loverboy over there has plans for you."

"He best make other plans." Bo smirked, rubbing his ass.

"Ain'tcha goin' to the party, birthday boy?"

"Nah." He drained whatever this shit was in his plastic cup. Tasted like the smell of window cleaner. "We're pulling out early and I want to spend the rest of today with Emmy."

"She's probably asleep by now, man." Sloan hooked an arm around his neck. "C'mon, it's your birthday. You don't want to disappoint what's-his-name. Have a good time. Get your dick sucked or something."

They'd wheeled out a cake lit with sparklers for him on stage. Sloan and the boys and the crowd sang "Happy Birthday". He was thirty-fucking-four years old. That was more than enough celebrating for him.

"Pass."

"Oh, I get it." Sloan bobbed his head up and down. "Gonna have a private party with the babysitter."

*I wish.*

"Shut up, asshole." Bo elbowed Sloan in the ribs. He leaned over to Taylor. "We done here?"

"Go on." Taylor squeezed his shoulder. "Happy birthday."

Holding his hand up in a wave, he dipped out of the line, grabbing some beer from a trough of ice on his way out.

She was sitting on the sofa watching TV, Emery asleep beside her, when he walked in. Bo set the beer on the counter and leaned over to kiss his daughter.

"I tried to keep her up. She wanted to sing to you," Ava said, smiling as she shrugged. "We baked you a cake."

"You did?"

Besides his mother, no one had ever made him a cake for his birthday before.

"Yeah, we did."

Emery sat up, rubbing her eyes. She reached for him. "Hi, Daddy."

"Hi, baby." Bo hugged her tight. "Ava tells me the two of you baked a cake. Is that right?"

She nodded against his shoulder.

"Why don't we sing to Daddy now, then you can go back to sleep?"

Ava got up and went to the kitchen.

Bo sat down with Emery on his lap.

She carried the cake on a platter. Alight with candles, Ava set it down on the low-set table and began to sing. Emery bounced on his lap, clapping.

She'd decorated the cake to look like a snare drum.

"Blow out the candles and make a wish."

*I wish...*

Dare he? He shouldn't.

*...you could be mine.*

But he did anyway.

Ava retrieved a sleeping Emery from his arms and tucked her in her bed. He opened two of the bottles and cut them slices of birthday cake. Not two minutes later, she returned, sitting down on the sofa beside him.

"You really made this?" Bo took a bite. "It didn't come from a bakery?"

"I really did." She blushed. He loved making her blush. "At school, when I'm stressed, I bake. It relaxes me."

"This is the best cake ever. Thank you, Avie." Bo leaned up against her to whisper in her ear, "Where's my kiss?"

She pecked his cheek.

"It's my birthday and that's all I get?"

"Course not." Ava smirked. "Stand up."

He did and she playfully spanked him on the ass.

Bo rubbed himself. "Baby, I'm really trying to behave here, but you make it so damn hard."

Ava giggled and he sat back down with his arm around her shoulders, handing her a beer. Bo watched her lips surround the glass neck as she held the bottle and tipped it back, the muscles of her throat working as she swallowed. God, he needed out of these leather pants.

"How was the show?" With her head on his shoulder, she settled against him.

"Good." He twirled a piece of her hair. "It was good."

"How'd you guys get together anyway?" She moved to stretch out across his lap, her head on the arm of the sofa.

*Fuck me.*

"We've known each other since we were in diapers, you know. Lived on the same block." Bo tucked a throw pillow behind her. "My mom let us play in our basement. We didn't get serious about it until we were fourteen, though. That's when Taylor moved here from London."

"You've been together a very long time."

"As a band, twenty years now." Bo ran his fingers through her hair. "As brothers, always."

She looked up at him. "Not many bands stay together that long."

"Not without changing a member or two, no." He took a sip of beer. "That's almost unheard of. Venery is special and what we have is rare. See, we made a pact and stuck to it."

"What was that?"

"Music and family first." Bo paused, his hand cupping her face. "And make no mistake, Ava, we're a family. You're one of us now."

"I am?"

"You are." He leaned to the side. Pulling his legs up on the sofa, he rested his head next to hers. "You should know, the band has two rules."

"And what are those?" Ava asked.

"No drugs."

"But..."

"Weed doesn't count. Hell, Sloan pops gummies like candy." He chortled.

"I was gonna say." She giggled. "And?"

"No fucking on the bus." Bo exhaled a sigh. "Me and Tay broke that rule one time. That's how Emery came to be."

"Oh."

Bo turned her face toward his, their lips so close to touching. "We're lucky, Avie."

"Why's that?"

Pressing her closer, he burred in her ear, "We're not on that damn bus."

And his phone vibrated on the table.

*Fuck.*

He sat up. "That's my mom. I have to get it."

"How do you know?"

"It's eleven twenty-eight," he replied, reaching for his phone. "She always calls me on my birthday at the exact moment I was born."

Ava got up from the sofa.

Bo motioned for her to stay.

"Hi, Mom."

She leaned over, kissed his forehead, and spoke in a whisper. "Goodnight."

*Cockblocked by my own mother.*

"Happy birthday, Robert!"

*To hell with it...never mind.*

# Seventeen

The City of Roses.

Portland, Oregon was a pretty cool place. Vibrant. Scenic. Extraordinarily unconventional, Bo could happily live here if he didn't love Chicago so much. Its character reminded him of home in so many ways.

Venery was headlining a festival gig here. That meant a helluva lot of sun, sweat, and beer. Oh, and groupies. How could Bo forget about them? Promotional appearances all damn day. Live radio station interviews, meet and greets, and an after-party they were obligated to at least show up for. There was a time he lived for this shit. Now, not so much.

Apparently, some of his brothers still enjoyed the perks.

Bo walked into the large hospitality tent on the festival grounds that was at their disposal. All of the performing bands hung out there between sets and appearances. Outside of the cramped tour buses, it was where they ate, stretched out, and relaxed. It was where a lot of them got high, and a lot of them got laid.

Kit lounged on a sofa, arms spread across the back, thighs splayed wide, a girl on either side of him. They joined together, stroking his bandmate's dick with their wet tongues. One took possession of the head, sucking it into her greedy little mouth, while the other owned his balls.

"Heh." Matt came up beside him, draping an arm across his shoulders. "Dude can never fuck just one, can he?"

*Truth.*

Bo chuckled. "Nope."

Lifting his head from the back of the sofa, Kit gripped the hair of the girl sucking his dick. He tipped his chin at Matt. "Care to help me out here, brother?"

"You got this, man." His tongue dragged across his lip, and he snarled low, "Too easy. I like to pursue my dinner."

"Snacks, man." Bo tickled his ribs. "Where's Sloan? I've been looking for him."

"Dunno." Matt grabbed each of them a beer. "He was holed up in his bunk last I saw him."

"I checked the bus. He wasn't there."

"He's somewhere getting his dick ridden then." Matt took a swig. "Don't worry about him."

But he did.

"C'mon, let's get out of here." He turned them around, and glancing back over his shoulder, he yelled, "Fifteen minutes, Christopher."

It looked like he'd worried for nothing. When they got to the staging area, Taylor and Sloan were already there. Kit sauntered over, tucking his shirt in his pants, five minutes before they were due to go on.

With his mind quiet, he thought of his girls. Bo pulled out his phone, sending Ava a quick text while he had a moment. He liked it. It was nice having someone to check in with, to have someone waiting for him when he came home. And he liked that someone a whole helluva lot. More than he should.

"Venery," someone shouted. "Showtime."

Surrounded with security, the after-party was being held in yet another tent, set far off behind the stage. Filled with models brought in by the promoters, starlets, and beautiful people, these parties turned into hedonistic, MDMA-fueled lustfests before they were over. Usually at dawn. Some people will do anything, fuck anyone, to move up from the B-list. And some people just needed an excuse to party and fuck.

*Been there. Done that.*

Bo just wanted to go home.

"We'll have a beer, show our faces, then split." Taylor squeezed his shoulder. He didn't want to be here either.

"Sounds like a good plan to me," he agreed. "I'm getting too old for this shit."

"Heh." Taylor arched a brow. "Oh, I wouldn't say that."

Sloan surrounded himself with a bevy of nubile females vying for his attention. Matt took off, Kit following along behind him, to hunt down his next meal.

Someone put a beer in his hand. The rigger. What's-his-name. "What the fuck are you doing here? Shouldn't you be, I dunno, rigging or whatever it is you do?"

"Nah, man. I'm done. This was my last gig. Goin' home in the morning."

"Oh, so you came to say goodbye?" Bo snickered, taking a pull of his beer.

"Something like that." His smile was somewhat timid. "I like you."

"So you want to suck my dick again?"

"No." And that timid smile turned into a salacious grin. "I want to fuck."

Taking another swig, Bo shook his head. "I'm not feeling it, man."

"No?" The rigger grabbed between his legs. "I can make you feel it."

"Sure, you can get my dick hard." Bo chuckled. "Breathing gets my dick hard."

"C'mon, baby." He furiously rubbed the leather placket guarding his cock. "Please, let me in that ass. I promise to fuck you sooo good. Your girlfriend can't do that, but I can."

"Trust me, if she was my girlfriend, I wouldn't even be talking to you."

"Be my pussy for me then. Let me wreck that hole," he pleaded.

Bo smirked. "Maybe I'd rather tear apart yours."

"I'd love it, baby."

"Oh, yeah?" Bored with this shit, he was getting annoyed. "Suck me off then. Right here. Let everyone see how much you love choking on my dick."

Unzipping his pants, the rigger pulled him out.

"Jesus Christ, I was kidding."

Zipping himself back up, Bo turned away, leaving what's-his-name standing there. He waved to Taylor. "I'm out."

What the fuck was wrong with him? He'd never acted like such a self-entitled, A-list prick before. And he rarely turned down a good fucking either. So now he was walking to the lot with a raging boner in his pants and no one to give it to.

*Hello, right hand. My old friend.*

He was in desperate need of a long, hot shower anyway. Coated with the day's grime and sweat, his skin itched.

Bo sensed the dude was behind him. Stopping near Venery's bus, he turned around. "You're not gonna give up, are you?"

The rigger's answer was to pull him by the hair to his mouth. Thrusting his tongue inside, Bo kissed him back. Someone else rubbing his dick felt sublime. He reached inside the rigger's pants to reciprocate.

"You want my cock, Bo." He licked up the side of his neck. "I know you do. Try to deny it."

"I can't."

Bo kissed him again. Harder. The man's dick throbbed in his hand. With the thought of it splaying his ass wide open, ramming into that spot only another man can hit, he gave in.

Precum flowed. Bo licked it from his fingers.

"Please, man. I'm dying here."

"Just make it quick."

He pushed the dude to the other side of the bus, where no one could witness their frenzied debauchery.

"What's your name anyway?"

"Paul," he answered, proceeding to pull Bo's leather pants down. Sticky from sweat, it felt like they were being ripped from his skin.

"Fuck me with your tongue, Paul." Fingers rubbed between his cheeks. "Yeah, that's a good boy. Open that hole with your fingers, spread it wide, and get that tongue all the way in there."

*So fucking good.*

Next to sinking his dick in a tight, hot pussy, there was nothing he loved more than getting his ass worked. And Paul was doing a thorough job of it.

"Suck that asshole. Get it good and wet." He hissed through his teeth. "Mm, just like that."

"You taste so good, baby." Paul replaced his tongue with his fingers. "I could eat your ass all night, but I can't wait to shove my cock inside you."

*Fuck.*

His own precum leaked into his hand. Loving the taste of it, Bo lapped it from his palm. He stroked himself with the other. "Don't wait then."

The bulbous head pushed through the ring of muscle. He loved the burn, that sensation of being split open.

Paul kissed up his spine. Sucking on the side of his neck, he groaned, "Fuck, baby, this is heaven."

*Heaven?*

No. Heaven was an angel with long blonde hair and big blue eyes. A beautiful girl who hid behind her glasses. Who baked cakes and loved his daughter.

If only Ava could learn to love him too.

He could love her back.

But then, why would she? No one else had ever chosen him to love.

Except for a sliver of light coming from the bottom of her door, it was dark when he stepped inside. Bo tiptoed into his room, saw that Emery was sound asleep in her bed, grabbed a pair of clean sweats, and headed into the shower. He went through his cleansing ritual, sans jerking off, since that had already been taken care of. Why did he feel so...guilty? Regretful? He'd never felt like this before, but he was out of sorts, and he didn't like it.

Ava was on the sofa, watching TV, when he came out of the bathroom. She glanced up at him. "Hey."

"Hey, Ava." Bo grabbed a bottle of water out of the fridge. Yeah, it was definitely guilt he was feeling. And regret. Remorse. But why?

She wasn't his girlfriend. They hadn't fucked. He hadn't even kissed her, for chrissakes.

But he wanted to.

"Did you and Emmy have a good night?"

"Yeah, with *Peppa Pig*." She smiled at the TV, but didn't look at him. "And no accidents again today. I think she's ready for her big-girl panties."

"That's good." Bo took a seat next to her on the sofa. "What are you watching?"

"Catching up on *The Handmaid's Tale*." Ava shrugged, pursing her lips. "I heard June rips Fred to pieces in this episode. Fucker deserves it."

She wasn't her usual self. Ava was out of sorts too. He could feel it.

"Are you okay?" He placed his hand on her arm.

"Yeah, I'm fine."

*Uh-oh.*

According to Dillon, fine never means fine.

"Want to talk about it?"

"Talk about what?"

"I feel the tension, Avie." Bo laced their fingers together. "And I don't like it."

She licked her lips and exhaled. "I had this boyfriend my senior year of high school. He was perfect, ya know? Hot, played football, nice car, and he treated me like a queen. We went to prom, I gave up my v-card because I thought I loved him, and the next day he broke up with me."

"He was a fucking idiot."

She turned her head to look at him. "He broke up with me for a guy."

*Shit.*

"I'm sorry."

Ava laughed, but a tear rolled down her face. "I couldn't even be upset about it. I mean, I was upset, but he wanted a penis and I didn't have one, so I couldn't compete with that, now could I?" She snickered. "At least he didn't dump me for another girl."

"You saw me, didn't you?"

Chewing the corner of her lip, she nodded.

Bo was grateful that at least the deed had been done on the other side of the bus. The only thing Ava could have seen was kissing. His hand down the rigger's pants. But that was enough.

He didn't know why he felt the need to explain, but he did. "I don't see gender, Avie."

She looked up at him.

"Never have. I see the person. Bisexual. Pansexual. Call it whatever you want, I don't do labels either."

"I…I…"

"Are you thinking I can't possibly be attracted to you because I was with some dude?"

"No."

"Good." He tipped her chin up. "Because you know that isn't true. So, tell me why you're upset?"

*Claim me, angel. Please. You're making me crazy.*

"Triggered some memories, that's all." Ava leaned forward and kissed him on the cheek. "I'm not upset, just hormonal."

"Okay."

But he didn't believe her.

"When are we leaving for Oakland?"

"As soon as they have everything loaded. Before the sun comes up, I imagine."

"Okay."

He pulled her closer. "C'mere, I want a hug."

She straddled his lap. Bo stared into her big blue eyes, drowning in them. And he held her.

Ava nestled against his shoulder. He kissed her hair, breathing raspberries and jasmine petals. "And just in case you were wondering, pretty girl, yeah, I want you."

She squeezed him tighter.

*More than you'll probably ever know.*

"And I'm sorry."

# Eighteen

Ava chewed on a fingernail. She shouldn't. They looked like shit already, just like she knew they would. She cursed herself for not slipping away to a salon with Emery when they were in Oakland. Bo wouldn't have minded. Hell, he probably would've called for a car to come take her. There had to be someplace where she could go around here. This was Hollywood, after all.

She had to admit, she was a bit disappointed. Los Angeles didn't look anything at all like it did on TV. Seeing the Hollywood sign was cool, though. And the donuts at Randy's were amazing. Ava, Bo, Emery, and the boys even took a photo together in front of the iconic landmark. Maybe they just hadn't been to the good parts yet.

Venery's show at the Hollywood Bowl was going to be huge, and since Bo's family lived here, they were staying a few days. And not in the motorhome. They had a two-bedroom suite in a posh, historic hotel, built in 1939, less than a mile from the venue. A magazine was coming to do a photoshoot of them here for an article. It was a big deal, at least according to CJ. The band seemed quite blasé about the whole thing.

"Ava?" Bo casually strolled into her room like it was something he did every morning. He didn't. "I'm gonna order us some breakfast. What do you want, baby?"

*Baby?*

"Naked here."

"Doesn't look like you're naked to me." Warm hands caressed her shoulders.

"I'm in my underwear." She glanced down at her lace-covered breasts. "You might've knocked."

"Your door was open." He kissed the top of her head. "And you see me in my underwear all the time."

*Lucky me.*

"Oh, I know."

"Fair is fair." She looked at him in the mirror. He winked. "So, what's for breakfast?"

"Uh, surprise me."

Bo grinned. "I'm good at that."

Ava finished putting on her makeup and got dressed, thankful now, that salesgirl at Akira had been so convincing. The off-white, rib-knit bodycon dress reached just past mid-thigh. Sleeveless, she paired it with a cropped denim jacket, and slipped into a pair of trendy thong sandals that annoyingly rubbed between her toes. She'd deal with it. The mirror told her the outfit was on point.

Room service was setting up their breakfast. Bo signed the check and tipped the man, holding a squirming Emery. Seeing her, the little girl broke free. "Mommy."

She scooped her up. "Ava." But it didn't seem to matter how many times she and Bo corrected her, Emery had bestowed her with the title, and that was that.

"Wow."

"What?"

"You're so beautiful." Without taking his eyes off her, Bo pulled out a chair. "Breakfast."

Ava sat down. It looked like he'd ordered her everything on the menu. A bowl of Greek yogurt, granola, and fresh berries, Pears Tartine, and French toast topped with roasted apples, pecans, and whipped cream were laid out in front of her. It was her turn. "Wow."

"Did I surprise you?"

She took a sip of coffee, her eyes widening. "Caffè misto."

"Almond milk and lavender syrup." Cutting into his steak and eggs, Bo winked at her. "I pay attention."

"And yeah, you did it again, Bo Robertson."

The corner of his mouth tugged up and he tucked into his food.

"Robert!"

Shortly after breakfast, Ava came out of her room where she'd retrieved her bag. Two blonde women, one older and one younger, rushed at him, smothering Bo in hugs and kisses. A gentleman with a full head of graying hair held the door open, waving more people inside, then closed it.

"You look so good, sweetie." Taking a step back, the older woman touched his cheeks. "Where's Emery? She's probably already forgotten who I am."

But she hadn't.

"Gamma!" The toddler bounced on Ava's hip.

Everyone stopped to look at them. Bo came over to her, and slipping his arm around her waist, drew Ava to his side as he brought her to meet his family. At least she presumed that's who they were.

"Mom, this is Ava."

"Robert's told me so much about you." Emery fell into her grandmother's arms as the woman hugged Ava, kissing her on the cheek. She winked at her son. "She is lovely, dear."

And he blushed.

Without letting go of her waist, he introduced them all. "Ava, my mom, Cynthia. My dad, *he's* Robert," Bo emphatically stated, his brow raising. "My sister, Allie, and her husband, Ryan." He ruffled the dark hair of the youngster closest to him. "And their boys."

"Ryan, Logan," Cynthia called her grandsons over to her. "Come here and say hello to your little cousin."

Now that Emery had everyone's attention, squeezing her waist, Bo leaned into her. "Going somewhere?"

"Yeah." She adjusted the strap of her bag on her shoulder. "I thought I'd grab an Uber and go get my nails done. Give you some time with your family."

"Don't be silly," Bo's mother chimed in, having overheard her. "I can take you."

Softly chuckling, he whispered in her ear, "She likes you."

And that's how she came to be in this little hole-in-the-wall nail salon with Cynthia and Allie for some *female bonding time*, as Bo called it. Ava couldn't understand why he was so eager for them to get to know each other. The day after tomorrow they'd be back on the road and she'd likely never see them again anyway.

With her feet soaking in a whirling pool of water that was almost too hot, Emery sat on her lap, giggling at the motion of the massage chair. Ava closed her eyes, relaxing and stroking the child's hair, in the hopes she'd take a little nap while they painted her toes. Bo's sister was in the chair next to hers, and his mother in the one beyond that.

Allie rolled her head to the side, facing her. "Has my brother taken you to In-N-Out yet?"

"No, what's that?"

"Only the best burgers on the planet." She rolled her head the other way. "Mom, you should take Sunset on the way back. We can stop in and get some."

"We'll see, dear," Cynthia answered. "I told your brother I'd have us back in time to watch the photoshoot. He wants us to be there."

"What the hell for?" She giggled, turning back to Ava. "I think it's really you he wants there."

"Me?"

"I know my brother, and he couldn't care less if we see him get his picture taken." Allie winked. "He likes you."

Ava snickered. "He likes everybody."

"True."

They didn't stop for burgers, which was more than okay with Ava. After such a decadent breakfast, the last thing she needed was to eat again. There were gardens tucked away on the hotel's grounds.

Lush, foliage-covered alcoves with chaise lounges and fire tables that burned at night.

One of the garden alcoves was cordoned off. A photographer was set up on the perimeter with Venery inside it. The band posed, taking direction from the man behind the camera. All of them in ripped-up jeans, with the exception of Bo in his leather pants. None of them had shirts on.

Bo's father, Ryan, and the boys stood off to the side, watching. A woman sat on a stool opposite them, an iPad in her lap. Long, dark hair. Stiletto boots, tight jeans, and a daring halter top. Ava caught the guys stealing glances at her in between shots. All the guys. From little Logan to his grandfather.

Allie leaned into her ear. "Don't know how she's managing to keep her tits from falling out."

The photographer stopped shooting to change the lens on his camera, prompting the boys to relax their muscles. Bo glanced up, and with a smile, he waved them over.

Tapping on her iPad, the woman looked over at them. She was beautiful up close. Rocker chic. Late twenties, maybe. Her makeup was perfect, her hair, her clothes. Everything about her was fucking perfect. She gave them a brief nod, and smiled at Bo. "Is that your baby?"

"Yeah."

"She's so cute," the woman commented, tapping away on her iPad. "Do you want to have more children?"

Bo looked right at Ava. "I'd love to have another baby someday."

Ava swallowed nervously. A sheen of sweat rose on her skin as her heart dropped into her stomach. Miss Perfect stopped her tapping to glance at her, then cast her attention at Taylor. "What about you?"

"I already have two, Vanessa. My daughter's only six months old. Not thinking about a third."

*Vanessa. Of course, that's her name. It's perfect for her.*

Bo proudly introduced Miss Perfect to his mom and sister. He was beaming. Indigo eyes shining, his smile wide. "And these are my girls. My daughter, Emery, and my beautiful Ava."

Vanessa plastered on what Ava was sure was her often-used fake smile. "You make such a lovely couple."

"Oh, no," she corrected her. "I'm just the babysitter."

And the smile fell from Bo's face.

The cerulean sky deepened to a muddled purple tinged with magenta in the California twilight. Alone with her thoughts, Ava wandered the hotel gardens. Guests gathered at tables, now alight with dancing flames, laughing and sipping on fancy cocktails.

Bo and Emery had gone to dinner with his family. Cynthia asked her to go with them, of course, but she begged off, insisting they deserved some private time together. He didn't protest. In fact, he'd barely spoken since the photoshoot.

"Little Bo Peep has lost her sheep."

The slurred voice came from an alcove tucked away in the corner of the garden. Sloan reclined on a double lounger, the fire reflecting in his eyes, a bottle of whiskey in his hand. He smirked and brought it to his lips.

"Sloan, what are you doing here?"

"Getting drunk." He took a swig. "Though, I should be asking you that question. Why aren't you with your flock, little miss?"

"Family time, you know?" She shrugged. Sometimes Ava didn't know how to interpret his sarcasm.

Sloan moved over, patting the space beside him. Hesitating for a brief moment, she tentatively stepped into the alcove and sat down on the edge of the lounger.

"I won't bite. Unless you ask me nicely, of course." He handed her the bottle. "You look like you could use a drink."

Ava took a swig. Sputtering, she returned it to him. "That's awful. How do you drink this stuff?"

"It's an acquired taste, I guess." Sloan chuckled softly, tipping the bottle back. "I can get you something else. Pick your poison, baby."

"No, thanks." She tucked her hair behind her ear. "I'm good."

"C'mon, Ava, have a drink with me." Sloan rested the arm holding the bottle on her shoulder. "You're all mopey and shit."

"Am not."

"Are too."

She was. Ava had the night off. It's not like she had anything else to do, besides stare at the walls of an empty hotel room. "Fine. I'll take a glass of pinot."

He got her the whole damn bottle.

"So, why so glum, Miss Bo Peep?" Sloan toyed with a lock of her hair.

"Told you, I'm not." Ava cautiously sipped on her wine, pacing herself. "I suppose I could ask you the same question, though, couldn't I?"

"You could." With a nod, he swallowed more whiskey and smirked. "But you wouldn't get an answer."

"Why not?"

"We're talking about you, little miss." He tugged on her hair. "You like him, don't you?"

"Sure, I like him."

Grabbing her shoulder, Sloan turned Ava toward him. "I mean you *really* like him."

She didn't answer, but then she probably didn't have to. It didn't matter anyway.

His fingers skimmed her cheek. "Tell me, has my boy fucked you yet?"

Ava gasped. Her heart rate accelerating, she was finding it difficult to catch a breath.

"Have you asked yourself why?" Sloan challenged, the corner of his mouth slyly lifting. "It's obvious to everyone he wants in that pussy of yours."

"Bo doesn't know what he wants."

"Beautiful Ava." He snickered. "C'mon now, you're a smart girl. Bo wants what we all do, baby."

"What's that?"

"Doesn't everyone just want someone to love? Someone who loves every fucked-up part of them. Exactly as they are."

Their lips a breath apart, Ava swallowed. "Is that what you want?"

"Not all of us deserve it." Sloan turned his head, staring into the flames. "He does, though. Make him happy."

"He is happy, all the time."

Sloan looked at her then, a haunted smile on his face. "Don't be fooled. Pain often hides in plain sight."

She opened the door to her posh hotel room and flipped on the light. Bo sat at the table, a bag from In-N-Out in front of him. "Where were you?"

"Having a drink with Sloan."

Standing up, he nodded. "I brought you a burger."

"Thanks."

"I was worried." Indigo eyes stared into her own. "Why'd you say that?"

"Say what?"

"That you're just the babysitter."

"Because I am."

"I see." He chewed on his lip, and with his gaze lowering to the floor, Bo left the room.

*No, you don't.*

Holding Emery, Ava stood with Bo's family behind the stage. Twenty thousand fans filled the Hollywood Bowl, screaming their names. She only heard one, though. His.

Vanessa crooked a finger at the photographer, yelling over the music into her phone. "Yeah, I'll get him. Tell CJ thanks for hooking me up."

That's who Bo should be with. Miss Perfect, or someone just like her. Ava would never be able to give him everything he wanted. She couldn't be what he needed. Maybe Vanessa could.

The music ended and the crowd roared. The boys came off the stage, Bo rushing directly over to her. His hands gripped her shoulders hard. "You're not."

"What?"

He planted a kiss on her lips.

"You're not just the babysitter."

# Nineteen

They pulled into a Buc-ee's, traveling east on I-10, somewhere between San Antonio and Houston. The bus needed to refuel and Bo suddenly craved a bag of Beaver Nuggets. After midnight, Emery had long since been tucked in her bed and Ava nodded off in the middle of the movie they were watching. He chuckled to himself. She was always doing that.

Swinging himself over the steps, his feet landed with a thud on the pavement. On the other side of the gas pump, Matt and Kit stood stretching their limbs. "Going in?"

"Nah, man," Kit replied. "I'm good."

"You?" Bo tipped his chin at Matt.

"I'm going to bed." He shook his head and grinned. "You know, it's amazing how much better I sleep without having to listen to you snore."

"I don't snore, asshole."

"Yeah, you do." Kit nodded. "But so does Tay, so the sleeping's still shit."

Bo sniggered. "Want anything?"

"A breakfast taco." He pondered for a moment. "And Beaver Nuggets. The cheese ones."

"You got it, brother."

"I love you, man," Matt shouted from across the parking lot.

Flipping him off, Bo went inside the mega-convenience store.

Bo ordered Kit's taco and began filling his basket up with goodies. Those sweet puffed corn nuggets he was craving, some dried pineapple slices, and chocolate-covered pretzels for Ava, because he knew she loved them, and a bag of gummy worms for Emery. On impulse, he threw in a jar of cinnamon honey butter just because it was fucking delicious on toast.

"Hey, Lon." Bo patted Venery's driver on the shoulder. He looked tired. "Doing all right?"

"We'll be in Pensacola by eight." He grinned. "I'm okay."

He walked the bus, peeking in on a snoring Taylor, and tossed a bag to Kit. "Thanks, stud muffin."

"See you in the morning." Bo ruffled Matt's hair in the bunk below. Dude was already snoring. "Sweet dreams, asshole."

Plunking his bag of snacks on the banquette, Bo saw the sofa was empty, the TV turned off. He opened the Beaver Nuggets, popping a handful in his mouth. Ed climbed the steps and got into the driver's seat.

"Want some?"

"Thanks, Bo." Ed held up a bag of his own. "Got me some beef jerky."

*Gross.*

"Where's Ava?"

"She woke up and went to bed, I think."

*Duh. Stupid question. Where else could she go?*

"You good, man?"

Ed started the engine. "I'm good."

Bo figured he might as well take a shower and go to bed. He usually slept well when they were driving, the sound of wheels on asphalt a lullaby, and they had a nice, long stretch of highway ahead of them.

He opened the bathroom door and there she was.

Naked. Wet. Beautiful.

She took his fucking breath away.

Her back was to him, so Ava didn't see Bo standing there. One foot on the rim of the tub, she was drying herself off with a towel. He stared at her shapely ass, the dip in her spine, the water beading down her back. Nothing on Earth could have stopped him from watching her.

Dropping the towel, Ava picked up a bottle and began rubbing oil into her skin. She massaged it into her calf, fingers slowly gliding over wet flesh. Bent over as she was, Bo could see the puffy, fat lips of her pussy. He wondered if she ever touched herself while thinking of him.

Bo didn't even realize he'd moved in closer. So close, all he'd have to do is move his hand forward a few inches to reach heaven. His fingertips grazed the back of her thigh, while his lips caressed the nape of her neck. Bo groaned at the sizzling contact. Ava emitted a squeak, goosebumps sheeting her skin.

She didn't shriek or scream or push him away.

He wrapped his arms around her.

Maybe she wanted him too.

Bo turned Ava around. He stared into her big Bambi eyes, the pupils blown. Yeah, perhaps she did.

Reaching down for the towel, he covered her, but not before he gazed upon those perfect tits. They'd be home in a couple weeks. What then? Would she want him still, or would she make a graceful exit from their lives?

He should just snatch that towel from her fingers, push her onto the bed, and fuck her senseless like he'd been dying to for weeks. So why the fuck was he holding back?

Because she mattered to him.

And he needed it to be real.

After Pensacola, there was Jacksonville. The East Coast, the Atlantic Ocean, and the final leg of Venery's tour. From here they would travel north, as far as Richmond, before heading back toward the Midwest, and home.

As much as he couldn't wait to be home again, Bo didn't

want this to come to an end either. He looked over at Ava, playing a game with his daughter, teaching her colors. She kissed Emery on the head, praising her for knowing the color red, and with a smile that lit up his insides, she glanced at him. Here, she felt like his. But when they got there? He only hoped he could keep her.

A twenty-five-foot-tall ice cream cone came into view. They were in Florida, weren't they? That could only mean one thing. Twistee Treat. "Ed, we're making an unscheduled stop."

He, Ava, and Emery were already standing in line when Venery's bus, having had to make a U-turn, pulled in. His boys came out, Taylor leading the way. "What the bloody hell are you doing?"

"Getting ice cream, obviously." Bo squeezed Emery in his arms, kissing her forehead. "Emmy wants a baby cone with sprinkles, don't you, darling?"

"No." Giggling, she emphatically shook her head.

"No?"

"Big girl."

"That's right. You're not a baby anymore." With a wistful smile, he brushed the hair out of her eyes. "Big-girl cone with sprinkles then?"

"Yes."

Bo dropped his forehead to hers. "Think you can handle it, sunshine?"

Giddy with excitement she couldn't contain, her nod was exuberant.

"All right then." He slipped his arm around Ava. "How about you? What's your favorite?"

"*Mine's cherry vanilla—the kind with chunks of dark chocolate and nuts in it.*"

Shelley. He smiled to himself, remembering her and that day. He'd always be grateful for the time he was given to spend with her and the memories he could share with Emery.

"God, there're so many." Ava studied the list of flavors. "Um, salted caramel."

"Yeah?"

"Yeah, that's my favorite." Holding onto his arm, she gazed up at him

"Well, what do you know," he said, squeezing her waist. "It's mine too."

Emery was still working on her big-girl cone, and making a fine mess of it, when Ed parked in their designated space at the Jacksonville arena. Ava scooped the last of the salted caramel out of her cone with her tongue before popping it in her mouth. Bo swallowed as she did.

"Emmy, darling, are you sure you don't need Daddy's help with that?"

Her cone soggy, the ice cream was melting faster than she could lick it. She handed it to him. "All done."

"Good job, my big girl." He licked the dripping mess. "Daddy'll finish it for you."

"Oh. My. God," Ava shrieked, moving to sit next to him. "Did you see this? Katie just sent it to me."

An image of him, his lips on hers, taken just after he came offstage at the Hollywood Bowl displayed on the screen. The caption below it, "*Venery's drummer in torrid affair with his daughter's babysitter!*"

"Warned you." Bo chuckled. "*TMZ* strikes again."

"You're not upset?"

"Not this time." He smirked. "Are you?"

"But it isn't true."

*Not yet.*

"We have to do something about that then, don't we?"

But they didn't, and their time together was running out. Each day slipping by faster and faster.

They were driving though Pennsylvania. Bo thought that's where they were anyway. He knew it was Thursday, the first day of September, and the next gig was Columbus. He sighed. Summer was almost over. Labor Day weekend had come much too quickly. They'd be back in Chicago on Tuesday.

Ed followed Venery's bus into the parking lot of a roadside diner. "Guess we're stopping for breakfast." Bo turned to Ava, who'd just come out of her room, still in pajamas. "You want to go in or should I get us something to-go?"

"Emmy's still sleeping." Stretching her arms, she yawned. "Better make it to-go."

"You got it, baby." He patted her curvy bottom as she reached for the coffeepot. "What do you want?"

She winked. "Surprise me."

Taylor was tapping away on his phone when Bo walked in, no doubt texting Jesse or Chloe. He knew being separated from them had taken a toll on him. Crazy as it sounded, he envied him for that.

Bo slipped into the booth. "Hi, Chloe."

"It's Jesse." Taylor smiled. He didn't do that very often. "He's at the office. Chloe's going to the shops."

He placed his order with the waitress. One by one the boys trickled in. Sloan slid in beside him. "Where's Miss Bo Peep?"

"Who?"

"Ava," he answered with a smirk.

Cocking his head, Bo glared. "She's staying with Emmy."

"Well, shit." Sloan tilted his head to match him. "Looks like you're stuck with me then."

Taylor cleared his throat to get everyone's attention. "CJ mentioned *Revolver* wants to do a follow-up article on our lives at home."

"What the hell for?" Kit didn't seem to care for the idea.

"Bands on and off the road, or some such nonsense." Taylor's nostrils flared. "I'm not too keen, but I told CJ we'd think about it. It's an intrusion into our private lives and I'm not sure it's worth it, to be honest."

"Are they sending Vanessa?" Matt waggled his brows, cupping his hands to his chest.

Shaking his head, Taylor raised his gaze to the ceiling. "Yes, actually. It was her idea."

"Then I'm in." Matt tipped his chin toward him. "What do you say, man?"

"I think I'm with Tay on this one." The waitress brought him his order. He stood up to leave. "But I'm okay with whatever all of you decide."

Sunday. Louisville. Venery's penultimate stop on their tour. When they left here in the morning, it was a short two-hour drive to Indianapolis, one last show, one more night with her, and a three-hour drive home.

Bo came out of the shower, washed clean of the stench of their twenty-ninth gig, in a pair of gray sweats. Ava waited for him on the sofa. "We gonna watch a movie?"

"Gonna stay awake for it?" He chuckled, grabbing a beer out of the fridge. "Want one?"

"Yes." She stuck her tongue out at him. "To both."

He handed Ava a beer, and sitting down beside her, stretched his arm out along the back of the sofa. Moving closer, she tucked herself beneath it like she usually did, snuggling against him. Combing his fingers through her long blonde hair, Bo watched her drink her beer. He liked to watch her, imagining that bottle between her lips was his cock. All the things he could do to her with it.

"Pick a movie, pretty girl." He passed her the remote.

Ava settled on some action flick he'd never heard of on HBO. The movie didn't matter to him so much. She did. Fifteen minutes in, she pulled her feet up. And fifteen minutes after that, her head on his chest, she fell asleep.

"I knew it." He chortled.

But he watched the movie anyway. Kissing her hair. Stroking her skin. He wanted every moment he could have, because there weren't many left. Not like this.

Her eyes fluttered open as the end credits rolled. Bo

skimmed his lips across her cheek. "I almost don't want to go home."

She sat up to look at him. "Why?"

"I'm going to miss this." He picked up a lock of her hair. "Being here with you."

"Me too."

With her hair in his fingers, Bo pulled her closer. He brushed her lips with his, and then moving Ava onto his lap, fingers stroking her cheek, he kissed her. Lightly. Gently. Her lips warm and soft beneath his. They parted for him and his tongue slipped inside.

*Heaven.*

An angel and she felt like heaven.

Soft kisses to her neck, he inhaled fragrant skin. Threading his fingers in her hair, his thumb grazed the side of her face, rubbing back toward her ear. Bo kissed her cheeks, her eyelids, and her forehead, before returning to her mouth. Little nips. He sucked her bottom lip, gently pulling on it with his teeth.

She made that soft squeaky sound and he groaned. With his hand on the small of her back, Bo lightly pressed himself into her. Panting, Ava dropped her forehead to his. He looked into her big blue eyes, then scanned her entire face, stroking her temples with his thumbs.

"You're a really good kisser," she breathlessly murmured into his mouth.

He brushed his lips with hers again. "I love kissing." *You. I love kissing you.*

"Why?"

"Besides how good it feels"—he kissed the tip of her nose—"I love how intimate it is."

"What's your favorite part of a woman?"

Bo shifted himself beneath her. "You ask a lot of questions."

Biting her lip, Ava smiled. "I know. It's how we learn."

"Her neck." Nestling his nose in the curve of hers, he kissed the sensitive skin there. "Not what you thought I'd say, is it?"

"No, but then you're always surprising me."

"Just so you know, I love all the other parts too." Trailing his fingers from Ava's neck to her breast, Bo let his palm rest there. "What's your favorite part of a man?"

She glanced downward. "His hands."

*Oh, yeah?*

He squeezed.

# Twenty

A va rolled over, curling into the silk sheets of her sumptuous bed, memorizing the luxurious feel of it. She was going to miss these sheets, watching the ever-changing scenery outside her window, hanging out with the band, takeout food from greasy spoon diners, and soft-serve ice cream. But most of all, more than anything else, she was going to miss her darling girl, Emery, and her drummer boy.

They weren't really hers, of course. Ava knew that. She liked to think of them that way, though. And for the past six weeks they had been. Waking up to see Bo in his underwear. Teaching Emery her colors and numbers. To use the potty like a big girl. Sharing everything from movies and meals to hugs and kisses.

*God, that man can kiss.*

She squeezed her breast.

She wanted him to do it again.

Ava wondered if he would. She wondered if she would still see him after they returned to Chicago. Bo wanted her now, but would he still want her then? They were in a fantastical bubble, here in this rolling palace on wheels, where the real world didn't exist. She wished she could lock herself inside it. She wished she could keep him. Foolish wishes. She'd never be enough for a man like him. Still, Ava wished she could be, but then she'd lost her mind weeks ago.

Turning to the other side, she opened her eyes. Sunlight

streamed in through the window. She blinked a few times and abruptly sat up. "We're not moving. Why aren't we moving?"

Whipping off the covers, she got up and peered through the glass to gaze at the Indiana sunrise. They should be close to home by now, but they were parked on the lot at the venue.

He was standing at the toaster in his underwear.

"Bo, what's going on?"

His head turned, and slowly scanning her from head to toe, that wicked grin appeared. "It's a fucking beautiful morning." He pulled her to him. Fingers kneading her ass, he kissed her below the ear.

It tickled, making her giggle. "Why are we still here?"

"Bus needs a fuel pump or something," he murmured, trailing his lips down her neck. Bread popped up in the toaster. "We're not going anywhere."

"No?"

"No, do you mind?" Bo slipped his hands inside the back of her boy shorts. Squeezing the globes of flesh, he pressed the hardness in his boxers against her soft belly.

"Uh-uh."

His lips found hers and he kissed her. Bo melded their mouths together, pillowy-soft, yet demanding, with a building urgency. Her stomach wasn't just doing somersaults. It had taken a ride on the goddamn tilt-a-whirl and her entire world was spinning. Dizzy. Ava held onto him, spiraling further out of control with every nip of his teeth, every sweep of his tongue, every push of his cock into her belly. She wanted to feel him inside her.

Even if it was just this once.

She'd have the memory of him.

And that could last a lifetime.

A hand traveled from her bare bottom, to squeeze her hip, and brush over the skin of her belly. Down. Down. Down. Bo cupped her pussy, then squeezed it, pressing into the lips with his fingers. He drew one up through her slit and groaned into her mouth, halting at her clit.

"Wet and bare." He nipped her lip. "So fucking perfect. Spread your legs for me."

She did.

And Bo pushed that finger inside her.

Biting her lip, Ava moaned with his penetration. She needed it and wanted more.

"Yeah, that's it." With his thumb on her clit, he withdrew and pushed two fingers back inside. "You're going to make a big mess for me, aren't you, baby?"

"Yes." His words alone made her gush.

"I know you will." He stroked deep inside her and she whimpered. "Because I want you to. Aren't you gonna ask me why?"

But his thumb was pressing into her clit and she found it difficult to speak. "Why?"

"So I can clean it up with my tongue."

"Fuck."

Kissing along her jaw, Bo whispered into her ear, "You're gonna come so hard."

"Daddy?" The sleepy voice came from the bedroom.

Withdrawing his hand from inside her shorts, Bo pulled away from her. "Shit."

"Uh, I'll go get her." Ava tucked her hair behind her ear, turning toward the bedroom.

He pulled her back and kissed her on the lips. "To be continued." Then he winked, licking her from his fingers.

*Yeah, sure. When?*

She wasn't counting on it. She'd be home in her own bed tonight. Alone.

"Avie?" He peeked his head in her bedroom. She was tossing stuff in a bag. "Bus is ready. We're going."

"Okay."

She'd been quiet since this morning. Distant. She almost seemed sad. What was going on inside that pretty, little head of hers?

Bo sat next to her on the bed. Glasses on, her hair was back up in a pile on her head. He skimmed his fingers along her cheek. "What's wrong?"

"Nothing."

"Don't lie to me." He grasped her nape. "It's the one thing I can't tolerate. Something's bothering you, I can tell."

"I'm just." Ava let out a breath. "I dunno."

"Sad?"

"I am…"

Bo wrapped his arms around her, strumming her back with his fingers.

"…but it's something else too."

"What?" He pulled his head back to look at her.

"I couldn't explain it even if I tried." She shrugged. "It's like nothing will ever be the same again."

Bo kissed her on the lips.

And Venery's bus pulled out beside them.

"C'mon." He took her hand. "Let's go watch I-65 through the window."

Ava rolled her big blue eyes. "That sounds fun."

"Or we can make out on the couch until Emmy wakes up. Your choice."

She snorted. "Guess we'll be looking out the window."

"That isn't what you wanted this morning."

They didn't bother turning the TV on. Ava lay with him on the sofa while he played with her hair, holding her and kissing her, rubbing his cheek against hers. "You should stay with me tonight."

"I have class in the morning."

"I can take you to school."

She didn't get a chance to respond to that. His phone vibrated on the table as sounds of Emery stirring came from the other room.

"Let me get her."

Bo read the text. "Hey, Ed. Tay wanted me to tell you to get off at the next exit."

"Will do."

Ava came out with Emery just as they pulled off the highway. "What's going on?"

"I dunno." He shrugged, getting a juice box out of the fridge. "Bus must be acting up again. Tay said to take the next exit."

She stood there, looking past him, through the window. "Yeah, I suppose that makes sense."

"Did you have a nice nap, sunshine?" Handing Emery the juice box, he kissed the top of her head, then Ava's cheek.

"Bo." Ava grabbed his hand and squeezed it. "It's something bad, Bo."

"What?"

She pointed out the window. "Look."

Taylor paced in circles, pulling at his hair, while Sloan solemnly stood there, frozen. He looked shell-shocked or something.

"What the fuck?" Bo looked back at Ava. "Stay here."

He raced down the steps to the truck stop parking lot.

Matt and Kit exited the bus, eyes red and glassy.

"What the hell happened?"

"Kyan." It was Sloan who spoke.

Taylor doubled over, and clutching his knees, began to sob or scream. Maybe both at once. It was a pained, mournful cry he'd never heard before.

"Jesse called."

*No.*

"There was an accident."

*No. Oh, fuck. Linnea. No.*

"Kyan's gone, man."

*"Love you, brother."*

*"You got this…Love you."*

Bo sat right there on the ground, rocking with his head between his knees. "No, no, no, no, no."

He felt a hand squeeze his shoulder and looked up. "You were right, Avie. Nothing will ever be the same again."

"C'mon, brother." Kodiak tapped him on the shoulder. "Help us get him out of the car."

Bo opened his eyes. Head tipped back, Dillon was pounding his chest on the seat beside him. He looked like he couldn't breathe or he was going to be sick.

"He's trashed, man."

It sounded like Matt, but Bo couldn't be sure. He was wasted too.

"Jesus, he's going to vomit." Kelsey opened her door and got out. "I can't believe he let himself get like this."

*He just buried his brother, you fucking bitch.*

"You're gonna be okay, Dill." Bo hooked an arm around him. "We got you."

Somehow, he, Matt, and Kodiak got him out of the Uber and into his bed, while Dillon's sorry-ass excuse for a girlfriend just stood there and watched.

Kodiak pulled off Dillon's shoe. Kelsey pushed him out of the way. "Thanks, but I can take it from here."

Bo stood on the sidewalk. He debated if he should go across the street or down the block. The wind blew. It smelled like rain.

Matt shook his shoulder. "You all right, man?"

"I hope Linn didn't see that. I don't know where to go." He held his hands up. "Where's Ava? I need my angel."

"Your house."

He started walking. "I'm coming, baby."

Bo opened his front door, and tossing his black suit jacket on the floor, sat down on the sofa. He didn't trust himself to climb the stairs just yet. Tipping his head back, he closed his eyes, but he didn't like the images he saw.

Shelley choking on her final breath.

Kyan not breathing at all.

*What in the actual fuck?*

Maybe he should have another drink, pass out, and not remember anything until tomorrow. He couldn't do that, though. Ava and Emery were upstairs. He opened his eyes, staring at nothing in front of him, but he couldn't silence the sounds.

Sobbing.

Choirboys.

Bagpipes.

They were just so fucking loud. Bo wanted to cover his ears, but he couldn't. He had to carry Kyan's casket to his grave.

Taylor looked over at him and nodded. "Count us off, Bo."

"One, two, three…"

It was the longest walk he ever took, the heaviest burden he ever carried.

He felt the tickle of hot saline trickling down his face. He didn't care. Let the tears come. Bo blinked them from his lashes.

*Life is short, eat the cookie.*

*You got this…Love you.*

*The beginning is always today.*

He wanted her. Where was she? Beautiful Ava. She loved his daughter. Maybe she could love him.

"Ava?"

*I'm so fucked. And so fucked up.*

He felt her fingers in his hair. "Bo?"

"Is Emmy asleep?"

"Yeah." Nodding, Ava sat down beside him.

"I don't want her to see me like this."

"Are you okay?"

"No." Bo looked at her then. "I need you."

And grabbing her shoulders, he took her mouth. His kiss wasn't soft or gentle. It was do or die. A burning need to taste her, to claim her, to win her. Bo was done fighting it.

Biting and nipping and sucking her sweet lips, he pushed her into the sofa. He yanked her shirt up and squeezed those perfect tits, sucking her nipples into his mouth. Ava deserved better than him, more than he was capable of at the moment, but he couldn't wait another minute.

He fumbled, unfastening his pants.

"What are you doing?"

"I fucking need you."

Her lips parted with a nod.

Bo pulled her panties to the side, and with a swift, hard thrust he was finally home.

*Fucking Christ.*

It felt so good to be inside her. He pulled himself out and thrust in again. Tethering himself to her nipples, Bo held onto them. Over and over. Harder and harder. Faster and faster. He fucked her as if his life depended on it, like he'd die if he wasn't inside her.

And she gave him back everything he gave her.

Ava took his nipples between her fingers and pinched. She pulled him by the hair to her mouth, kissing him with a feverish intensity he'd never in his life felt before. Her hips smacked into his with every thrust.

She let go of his hair, her hands reaching around him, finger-nails sinking into his ass. "Fuck, Bo. Please."

The sofa thumped against the wall, mingling with her cries. Bo lowered his forehead to hers. "Do you need me?"

"Yes."

"You need to come, baby?"

She panted beneath him. "Yes."

Rubbing her clit, Bo drove into her pussy, as hard and as deep as he could go. She screamed, and he let himself come inside her.

*I could love you.*

He kissed her, and wrapping his body around hers, he held her.

*I think maybe I already do.*

# Twenty-One

She lay gasping beneath him—with the weight of his body on hers, Ava was struggling to breathe. Not that she minded. She didn't mind the whiskey on his breath, their comingled cum dripping between her legs, or Bo nuzzling on her neck.

He took her face in his hands, stroking her temples—she loved how he did that—and tenderly kissed her. Slower. Softer. There was no urgency to it like before. It felt different. More intimate. Like he was making love to her mouth.

"I'm sorry."

"What for?"

Bo didn't answer. Instead, scooping her from the sofa, he carried her upstairs to his bed. Kicking off his shoes, he unbuttoned his shirt and tossed it. His pants, unzipped and hanging precariously off his narrow hips, fell to the floor.

Ava watched him from the bed. He stood there for a moment, gazing at her, completely unaffected by his nudity. She'd seen him in his underwear plenty of times, so she wasn't shocked by it, but seeing a naked Bo was a completely different story.

He caught Ava looking at that part of him he'd just had inside her, and with a smirk, climbed into bed. Bo stretched out on his side next to her and started playing with her hair. "You deserved better than that."

*Better?*

Was he out of his mind? Her pussy was raw, her clit swollen and throbbing. Ava could still feel him inside her. Not to mention, she had an out-of-this-world orgasm she didn't have to give herself.

"I'm clean, I promise." His fingers swirled through the mess coating her inner thighs, rubbing it into her skin. "You're on the Pill or something, aren't you?"

She hesitated. "Yes, of course."

It was easier than explaining, and most likely it would never matter anyway.

"I wanted to make love to you our first time." Bo kissed below her ear, moving his mouth along her jaw. "Please, let me make it right."

His lips met hers, and he kissed her, stealing her breath along with her reason. Ava couldn't think straight when he was near, reality slipped away when he touched her. Lifting the hem of her shirt, Bo tossed it. She decided sanity was way overrated.

"You're so perfect," he whispered, fingertips softly brushing the swell of her breast.

She'd always thought they were too big, and her ass too fat, for her slender frame.

Her chest heaving with every breath, he placed a light kiss on her nipple and sucked it into his mouth. Ava held his head, fingers tangled in his hair, as Bo nuzzled between her breasts, squeezing them, kissing her skin, before lavishing his attention on the other one. He wasn't in a hurry, taking his time, driving her crazy with every sweep of his tongue, every pull of his mouth, every nip of his teeth.

No one had ever done that to her before. It was usually a quick grope on the way to the main event. Ava never thought her nipples were particularly sensitive. She must have been wrong, because the way Bo worshipped them ignited a fire between her thighs.

She found herself pressing her body into his, seeking... something.

Bo groaned, a hungry sound, as he kissed his way down her abdomen, peeling her ruined underwear down her thighs. Kneeling between her legs, his thick cock bobbed at his navel, the silver metal piercing its head winking at her. He brought her sodden panties to his nose, inhaling them like chocolate chip cookies right out of the oven, and her eyes widened.

"I've been dying for this." He lifted her leg over his shoulder. "I just know you're going to taste even better than you smell."

*Oh, God! He can't mean to…*

He came inside her. She was a mess down there. "Bo, you can't…"

"Can't what?"

"You know." Embarrassed, Ava looked up at the ceiling. "We had sex, so I need to—"

"Do you think I care?" Bo dipped his finger inside her and sucked it into his mouth. "Any man who's afraid to taste his own cum doesn't deserve to have you."

Bo was not afraid. Not. At. All.

He cleaned the mess from her thighs with his tongue, caressing her pussy. Running his fingers over the bare, swollen lips, Bo parted them, spreading her wide with his thumbs. Then his mouth was on her, tongue lapping at her hole, dragging up and down her slit, spearing it inside her. Groaning as he did so.

She was holding her breath, anticipating the moment his tongue would touch her clit. It was his lips she felt kissing her there first. Ava clutched his hair. He circled around the swollen nub, teasing her, but not quite touching it. She lifted her hips, trying to get his tongue where she needed it to be.

Bo chuckled against her pussy. His hand on her thigh, he pushed her legs wider apart. She felt it then. "Fuck."

That velvety, wet tongue slowly stroked her clit. Up and down. Side to side. He slurped on it, laved circles around it. And just as slowly, she was dying.

He slipped a finger inside her. "Now, what do I want, baby?"

"I don't know," she panted. "What?"

"Yes, you do." Adding a second finger, Bo hooked them inside her. "Make me a big mess."

*Oh, fuck.*

And he sucked on her clit, his fingers pressing on her walls, stroking a sweet spot she hadn't known was there.

Ava pulled on his hair, her head rising from the pillow. Torn between pulling him off her or pushing him even closer, she screamed, the sensation wickedly intense.

The orgasm jolted through her, and as it slowly subsided, Ava let go of his hair, her head returning to rest on the pillow.

Bo crawled up her body and kissed her. "See how delicious we are together, baby?"

She tasted their combined flavor on her tongue, and swiping it across her bottom lip, she smiled.

He smiled back and kissed her again.

She blinked her eyes open. Waking from an orgasm-induced sleep, Ava panicked, thinking she was late for class, until she remembered it was Sunday. She almost thought she'd been dreaming. Except her body ached and she was sore between her legs. Bo gripped her hips so tight, she probably had imprints of his fingers on her skin.

Not that she was complaining.

He'd given her memories that would last a lifetime, all right.

They'd fucked and made love—Bo did *not* use the terms interchangeably, insisting there was a difference between the two—so many times she lost count. Ava wasn't sure how she was even awake.

Rain tapped against the windows. The bedroom was semi-dark, cast in muted colors from gray light through stained glass. Softly snoring, Bo slept soundly behind her, his arm wrapped around her middle. Ava glanced at the monitor on the bedside table. She should slip away now, before he and Emery woke up.

The light of day always brought reality with it. He'd been drinking, and after the tragedy of Kyan's death, the wake, and the funeral, Bo sought comfort in her. That's all this was. Ava knew that. And she was okay with it. So, to spare them both the awkwardness that comes with the morning after, she should just go.

"Stop it, Avie." His arm tightened around her.

"What?"

"Thinking so much." Fingertips grazed her skin. "Your brain is going a mile a minute. I can tell. This only gets weird if you make it that way."

She rolled over to face him. "I'm not trying to."

"Good morning, baby." And he kissed her, morning breath and all. "That's better." Bo held her against his chest, running his fingers through her hair, rubbing her back. His touch gave her goosebumps. He pulled the blanket over them. "Are you cold?"

"No."

"Oh." He looked down at her with a knowing grin. "Don't even think about going anywhere. You're mine now."

"We had sex, so I'm yours? That's your logic?"

"Uh-huh. All mine." Bo kissed her forehead, squeezing her tight.

"I see." Ava smiled against his shoulder. "Does that make you all mine then?"

"Absofuckinglutely." He tipped her chin up. "I don't want anyone else. Do you?"

"No."

"Good." Bo kissed her on the lips this time. "You should move out of your room. Live here with me. And Emmy."

"Why?"

"Why not?"

He was rubbing his cheek against hers, making rational thought difficult. "It's a little too soon for that, don't you think?"

"We've been living together for six weeks already, so no, I do not think."

Ava chuckled. "That was different."

"How so?"

"I was just the babysitter, I had my own room, and we weren't having sex," she replied, having come to her senses.

"Baby, we're gonna have lots of sex no matter what, so you'll have to get used to sharing a room with me." Bo framed her face in his hands, and cushioning her lips between his, he kissed her. "And, Avie?"

"Yeah?"

"You were never *just* the babysitter."

*Gah! This man…*

"I'll think about it."

"You and me." He hooked his pinky with hers. "Together."

She was so fucked.

*I could fall in love with him.*

Who was she kidding?

She already had.

# Twenty - Two

She hadn't moved in.

Not officially anyway. But when she wasn't at school, Ava spent most of her time with him and Emery. She had clothes hanging in his closet and kept a toothbrush by the bathroom sink. That was something, right? They'd only been back a few weeks, though. Bo was still working on her.

Sorrow veiled Park Place, and it wouldn't be lifting anytime soon. Kyan's death had devastated them all, his absence painfully felt, and for none of them more so than Linnea and Dillon. They all did what they could to help them, and each other, navigate their way to a new normal.

Linnea needed the space to grieve in private right now, and he respected that. Kodiak saw his sister and her brother-in-law daily, and kept him updated, but Bo still worried about his seraph and Dillon. Death has a way of forcing the ones left behind to question life. Love. Family. All the things that truly matter. Redefining them. Shelley's untimely death had changed him, and so had Kyan's.

Life really is short.

And Bo planned on eating all the fucking cookies.

Taking his daughter by the hand, Bo and Emery made the short walk to the opposite end of the street. There was a crispness to the October air that hadn't been present yesterday. The leaves were already turning colors, falling from the trees in an autumnal dance to skitter with their footsteps along the sidewalk.

Bo poked his head inside the first-floor office. Brendan was the only one here, the vacant seats glaringly empty. "Hey, B. How you doin', man?"

"Everything just feels off." He lifted his shoulder, releasing a breath. "If it weren't for Katelyn and Dec, I'd…I don't think I'd be able to get through it."

He squeezed Brendan's shoulder. "Where's Jess and Dill?"

"Dillon went over to Linn's," he answered, absently chewing on the corner of his lip. "Jesse's here. He's downstairs with Tay."

"You know…whatever you need, Bren."

"I know." He glanced to Emery then, and smiled, reaching for her hand. "Hey, sweetheart. No hello for Uncle B?"

She climbed into his chair. "Hi, Unkey B." And wrapping her arms around his neck, Emery squeezed him tight. Maybe she sensed he could use a hug right then.

Hugging her back, Brendan glanced up at him. "We're the lucky ones, brother."

"The luckiest."

Jesse came upstairs from the studio, Taylor alongside him. "Oh, good. You're here. I have something for you." He handed him some folded sheets of music. "Take a look, will you? I think it needs keys."

"I can do that." Bo stuffed them in his back pocket.

"CJ is still on me about that bloody *Revolver* article," Taylor informed him, sliding his arm around Jesse. "You know I'm not keen on it. I told him now is not a good time."

*Asshole should already know that, so why in the fuck is he even asking?*

"Tell him maybe we'll consider it after the holidays." Bo shook his head with a snicker. "If we're lucky, he'll forget about it by then."

Brendan chuckled, kissing Emery's button nose. "Fat chance of that."

It was Friday, and he looked forward to Fridays now. Before Ava, every day was the same as any other, and it didn't matter what day of the week it was. But just like when he was a kid, Friday signaled the end of the school week, which meant the beginning of a leisurely weekend with his girls.

Parked at the curb where she was student-teaching, Bo was here to pick up Ava. Emery impatiently waited, peering out the window from her car seat. She'd been missing her since they dropped Ava off this morning. "Mommy, Mommy!"

*One day, darling.*

Bo smiled to himself, watching her emerge from the building with her backpack and a large tote bag. Ava greeted Emery first, giving her hugs and kisses, before getting in the seat beside him. Leaning over the console, she kissed him, slipping her tongue into his mouth.

"How was school today, baby?"

"Let's just say I'm really glad it's Friday," Ava replied, kissing him on the cheek.

Right then and there, Bo decided it was pizza night. He'd order from Rossi's as soon as they got home. After dinner, they'd read Emery a story. Tuck her in for the night. And then, he was going to take extra special care of his girl.

A sausage and pepperoni pizza, two episodes of *Puffin Rock*, and an entire chapter of *Frankenstein* later, Bo and Ava snuggled together in bed with the original *Top Gun* on the TV and slices of Italian rum cake in their laps.

He swallowed a forkful. "Are you a dog person or a cat person?"

"Both, I guess," Ava answered, glancing away from the TV. "Why?"

"I want to get us a dog."

"Yeah?"

"Yeah." Bo grinned. "I've been thinking about it for a while."

"Well then..." She dabbed whipped cream on his nose. "...I guess we're getting a dog."

Bo took away her plate, setting it along with his on the side table. He pulled the playful blonde vixen onto his lap. "You best be planning to lick that off me."

Ava kissed his nose, while scooping more whipped cream from her plate. She smeared it across his mouth, then licked it from his lips. Grasping her by the nape, Bo devoured the sweet cream on her tongue, blindly reaching into the Italian cake.

He trailed gooey fingers from her neck, down to her nipple. Twisting it, his tongue followed, licking up every trace of the rich pastry cream. Bo squeezed her perfectly round tits, sucking that delectable morsel into his mouth. Ava whimpered, a fucking delicious sound that made him insane. He bit into her, and letting go of her nipple, grazed it with his teeth.

Not to be outdone, she reached into the plate and covered his dick in rum syrup and chocolate cream. Ava knelt between his legs, and swiping her tongue across her pretty, pink lips, she leaned down and began to lick him clean.

Squeezing the base, she swirled her tongue around the pierced head. His fingers went to her hair, and making a mess of it, Bo held her to his dick. "Take it all, pretty girl," he rasped, pushing himself deeper down her throat. "Yeah, fuck."

Gagging and sputtering—the hottest sounds ever—Ava swallowed him and sucked. Her head bobbing up and down on his cock, she squeezed his balls and massaged his taint with cream-covered fingers. "I'm gonna come in your mouth, and when I do, you're gonna hold it. Got that?"

She made a garbled noise he took as a yes.

With the burn at the base of his spine, his balls tightened near to the point of bursting. "Don't swallow...fuck," Bo groaned out, exploding. He filled her mouth, then brought her lips up to his.

And he kissed her.

Salty and sweet. Thick and delicious. Cum and Italian rum cake.

Ava woke up at the first sign of light. She wanted to sleep in like most people do on the weekends, but ever since the tour, her internal clock wouldn't allow it. Bo had no such problem. With his arm draped across her, his breath fanned her hair. Rubbing her fingertips on his smooth skin, she studied the beautiful face of the man she'd fallen in love with.

Yes, she was sure of it now.

There was no denying it anymore.

She could list a gazillion adjectives to describe him. Silly, sweet, and sensual. Kind, thoughtful, and caring. Bo was everything. How could she not love him?

He was so open and uninhibited—free of constraints. She'd never felt as comfortable with anyone as she did with him. Bo made it so easy for her to express her sexual self. Looking at her as if she really was beautiful. And the way he kissed her and touched her made Ava feel so cherished and adored.

"What are you thinking about, baby?" His lips grazed her forehead.

"You."

"Yeah?" Ava felt his smile on her skin. "I was dreaming."

"What did you dream about?"

"You."

Maybe he did love her a little. For now, anyway. She'd bask in the feeling as long as she could. Eventually, her heart would be broken. Along with the rest of her. It was inevitable.

"Go back to sleep, angel," Bo whispered, stroking her hair down her back. Ava closed her eyes. "You're going need it."

He wasn't kidding.

Five adults and five children under the age of three gathered around the big marble island in the center of the Peters' kitchen, ready to transform five orange pumpkins into jack-o-lanterns. They were having a little Halloween shindig of their own, while everyone who wasn't here went to a masquerade ball at the club Katie's husband and his cousins owned.

She and Bo held an excited Emery perched between the two of them. Monica and Danielle corralled three boisterous boys. And a subdued, pregnant Linnea patted the back of baby Ireland, who slept on her shoulder. This was the first time Ava had seen her since Kyan died, and she didn't know what to say.

While Bo was preoccupied with his pumpkin—translation, trying real hard not to carve his own flesh—Linnea leaned into her ear. "Are you two a thing now?"

"A thing?"

"You know." She dropped her shoulders, kissing Ireland's cheek. "Together. A couple."

"Oh." Biting her lip, Ava nodded. "Yeah, I guess we are."

"I'm happy for you." Her lips twitched up a little. "We all hoped that would happen. Bo is…he's good down to his soul with a heart of pure gold, you know?"

She knew.

Ava hesitated, pursing her lips to the side. "I'm so sorry about Kyan. I wish I knew what else to say."

"It's okay, sweetie." Linnea linked an arm through hers. "No one does."

Glancing up from his pumpkin, Bo smiled at them.

"Just love him well."

She walked away then to lay the baby down in a portable crib in the den.

"I'm glad she agreed to come over," Danielle said, watching her. "I was afraid they'd talk her into going to the club with them."

"Yes, me too," her wife agreed. "The Red Door is the last place she needs to be right now."

"Kodiak never would have allowed it anyway." Scooping the guts out of his pumpkin, Bo snickered. "Or Dillon either, for that matter."

"It's just a costume party. Why not?"

All three of them stopped what they were doing to look at her, but it was Danielle who answered, "At a sex club."

*Oh.*

*What?*

Ava turned to Bo. "The Red Door is a sex club?"

"Sex positive." Rubbing her belly, Linnea returned to stand beside her. "Charlotte's awake."

Bo grinned. "She's kicking?"

"Yeah," she said, a smile on her sad face.

"There's a baby in Auntie Linn's tummy," he explained to a bewildered Emery.

Linnea took the child's hand, placing it on her belly. "Want to feel her?"

"Baby." She gasped with the hugest grin Ava had ever seen.

Standing behind Linnea, Bo gazed at her and winked. "You want a baby brother or sister one day, Emmy?"

"Baby."

He placed his hand beside his daughter's. Feeling the baby kick, his indigo eyes filled. Bo kissed the top of Linnea's head, tears rolling down her face. "A part of him will always be with you, baby girl."

Danielle was crying. Monica was crying. Hell, she was crying too. For the man who never got to meet his daughter, for the wife who mourned him, and the unborn child he left behind.

"Dillon got to feel her kick." Linnea sniffled, grasping onto Bo. "But Kyan never did."

She watched him comfort her. Holding Linnea, Bo laid his head on hers, rubbing the baby in her belly. And Ava grieved for something she would never have.

A little hand tugged on hers. "Mommy. Potty."

Lifting his head, Bo blew her a kiss.

Monica smiled warmly and winked. "Down the hall. First door on your left."

Later that evening, after Emery was asleep, they cuddled together on the sofa, relaxing with a bottle of wine. Bo's jack-o-lantern stared at them from across the room. They'd set it out on the porch and light it tomorrow.

"What are you thinking about, Avie?"

She took a sip of her wine. "How did I not know it's a sex club?" It was the first thing that popped into her head.

"I figured you did." His fingers trailed down her arm. "Being Katie's your friend and all."

"Nope." Ava sniggered. "She forgot to mention that part."

"Maybe she wasn't sure how you'd react." Bo pulled her closer against him. "They don't hide what the club is, but they don't advertise it either. You won't even find a sign out front."

"Why?"

"To keep it private," he simply said. "Not everyone is accepting of what goes on in there."

"And what's that?"

"Anything you might desire." Bo winked. "I'll take you if you ever want to go."

"You could have gone with the boys tonight," she told him, looking down at her lap. "I wouldn't have minded."

*Liar, liar, pants on fire.*

"Now, why would I want to do that?" He tipped her chin up. "When everything I desire is right here."

"Me?"

"You." Bo kissed her lips. "Sex is everywhere, but the connection you and I have is so special and rare. That's everything, Avie."

The little voice in her head whispered, "*Tell him.*"

But she couldn't.

She wasn't ready to lose him yet.

# Twenty-Three

She walked in the front door to the rich, clear notes of a piano. It stopped, then started again, the melody haunting and exquisite. Tiptoeing down the stairs, Ava followed the sound.

His back was to her. Sitting on the bench, his eyes on hand-written sheet music in front of him, Bo's fingers swept over the ivory keys. Emery sat, swinging her feet, in the space beside him. Ava just stood there, transfixed, listening from the doorway.

He lifted his fingers from the keys, and picking up a pencil, scribbled something on the paper. Emery, turning her head, noticed her standing there then.

"Mommy," she happily shouted, sliding off the bench.

Ava picked her up, and rubbing noses, they both giggled. "How's my cutie-pie?"

She glanced up. With his back to the piano, having turned around, Bo watched them from where he sat, a jubilant smile on his face. He stood up, and wrapping her in his arms, Emery sand-wiched between them, he kissed her.

"I didn't know you could play the piano."

"Why else would I have one?" He chuckled. "Decoration?"

Ava looked around his music room. Framed album covers and band memorabilia hung on the walls. Guitars in stands. His kit in the corner.

Feeling her cheeks heat, she shrugged. "Well…yeah."

"My mom started me on the piano when I was three. Allie too." Bo sat back down on the bench and began to play.

"You're very good."

"Not really." He stopped. "I'm okay. I mean…technically, I can play, but I don't love it."

"I'm not following."

"To be really good at something, you have to love it." Bo swung his legs around and chuckled. "And the piano always felt like homework to me."

"How did you start playing drums?"

"Santa left one of those kiddie drum kits under the tree for me when I was five." He grinned. "And the rest, as they say, is history. Mom made me keep up with the piano lessons until I was thirteen, though."

"What were you playing?" Emery in her lap, Ava sat down beside him. "It's beautiful."

"A tune Taylor started writing. He thought it could use piano—keyboards—and I agreed. So, I'll finish it, and then Sloan will put lyrics to it."

She blinked. "And that's how it's done?"

"This time." Leaning in, Bo smacked a kiss on her lips. "Sometimes Sloan gives us the words first. Tay comes up with most of the music, but I've written a bunch of our stuff too."

"You did it again, Bo Robertson."

"What?"

Ava nipped at his full bottom lip. "You just keep on surprising me."

"I hope I always do." And he kissed her. "Hey, wasn't I supposed to pick you up from class at two?"

"Prof let us out early since it's Thanksgiving break."

"Oh, baby, what will we do?"

And that wicked grin she loved, appeared.

They did plenty. Apparently Bo had the entire week planned out for them. A train ride downtown with Emery to see the Magnificent Mile Lights Festival parade, the lighting of the tree in Millennium Park, and fireworks. A day at the zoo. Getting the house ready for Christmas. All the typical things families do during the holidays.

But after long, laughter-filled days, once Emery was tucked in her bed, the nights belonged only to them. Sky-gazing on the rooftop. Sharing a bottle of wine on the patio, wrapped together in a blanket. They fucked outside. Cold air feels amazing on hot, sweat-slicked skin. Peeling sweet potatoes in the kitchen, Ava smiled to herself at the memory of it.

Bo had music playing on the sound system while they prepped the contribution he was taking to Kit's for Thanksgiving tomorrow. He came up behind her, and wrapping his arms around her middle, kissed the tender skin beneath her ear. "Dance with me."

"I can't dance." Leaning into him, Ava giggled. "My sister dances. I have no rhythm."

"Yes, you do." He turned her around and kissed her. "I know it for a fact. So dance with me."

Her arms went around his neck as Bo pulled her from the counter. He held her to him, fingers caressing her back, as he led the steps. And laying her head on his shoulder, Ava followed. He kissed her hair as they swayed in the kitchen. She squeezed her eyes closed, praying the song would never end. There was nothing better than being right here in his arms.

It did end, though.

Everything does.

Lifting her head from his shoulder, Ava lost herself in the indigo eyes that stared into hers. She touched her lips to his, parting for him, needing his kiss at this moment as much as she needed air to breathe.

Pulling the hair down her back, Bo took possession of her mouth, their tongues twirling together in a dance of their own. His hands slid beneath her sweater, feeling their way up her back. Pressing her into him. Ava could feel the hard cock in his sweats against her belly and the beating pulse between her legs.

Gasping, she pulled her head back. "I want you."

"I always want you, Avie." Bo lifted her sweater, pulling it over her head. She wore no bra underneath. His fingertips brushed across her nipples. "Every way I can have you."

He lowered his head to her breast, long strands of silk sweeping her skin, to suck a nipple into his mouth. A soft whimper escaped at the delicious sensation. The pulse between her legs growing stronger, Ava grabbed onto his hair and held him to her breast.

Tugging on her nipple with his teeth, Bo guided her down to the floor. "You make me fucking crazy." He nuzzled her neck, nipping at her skin, grinding against her pelvis. "I want you naked."

Ava rubbed his nipples. "Let's go upstairs."

"Uh-uh."

"But…"

Bo pulled her leggings down her thighs, and running his fingers through her pussy, he groaned. "So wet, and it's all for me." His tongue swiped up her slit. "God, I love eating this pussy." And he proceeded to devour her, right there on the kitchen floor. Pointed tongue fluttering on her clit, fingers inside her.

Thighs shaking, Ava was so close to coming, but Bo didn't let her. He stopped. Pulling his tongue and fingers away, he kissed up her belly and rolled her over on top of him.

"Why'd you stop?"

"Floor's too hard for my pretty girl." He winked at her, pulling his sweats down his legs. "Put me in you. I want to watch."

Gripping his cock, Ava lined it up at her entrance and nudged the tip inside.

"Yeah, just like that." He reached up to tweak her nipple. "Nice and slow."

Lowering herself onto him, her thighs trembling, she cried out, "Oh, God." Why did he feel so much bigger this way?

"See how you stretch open for me, baby. So beautiful."

Ava glanced down, watching, as she impaled herself the rest of the way on his cock. She didn't have anything to hold onto, no headboard, nothing. So she gathered his hair in her hands like reins, and she rode him.

"Fuck, Avie. Nothing feels better than being inside you." His fingers tightly gripped her hips.

She leaned forward, her nipples brushing his chest, and kissed him. "I love the way you feel inside me."

*I love you.*

But she couldn't tell him that.

"Wanna fly, angel?" Bo traced her lips with his fingers. "Suck them."

Taking them in her mouth, Ava did as he asked.

She felt him probing at her bottom. He'd never touched her there like that before. Tensing up, she whimpered his name, "Bo."

"Shh, relax, angel," he soothed. "Let me in."

Sucking in a breath, she tried. His finger pushed through the ring of muscle while Ava screamed from the burn. Or perhaps pleasure. Because once he got past it, the sensation lessened, replaced by an odd, yet wonderful, feeling of fullness.

"You did so good, baby," Bo praised, kissing her lips. "So, so good."

With her shaking thighs splayed open across his body, both entrances filled, Ava rested her forehead on his. Slowly and gently, Bo began moving his finger. She needed to move, but didn't trust her legs to hold her. Using the strength in her arms, she lifted herself from his chest, and holding onto his shoulders, tremulously began to rock.

"My beautiful Ava." He cupped the side of her face with his free hand. "Look at me."

Her gaze locked with his.

"I wished for you." Bo rubbed her cheek with his fingers, and lifting his hips off the floor, pushed himself even deeper inside her. "And you're mine."

She raised herself higher, and never taking her eyes off him, Ava took what she wanted. And she wanted Bo. She'd wished for him too, and for however long this lasted, he was hers.

"Always," she whispered.

He grabbed her by the hair, and pulling her back down to his chest, Bo kissed her.

"Where are we going?"

Bo passed by the First Avenue exit that would take them home.

"You'll see." He reached across the console for Ava's hand and held it on his thigh. "It's a surprise."

He took the split off the Kennedy Expressway to the Edens, heading toward the suburbs north of the city.

"I guess we're not going to Woodfield."

"Nope." Bo chuckled, giving her hand a squeeze. "A shopping mall on Black Friday is definitely not on my to-do list."

"You have a list?"

He glanced at Emery, passed out in her car seat. Pressing her hand between his legs, he answered, "Absofuckinglutely."

"Jesus, one day I was gone." Ava giggled, snatching her hand away.

"Put that back." Bo returned her hand to his thigh, lacing their fingers together. "One day was one too many. I missed you." He glanced at her. "And Emmy missed you. Everybody did."

It surprised him just how much, but in the six months since that day in Brendan's backyard, along with his daughter, Ava had become his world. She went to see her family for Thanksgiving. He'd taken her to the station yesterday morning and kissed her goodbye. The realization struck him as soon as she boarded that train. Half of his heart was going with her.

They passed Libertyville. "Are we going to Wisconsin?"

"Not quite," he assured her, getting off at the next exit. "We're almost there."

He turned down a long drive, empty fields on either side. Emery woke from the sound of tires crunching on gravel. A white farmhouse with a big front porch came into view. Bo parked behind an old Ford pickup truck.

Ava glanced at him without turning her head. Only her eyes moved. "Why am I picturing Leatherface busting through that door with a chainsaw?"

"No more scary movies for you." Leaning over the console, he kissed her cheek.

She made no move to unbuckle her seatbelt. "It looks creepy."

An old woman stepped out on the porch and waved.

Ava finally turned her head. "It's Leatherface's grandmother."

"C'mon." With a soft chuckle, he opened his door.

Bo held Ava's hand and carried his half-asleep koala bear up the porch steps. The woman waited for them, cheeks reddened from the cold, holding her plaid flannel tight around her midsection with crooked fingers. A cat preened at her feet, while a chorus of barking could be heard from beyond the door.

"Hope you didn't have any trouble finding the place." She let go of the flannel, extending a gnarly hand. "He's ready and waiting for ya. Come on in."

Ava glanced up at him. With a breathy little gasp, her blue eyes got bigger. She was getting it now.

"Have a seat. I'll be right back."

"Bo," she said, squeezing his hand as they sat on a sofa covered in plaid. The old woman must have a thing for it. "What did you do?"

She returned carrying the puppy in her arms. White, brown, tan, and blue merle in color, with a wavy coat. Pink freckled nose. Bright blue eyes. A large spot of brown fur surrounding his left.

"Surprise." Bo leaned over and kissed her, hugging Emery. "Look, baby, Daddy found us a puppy."

"Puppy, puppy, puppy," she squealed, as the woman placed him on Ava's lap.

Wagging his little tail, he licked her face. "Oh, my goodness." She giggled. "He's so cute. What kind of dog is he?"

"Can't say for sure." The woman smiled down at the sight of Emery petting her new friend. "Someone left him on my porch. I run a small rescue here on the farm," she explained. "But he looks like an Australian Shepherd to me."

"Oh, Bo, I love him," Ava exclaimed, kissing him and the puppy's wet nose.

*Do you love me too?*

His lips quirked up, thinking maybe, just maybe, she might.

# Twenty-Four

Bo looked up at the overcast sky, sniffing the air. It smelled like snow.

Emery frolicked around the backyard, Chester nipping at her heels. That's what they ended up naming him. Goofy and cute, it fit. He looked like a Chester.

Ava had just finished the semester. Her brother was staying in Florida this Christmas, so she was staying right here with him. No goodbye kisses at the train station. With close to a month off from school for winter break, Bo was determined to use the time to convince her to make Park Place her official address. It puzzled him that she hadn't already—she practically lived here, for chrissakes—but something seemed to be holding her back.

"C'mere, Chester." Bo patted his leg and the puppy ran over to him. "Good boy."

Giggling and out of breath, Emery followed behind him. "C'mon, darling, we have to go in now."

"Why?"

"You have to take a bath and put on a pretty dress."

"Why?"

With a chuckle, Bo got down on his haunches. Did she get that from Ava? Everything was 'why' lately.

"Because we're going over to Uncle Tay's."

"Why?"

"So you and Chandan can play."

Emery smiled at that. "Okay."

The weekend before Christmas, and Taylor was having the boys over for a little holiday cheer before he took off with his family to London and Dublin. Each of them holding one of her hands, Bo and Ava swung Emery over every crack in the sidewalk all the way to his house. Luckily, she made a beeline for Chandan as soon as they got there. He could use a breather. And maybe a drink.

CJ and his whiny-ass girlfriend were here.

*Definitely calls for a drink. More like two.*

Bo ladled warm, mulled wine into glasses, giving one to Ava. "Here you go, baby."

She took a sip. "This is good."

He kissed her lips. "Mmm…sure is."

"I told you, no playing with the babysitter, Bo-Bo," CJ slurred, wagging his finger at him from across the room like his mother did when he was five.

He was over by the bar, chatting up Matt and Taylor. Obviously, he'd been here for a while already. Or he started early on his own. Fucker was soused. The whiny one sat on a barstool next to him, swinging her foot. She looked bored, but then she usually did.

Ava rolled her eyes. "I'm going to check on Emmy and see Chloe."

"He's an ass, Avie," Bo said, kissing her again. "Ignore him. That's what we do."

CJ might be drunk, but he was out of line. And Bo was going to set him straight.

Inserting himself between Matt and CJ, Bo leaned against the bar and cocked his head. "Tour's over, asshole." He poked him in the chest. "And she is *not* the babysitter. Got that?"

"So what." He snorted. "You're fucking her."

Matt grabbed ahold of his arm so he couldn't punch him. "CJ, don't be such a dick, man."

"That's enough, Curtis." Taylor made a stealthy move for his glass.

"Sorry." He reached for his drink that was no longer there. "And I need an answer for Vanessa. Two covers in less than a year, motherfuckers. You don't wanna turn it down."

"We'll think about it," Taylor placated him.

"You keep sayin' that, but Tay, shit, c'mon…"

Taylor flicked his chin at Matt.

Matt helped CJ up from his stool. "Let's go outside, bud. Get some fresh air."

"I'll just take him home." The whiny one drained her glass. "He's done. Second Christmas party today."

"Ava, baby, call me." CJ held his thumb to his ear, waving his little finger. "We gotta talk."

Bo glanced over to her, slowly shaking his head. She came to him. Slipping his arm around her waist, he kissed her temple.

Jesse closed the door behind them.

Kissing her husband, Chloe murmured with a giggle, "Merry Christmas."

Bo brought another stack of packages up from the basement, where they'd been kept hidden, to find Ava peering at the snow falling outside. In a red buffalo plaid robe, with her glasses on and her hair up in a messy pile, she created a stunning visual. He set the packages down by the tree to join her at the window.

"It feels so strange," she said, leaning into him. "I think we're the only ones here."

Dillon was at the hospital with Linnea and the baby. Charlotte made an early debut, arriving just after midnight this morning. Everyone else was away, spending the holiday with family. Only the three of them, along with Chester, remained here on Park Place.

"It's just us, and I like it." Holding her to his chest, he kissed her. "Now, let's finish playing Santa, I'll take the pupster out to do his business, and then we can go to bed. I might even let you get a little sleep."

"Oh, will you now?"

Bo smirked. "Probably not."

"Didn't think so," Ava quipped, leaving him at the window.

She sat beside the tree, smiling to herself, and began laying the wrapped, beribboned packages beneath it.

He came up behind her, hands kneading her shoulders. "Are you complaining?"

"Never."

"That's my girl." Inhaling raspberries, he kissed the top of her head, taking a seat on the floor beside her.

Chester got up from his bed by the fireplace, sniffed at the packages beneath the tree, and laying his head on Ava's lap, went back to sleep. She petted the dog's soft coat, arranging and rearranging the display of gifts from Santa. Leaning back on his elbows, Bo took it all in. Everything he'd ever wanted was right here.

Ava glanced back at him, Christmas lights twinkling in her eyes. "Is this all of it?"

"I still have to bring up the stuff Mom sent." He sat back up. Sliding his arm around her, Bo pulled Ava closer. "And her bike."

She giggled. "I can see Emmy and the boys racing around the block already."

"How fast do you think they can go on training wheels?" Running his fingers through her hair, he kissed her. "It's our first Christmas."

"It is."

"Shall we open our presents now?"

"If you want to." Pretty pink lips curving into a grin, Ava pointed to a very large package, propped up against the wall. "That one's yours."

Bo untied the silver ribbon and tore off the glossy green paper. Astonished, he gazed at an original studio-issued theater poster in a custom frame. "*Forrest Gump*."

"Signed by Tom himself." She smiled, lowering her lashes. "It's your favorite movie."

Coventry Park on a warm summer night, the smell of crying grass, his pinky linked with hers.

"It is." Fingertips grazing her tender skin, he brushed her lips with his. "And the first one I watched with you."

"I know," she whispered, then she kissed him.

"See that box over there?" Bo pointed toward an unwrapped package on the sofa. "That one's for both of us. Open it."

She peeled off the packing tape. He helped her unseal the flaps. With her blue eyes widening, she lifted the framed photo from a nest of brown paper. His lips touching hers, the moment he came off the stage at the Hollywood Bowl.

"Called a dude I know at *TMZ*. Told him the least he could do was send it to us, so he got in touch with the photographer."

With a shake of her head, she snickered. "Torrid affair with the babysitter."

"I love this picture."

"Me too." Ava gathered up the wrappings, then handed him the box that the photo was mailed in. She pointed to the return address. "Isn't that the guy who did the photoshoot for the magazine?"

He glanced at it. "Yeah."

*Sonofabitch sold the image to TMZ?*

"Vultures. Every last one of them." Smacking a kiss to her lips, Bo handed her his gift. "He did capture a perfect moment, though. I'll have to thank him."

"I won't ever forget it."

With her gaze lingering on him, Ava smiled, slowly loosening the ribbon. She lifted the lid, her lashes fluttering up, and whispered, "Bo."

He'd transcribed the notes he'd written for her onto vintage cotton paper. Mounted on velvet and encased in glass, surrounded by an antique frame. There were no words, just a title and a melody. A feeling she evoked in him, expressed with music.

*My beautiful Ava.*

She probably didn't realize it, but he'd given her his heart.

"I'll play it for you later." Bo reached for a lock of her hair, rubbing it between his fingers. "Maybe Sloan can put lyrics to it for me. I'm not so good with those."

Tears rolled down her cheeks. Ava flung herself into his arms. "You wrote a song for me."

"I did," he said, swiping beneath her eyes. "I got you other stuff too. You can open those in the morning with Emmy."

"I got you something else as well." She bit her lip. "You can open it now if you want."

"Shouldn't I wait?"

Ava loosened the tie on the buffalo plaid, shrugging it from her shoulders. "No, you really shouldn't."

She wore red satin beneath her robe. Round bottom swells peeked out from the bra tied across her breasts in a bow. Like a present. Ava was gifting herself to him.

Bo plucked at the satin, unwrapping her.

*I love you.*

"My beautiful Ava."

And he made love to her in the glow of sparkling, white lights from the tree.

# Twenty-Five

Not quite eight o'clock on New Year's Eve and the champagne was already flowing.

Ava didn't mind. She liked the way it tickled her nose and it went down easy. Too easy. With four hours to go until midnight, she better remember to pace herself.

*"Drink plenty of water and keep a full stomach."*

That's what her mother always said.

Shouldn't be a problem with the spread Chloe had laid out here. Ava popped another bite of boom boom shrimp in her mouth. As long as she stayed away from the crab dip she'd be okay. Just one taste of that mouthwatering deliciousness and she wouldn't be able to stop. Like Leo's muffins, dips of any kind were her weakness.

It was a cozy little soirée, as Chloe liked to call it. Monica and her wife, Danielle, were the only guests here, besides herself and Bo. And the kids, of course. Apparently, everyone else would be ringing in the New Year at the Red Door. Well, except Linnea, but then she had a brand-new baby at home.

Having filled his plate, Bo sidled up to her. "Try this, baby. It's so good." He proceeded to feed her a cracker slathered with crab dip.

"Oh, God." *Orgasmic.*

"That's what you sound like when—"

Ava swatted him on the ass. "Bo, get me away from this buffet table. Please."

"Can't wait until we get home, huh?" He waggled his brows.

"No…yes…" She burst into a fit of giggles. "God, you're so bad."

"But you love me when I'm bad." And he kissed her.

Tilting her head, she pursed her lips to the side. "Yeah, I guess I do."

Jesse was going from person to person, topping off glasses of champagne, while Chloe handed out plastic cups of sparkling white grape juice to the little ones. Sliding her arm around Taylor, Monica brought him to the center of the room and crooked her finger at his husband and his wife.

"I want to make a toast." She stood tall, almost as tall as Taylor, proudly smiling as she rubbed circles on his back. "Precisely three years ago, at this very moment, I had the absolute honor and privilege of officiating at your wedding."

Monica reached for Chloe's hand, bringing her and Jesse closer. "You have proven to everyone who knows you that love truly has no limits. Just look at this beautiful family you've made together." She glanced at Ireland in Taylor's arms, running her fingers through Chandan's shoulder-length black curls. "Not only is your cord of three not easily broken, it grows stronger by the day."

Jesse and Taylor gazed at the wife they shared, their adoration for her evident, as tears streamed down her face. Bo squeezed her hip. Ava glanced up to see him looking at her much the same way. He kissed her temple.

"We love you." Monica raised her glass. "Happy anniversary, and here's to many, many more."

Swallowing her champagne, Ava looked on as the three of them kissed. Most people are fortunate to find *one* person to love for a lifetime, and some never do, yet somehow they managed to find two. What they had was wonderful and special and rare, though not for everyone, she supposed. It had to be difficult. But in spite of society's prejudices and the odds stacked against them, or perhaps because of it, their love flourished.

There was a knock at the door. In came Dillon, impeccably dressed in black Armani. Having met him less than a handful of times, he was the one person on Park Place Ava didn't know very well. She stayed back while Bo stepped forward, bro-hugging him.

"Happy birthday, Dill." He planted his lips on the man's cheek with a loud smack and winked. "For twelve. That's the rule."

Chloe stepped in. "My turn."

One by one, each of them embraced Dillon, wishing him a happy birthday, but he didn't appear to be all that happy. Dressed to the nines, presumably on his way to the Red Door, and the poor guy looked so forlorn.

"Linn should be here soon. She just put Charlotte down and was going to get ready when I left," he murmured to Chloe with a sad smile, giving her one last squeeze before he went out the door. "Brendan's waiting on me. I've got to go."

"That's odd." Chloe glanced to Jesse, her brows pulling together.

"What?"

"I just spoke to Linn a little while ago. Tried to convince her to come over, you know?" She gave a shrug of her shoulders. "And she insisted she wanted to stay home."

"Maybe she changed her mind," Bo offered. "I'll run across the street and see, okay?"

"Yeah." Patting him on the shoulder, Chloe nodded. "Okay."

Bo turned to Ava then. Wrapping his arms around her, he pressed a kiss to her forehead. "I'll be right back."

He didn't even put his coat on.

Chloe slipped in beside her. "I could use a hand, sweetie," she said, steering Ava toward the kitchen. "Let's put that gorgeous cake out, yeah?"

She'd baked a small two-tiered white almond cake, frosted in a delicious, light buttercream, for the occasion.

"I still can't believe you made this yourself," Chloe exclaimed, setting the cake on a platter. "It's so pretty."

"Sort of a hobby I picked up." Ava tucked her hair behind her ear. "You can eat the flower too. It's white chocolate."

Pushing her hip up against the island, Chloe grinned. "Sweet."

"You didn't need any help, did you?"

"Not really." She giggled in that way of hers.

"Why'd you bring me in here then?"

"Girl talk, of course. Why else?" She let go of the weight in her shoulders. "Everything going okay?"

"Yeah. Everything's good." Leaning across from Chloe, Ava drew in a breath. "Can I ask you what's going to sound like a stupid question?"

"There's no such thing, silly." She play-swatted her hand. "Shoot."

"Hypothetically speaking, do you think a bisexual man can be, umm…satisfied by a woman, or would he eventually miss being with…"

"This is so *not* hypothetical." Chloe grabbed her hand and held it. "Bi means that you can be attracted to either sex, not that you have to be with both of them, you know."

"I know, but…" Chewing on her lip, Ava fixed her gaze on the white almond cake. "…it's just sometimes I think I'll never be enough. Because there's things I can't give him."

"Stop it. Right there." Chloe tightened the grip on her hand, squeezing it. "Your man. My men. Brendan, Dillon, Kodiak, Matt, Kit, and Sloan—all of them. They fuck hard, but they love even harder. And it's so obvious to all of us, Bo is very much in love with you."

*Maybe. Doesn't change things, though.*

"Is that it?"

*No.*

Exhaling, Ava nodded. "Yeah."

"There are things a woman can do, no penis required, if that's what you're concerned about, sweetie. Talk to him." She winked. "Now, let's have some cake."

Shortly after they left the kitchen, Bo returned alone. "Linn's not coming."

"Why would she tell Dillon she was?" Jesse asked.

Bo sat down beside Ava, pulling Emery up onto his lap. "So birthday boy wouldn't feel so guilty about going to the club."

They all exchanged a glance Ava didn't understand. And she wasn't about to ask, even though she wanted to.

"I got to hold the baby. She's so tiny and beautiful." Bo was beaming. He kissed the top of Emery's head. "It's hard to imagine my darling ever being that small."

Taylor squeezed his shoulder.

With a sad smile, Chloe passed out slices of cake. "Charlotte resembles Kyan."

"She does," Jesse agreed in a soft voice.

The room went silent for a moment, and there was no need for Ava to wonder why.

"I was thinking." Taking a seat between her husbands, plate of cake in hand, Chloe broke the silence. "Since I'm not pregnant or lactating this year, let's all go to the Eros party at the club on my birthday." Flicking her hazel eyes to Ava, she winked. "I'm turning the big two-five on Valentine's Day."

"Only you could make twenty-five sound positively ancient, little bird." Taylor snickered.

"It's a whole quarter of a century old."

"Yes, I'm aware." He shook his head, lifting his gaze to the ceiling.

"Anyway…" Her gaze snapped to Bo. "…I want you and Ava to be there."

Lacing their fingers together, he looked at her. With the question written in his eyes, a corner of his mouth rose into an impish smirk. Did she want to go? Yes, Ava was definitely curious to see inside the elusive Red Door. This could very well be her only chance to experience it. As much as the thought of it excited her, she was equal parts nervous and apprehensive too. The world on the other side of that door was this great, big unknown. But then, she'd have Bo to explore it with.

Another epic adventure, right?

Ava tugged at her bottom lip with her teeth. Then giving him a subtle nod, she smiled.

Bo grinned. "You got it, Red."

"Ah, Eros, the god of love and sex." Monica chuckled. "I can only imagine what Brendan is going to do this year."

Chloe tickled her husband's ribs. "Jesse, do you know?"

"Didn't ask." He fended her off, laughing. "And now I'm not going to."

"Please?" She batted her eyelashes at him.

"Maybe." Jesse kissed her and winked. "As long as you're a very good girl."

Bo trailed his fingers along her arm. He dipped his head to her neck. Brushing his lips across her skin, he softly whispered, "Fuck, I can't wait to get you home."

She took a shower while Bo put Emery to bed and took the dog out. There'd be no story tonight, so Ava had to make it a quick one. Her little cutie-pie had fallen asleep, along with the boys, well before the stroke of midnight. Bundled in a blanket, Daddy carried her to the house in his arms.

Ava toweled herself off. With her foot on the edge of the claw-foot tub, she rubbed lightly scented oil onto her still-damp skin. A hand skimmed up the back of her thigh, while warm lips kissed her nape.

"I wanted to touch you so bad that night," he whispered, fingertips stroking between her legs.

Leaning into his touch, she asked him, "Why didn't you?"

"I needed to be sure it was real."

She wasn't certain what he meant by that. If what was real? Feelings? His or hers?

"And is it?" Ava turned around. "Is it real?"

"Yeah, Avie." Bo held her naked body to his chest, and he kissed her. "It's real."

He took the clip from her hair. Tumbling in waves over her breasts, Bo combed his fingers through it. Indigo eyes locked on hers, he lifted her in his arms and carried her over to the bed.

Ava watched as he pulled off his sweater and tattered Levi's fell to the floor, his intense gaze never leaving her for a single second. Bo didn't climb into bed. He prowled into it, like a lion intent on its prey. Bending over her, his long mane hung in a golden halo, framing his beautiful face, sweeping her skin. She was caged beneath his body, caught between his muscled thighs, looking into eyes, wild and hungry, the pupils blown.

Clutching her head, fingers threaded in her hair, Bo lowered his face to hers, their lips a hairsbreadth apart. "It's real."

He took possession of her mouth, claiming her, like he was trying to prove something, or maybe to teach her a lesson. Stealing her breath, his tongue swirled inside her mouth. Bo devoured her. Crazed, feverish, and raw. Biting. Sucking. Pulling her lip with his teeth.

As his mouth moved down to her neck, she gasped for air, the rush of much-needed oxygen infusing her lungs. Bo licked and nipped at the tender flesh, while his fingers pulled at her hair and his cock prodded her thigh. She gripped his shoulders, and dropping a hand to his ass, Ava pressed him against her.

"All mine," he rasped, biting down on her nipple.

She yelped. Soothed by his laving tongue, the sudden sting turned into a warmth that flowed through her veins, setting every cell in her body on fire. Clawing at his skin, Ava nodded. "Yes, baby."

He sank his teeth into the other nipple. Hard. Ava screamed at the exquisite pain and moaned with the delicious sensation that followed it. Her clit was throbbing and he hadn't even touched her there yet. Reaching between her legs to ease the ache, Bo stopped her. He gripped her wrist, pinning her hand to the mattress.

"Oh, no. You don't get to touch that pretty pussy, baby. It's mine." He bit her again. "And these beautiful tits are mine."

Seeking friction, Ava raised her hips. "Please."

Bo plunged his fingers inside her, thumb pressing into her clit. "Fucking Christ, Avie, you're killing me. Just feel how wet you are, baby. All fucking mine."

"I am," she affirmed as he sucked her nipple into his mouth. "Oh, God."

Filled by his magic fingers, Bo fucked her with shallow, rapid thrusts. And right at the cusp of climax, he withdrew them and flipped her onto her belly. Hands gripped her cheeks, spreading them apart. His face rubbed up her back, sending tingles down her spine.

"I've never…"

"I know." He kissed her skin.

"Won't it hurt?"

"It doesn't have to, Avie." Stretching himself out on top of her, Bo kissed along her shoulder. "I'd never hurt you."

Ava took a fortifying breath. "I want you to."

"What?" he asked, his hand rubbing her back.

"Do it to me."

"You want me to take this sweet virgin ass?"

"Yeah."

That, at least, she could give him.

His dick twitched.

"Avie." Bo angled her face toward his. Softly, he kissed her lips. "Are you sure?"

He knew what she was offering, and he didn't take it lightly. Because even though Bo didn't want to cause her any pain, it would hurt a little. Okay, for her, maybe a lot. There was no avoiding it.

Even though Bo discovered his fondness for backdoor play, and his sweet spot, back in middle school—thank fuck for internet porn—it still hurt like a bitch the first time he took a dick in his ass. And he'd been shoving first his fingers inside himself, then objects, before graduating to toys, since puberty, so it surprised him that it did.

It was the summer he turned fourteen. Taylor had just moved into the neighborhood. They started playing around with the idea of putting the band together. Both of them being openly bisexual, everyone assumed they were fucking.

They weren't.

Jimmy Tascadero was a gay boy who liked to pretend he wasn't. He went to the Catholic high school and dated an older girl, whose name Bo still couldn't recall, who had a reputation for putting out. And boy, did she ever. Not that it was a bad thing. She knew what she wanted and owned it. And what Jimmy's girlfriend wanted was two cocks inside her. He was more than willing to help her out.

One day, Jimmy came by without her. They were downstairs in the basement. Taylor was due to come over and jam. Poor guy starts whining about how horny he is and the girlfriend isn't around. So, Bo unzipped the dude's pants and started sucking his dick for him. That's what a friend does, right?

Jimmy pulled him up by his hair, looked him square in the eye, and said, "I wanna fuck you." Then he kissed him.

*Well, all right.*

Taylor came down the stairs to Jimmy fucking him bent over a chair. His ass bleeding. He didn't say a word until they were finished, and snickered. "Bloody hell, mate. Try some lube next time."

Lube is sticky, disgusting stuff. And it tastes like shit. Bo didn't like using it, but he would, and plenty of it, if necessary. He knew how to make it good for her. He wanted Ava to love it, to crave the feeling of his dick in her ass, with his fingers in her pussy.

Ava stroked his hair. "I'm sure."

"Okay."

Bo reached into the bedside table drawer, blindly felt around inside it, and tossed the bottle onto the mattress. Pressing the heels of his palms into the dimples at the base of her spine, he pushed them all the way up her back.

Kneading her shoulders to relax her, Bo bent at the waist to whisper, "I have to get you ready to take me, baby. Pull your knees under your chest." He lowered a hand to her plush bottom, caressing the cheek. "That's my good girl. Now pop that ass up and open your legs. Show me that pretty pussy."

He sat up beside her.

Ava did exactly as she was told.

*So fucking perfect.*

Her pussy on display for him, the puffy lips glossy with her sweetness, he licked his lips. As much as Bo hungered to taste her, he refrained. Prepping a girl can be tricky, and if he wanted to forego the lube, he'd need every drop.

Bo inserted two fingers inside her, resuming his quick strokes from before, rubbing her clit at the same time, until he brought her back to the edge. Withdrawing his fingers, Ava whimpered in protest. Twice now, he hadn't let her come. She'd get her reward soon.

He positioned himself behind her. Covering his hand in her copious sweetness, Bo smeared it between her cheeks, teasing her clit with the opposite hand. "Take a breath now, baby. Relax for me," he instructed, as he pushed his finger, wet from her pussy, into her tight, little hole.

Ava mewled, the sound so lovely.

She screamed when he added a second.

"Shh." Bo rubbed her clit some more. "Breathe, angel. My dick is a lot bigger than two fingers."

Pulling his fingers out of her, he kissed the puckered flesh. Using all his saliva, Bo licked and laved her soon-to-be-fucked entrance, spearing his tongue inside her. Rubbing her back, he straightened. Then he gripped her hips, dipping his cock into her dripping pussy.

"Bo." Ava clawed at the sheets, her fingers searching for something to hold onto. "Please."

He fisted her hair in his hand, pulling on it as he thrust. "Getting my dick nice and wet for you, baby, so I can slide inside your ass."

Christ, she felt good. Bo was about thirty seconds from coming. If he didn't hurry up and do it now, it would be too late. Reluctantly, he pulled out of her.

Kissing up her spine, Bo held the pierced head to her back entrance. "Ready, baby?"

She nodded into the pillow.

"Take a breath."

Bo pushed through the ring of muscle. Ava screamed.

*I love you.*

Did he say that out loud? Maybe. He couldn't be sure. Bo was enraptured, fully sheathed inside her, where no one except him had ever been.

*All. Mine.*

Wrapping his arms around her middle, he lifted her up from the bed, holding her back to his chest. Bo nuzzled her neck, kissing her skin. "You okay?"

"Uh-huh," she squeaked.

He pulled out a little. Turning her face to his, he kissed her, pushing back in. Blood rushing through his veins, his body hummed. Bo breathed in her breath, his heart beating so fast, he didn't understand how it was possible he was breathing. Is there a place loftier than heaven? There had to be. Because he was sure he'd found it right here with her.

With Ava, Bo finally found that connection beyond the physical he'd been yearning for. She was his someone, his everything, and he loved her—mind, heart, body, and beautiful soul—exactly as she was. He hoped, that with him, she'd found the same.

When he imagined his future, he saw her. Emery. Maybe they'd have another kid or two. An amazing, beautiful life together.

If only she'd choose to share it with him.

Ava still hadn't changed her address.

*You will, angel. I know it. Because you're mine.*

Bo withdrew again, leaving just the tip inside, to slowly ease himself back in. He savored the euphoria of his bare cock moving within her tight, hot hole. An exquisite sensation he'd never experienced before, and one he would only ever feel with Ava.

Her limbs shaking, he held her to him tightly. Loving the sound of her little cries with every rhythmic penetration. Bo resisted the urge to go hard. Holding back, he kept his movements gentle and slow until Ava was ready for more. He'd know when.

"Bo." She grabbed at his hair. "Fuck, Bo."

Ava let go of him with one hand. Reaching her pussy, she rubbed her clit. And that's what he'd been waiting for. She was ready.

"That's my girl." Bracing her in one arm, his other hand slipped down her belly to join hers at her pussy. He plunged his fingers inside her. "Do you know how perfect you are?"

She threw her head back on his shoulder, frantically rubbing herself.

"My angel, you love having both holes fucked, don't you?"

He thrust himself into her harder, his fingers and his cock.

Her answer was an unintelligible, keening cry.

"Give me everything, baby. I'm gonna eat that pussy, and my cum out of your ass, when we're done."

And he did.

# Twenty-Six

I t was just the two of them. With Emery spending the night with Monica and Danielle, they had the house to themselves. "Come here."

She stepped out of the en suite in her panties, where she'd been putting on her makeup. "What?"

"Trust me?"

"Of course, I do."

Pointing to the bench at the foot of their bed, he grinned. "Sit."

Bo pulled the panties off her legs and spread them wide apart. He licked up her cunt, inserting his finger inside, sliding it in and out. "God, I love this pussy."

"Bo." She lifted her feet from the floor to the bench, opening herself up wider for him. "More, baby. Please."

Ava loved it when Bo fingered her. She especially loved it being done to both her holes at the same time. And he loved giving her everything she wanted.

"How many, my angel?"

"All of them." Teasing her nipples, she bit her lip. "I love your whole hand inside me."

She did. Ava loved to be filled.

"We don't have time for that now, baby." Bo scissored two fingers inside her. "We have to leave for the club soon, but I will later."

"Promise?"

"Count on it." Pulling his fingers out, he kissed her clit. "Now finish getting ready."

"Why'd you stop?"

"We have to go."

"But I didn't come yet." She pouted, reaching for her panties.

Bo winked. "I know."

"You're teasing me."

"I am."

That was the plan. To keep her on the edge all night long. Delayed gratification is a beautiful thing.

"Tell me about the club." Ava stood at the mirror, coating her lashes with mascara. "What's it like? Is there a sex dungeon in there?"

"Yeah." Bo stepped up behind her, trailing his finger down her spine. "Like that idea, huh?"

"Maybe."

"That's what the club is for." He kissed her neck. "Learning about what you desire."

"What do you desire?"

"You." Bo rubbed her hand on his dick. "Just you."

"What will we do there?" Ava turned around.

"Anything and everything you want." He kissed her. "Or we can just watch. There'll be plenty to see."

"So, if I wanted to kiss a girl or taste one, you wouldn't mind?"

"Every man's fantasy, baby." Bo sniggered. "Can I watch?"

"Why is that?" She snorted, tossing her mascara into a makeup bag. "I've never understood it. You only have one dick."

"True, but I do have two hands and a talented tongue to work with."

"Yes, you do." Ava got on her tiptoes to kiss his cheek. "For the record, I don't want to kiss a girl. Sorry."

"And that's okay too."

She slid her ass onto the vanity, swinging her legs with a mischievous smirk. "What if I wanted to kiss a boy?"

"Cool with me, as long as I can kiss him too." Bo stepped in between her legs, sweeping his thumbs across her nipples. "Look, I'm not a jealous guy, but what's mine is mine. Understand?"

"I don't want to kiss a boy," Ava assured him, holding his hand on her breast. "I want to watch you kiss one."

"Yeah?"

She grinned. "Yeah."

*Fucking hell, I love you.*

"I think I need to explain something to you." Bo exhaled, smoothing her hair over her shoulder. "The club isn't a swap meet, unless that's what you're into. There definitely are committed couples who are seeking a little…variety to spice things up. But the Red Door is so much more than just that. It's a community of enlightened people, just like you and me, who understand that safe, consensual sex, any way you happen to enjoy it, is natural, healthy, and good."

"Is that what sex positive means?"

"Yes, baby, exactly that." His lips brushed hers. "I should let you get dressed now."

She emerged twenty minutes later, a stunning vision in a little red dress that knocked the air right out of his lungs. "You're so beautiful, Avie." Kissing her, Bo fastened a delicate, diamond-studded chain around her neck. "Happy Valentine's Day."

"You did it again, Bo Robertson." Her fingers went to her throat, and she smiled, throwing her arms around him. "Happy Valentine's Day."

"C'mon, car's waiting." He offered her his arm and she took it. "Love the dress, by the way."

"Yeah? Red isn't my color, but that salesgirl at Akira is always—"

"Babe…" Bo stopped her at the curb. Ava tended to ramble when she was nervous. "…the dress is perfect, and so are you."

"Thanks." She smoothed the lapels on his jacket. "You're pretty perfect yourself. I like this look on you."

Armani. Black velvet. Silk lining.

The fabric felt rather nice against his skin.

Matt lowered the window. "Any day now, stud muffin."

His bandmates were waiting in the back of the limo. The driver opened the door and Bo assisted Ava inside. She slid into the seat next to Sloan.

"Miss Bo Peep," he drawled, his head lolling to the side. "This should be an interesting evening."

The driver took the back way, coming up to the red double doors from Ash Street. "It's so unassuming from the outside," Ava remarked. "You'd never know there was a club in there."

"That's the point, little miss." Sloan tipped his chin to Matt. "Stay close. Just in case."

"I know."

The car door opened. Kit got out first and Matt followed, waiting for them just in front of it. Bo went next and helped Ava up from her seat, holding her hand to his forearm. Sloan came out right behind her. He took her hand, flanking the other side.

"Ready?" Kit asked.

"We're good." Bo rubbed the back of Ava's hand, murmuring in her ear. "Keep your head down."

They walked as a unit, effectively shielding her. Two doormen, garbed all in black, opened the red doors as they approached, whisking Ava inside.

"What was that all about?"

"Paps," Bo explained. "Can't let them get a photo of you going into a sex club, can we? Try and explain that at school."

"Oh, I hadn't even thought of that."

"I got you, Avie." He kissed her temple. "Always."

"*We* got you," Sloan corrected him.

But gazing around the two-story entryway, her jaw slack, Ava wasn't paying either one of them any mind.

"You're not lost, Bo Peep." Sloan nudged her. "The world out there doesn't exist in here."

He wasn't lying.

Going through the red doors was like entering another dimension. Unencumbered by societal norms or judgment, members freely expressed their sexuality here. The environment of the club encouraged it. In this place, inhibitions disappeared and pleasure held sway.

"It's magnificent." Ava gaped at the massive chandelier.

"Just wait until you see all the way inside." He squeezed her hand on his arm. "I'll give you the grand tour."

Axel stood sentry at member check-in, waving them through. Bo escorted Ava up the stairs that led to VIP. He paused at the railing that overlooked the main club floor, her gaze flitting right and left, in an attempt to take it all in.

"When we were kids, this place was just one big, dusty old warehouse."

She smiled up at him. "Yeah?"

"Yeah. Everything along First Avenue from here and Charley's, all the way to Beanie's."

"Hard to imagine looking at it now."

But it was him Ava was looking at with her blue Bambi eyes, and the club faded away into the background. Bo brushed his fingers through her hair. She seemed luminescent, as if lit from within. Sometimes, he had to remind himself she wasn't a dream. She was real, and she was miraculously his.

"It was the beginning of everything. Kyan designed this place." He pointed. "See that empty booth way over there by the bar?"

"I see it."

"That was ours. Still is, I guess. No one else is allowed to sit there." His arm went around her waist, clutching Ava to his side. "We spent too many nights at that table. Lots of memories here."

He closed his eyes for a second.

And they all came flooding back.

"You miss him."

"I do." Nodding, his teeth caught on his bottom lip. He cleared his throat. "Those staircases go up to another bar and the dance floor." Bo caught her watching scantily clad people descend. "And down to the dungeon you're so curious about. That's where the themed rooms and the playpen are too."

"The what?"

Squeezing her waist, he softly chuckled. "That's where the orgies happen. Role-play. Other things. But you'll see some people enjoying themselves right out here in the open, while others like their privacy."

Club staff, nude, their skin painted gold, worked the main floor. Others took posts as living statues, frozen in their sensuous poses. From above, Eros pointed his bow and arrow at them all. "Well, I guess we know the theme of the party this year. Overwhelmed yet?"

"Maybe a little."

"C'mon, let's get you a drink and get settled in," Bo said, turning her away from the railing. "We have our own private space with a bar, staff...anything we could possibly want."

Chloe, in a short, shimmery gold dress, jumped up from her seat between Taylor and Jesse, the moment they came in.

*I guess she's been a very good girl.*

"There you are."

"Happy birthday, Red." Bo kissed her cheek, giving her a squeeze. That's when he noticed CJ smirking from the bar. "What are you doing here?"

"Uh, let's see." He strolled over. "There's a party, it's Chloe's birthday, and I am a member, you know." Dismissing him then, CJ eye-fucked his girl like she was dinner. "Hello, Ava. Why haven't you called me, baby?"

"She's not *your* baby."

Taylor got up and joined them.

"Tay tells me you guys finally agreed to do the article." CJ grinned, taking a sip of his drink.

Venery's lead guitarist stepped between him and their manager. "No photographer, though."

"I still don't see why not." The dude was actually pouting.

Bo poked him in the chest. "Maybe because last time, Vanessa's guy sold a shot to *TMZ*."

"Sorry, but this is our homes, our families, our private lives," Taylor added, his tone brooking no argument. "Vanessa can give you a list of what she wants. Danielle has agreed to shoot the photos. Take it or leave it."

"Fine. All right." He threw his hands up, sauntering back to the bar.

"Why does she have to come here anyway?" The thought struck him. "She can interview us over the phone or on Zoom, for fuck's sake."

Taylor shook his head. "No idea, mate."

Bo protectively tucked Ava between Matt and himself, in the corner of the plum silk U-shaped sofa. A nubile, gold-painted server brought them iced champagne, whiskey, and nibbles known for their aphrodisiac properties. Pomegranates. Imported chocolates. Figs dripping with honey.

Her legs crossed, Ava daintily sipped her wine. Bo ate a fig, tracing her lips with honey from his finger. "Relax, baby."

She sucked his finger into her mouth.

"That's my good girl."

Bo placed a pillow on her lap. Sliding his hand beneath her dress, he slipped her panties to the side and brought her back to the edge. Then he stopped, licking her from his fingers.

"Bo, please, I can't take it anymore," she protested, rubbing her fingers on the bare skin under his jacket.

"Shh." Giving her nipple a tweak, he winked. "I know you can."

Kodiak showed up, Brendan following behind him, with Hans and Brigitta bringing up the rear. White suit. Silver tie. Unusual attire for him. It glowed purple in the lights.

"Where's Katie?" Ava quietly asked. "And who are they?"

"Hans and his wife, Brigitta. They manage the club for Brendan. They're from Austria. Good people."

Taking a seat on the other side of him, Kodiak draped an arm around his shoulders. "Hey, brother."

"Hey, you came alone? Where's—"

"I can't stay." Kodiak leaned forward. "Hey, Ava."

"Why not?"

"She didn't want to be here tonight." He shrugged. "We have other plans, but I figured I'd stop by for a quick minute."

"Are you guys going to kiss again?" Ava giggled.

Grinning, Kodiak stood. "Liked that, did you?" And with a wave, he was gone.

"Baby, that ship has already sailed." Bo pulled Ava onto his lap. "Besides, I'd much rather kiss you."

And he did. Tasting honey on her lips, he slipped his tongue inside, and drifted in their magical rhythm. Whatever she'd done for him to crave her as he did, Bo didn't mind it. Madly in love, he was happily addicted to her.

"Last time you saw me kiss a dude it didn't go over so well, remember?"

*But I got to hold her after.* The corners of his mouth lifted at the memory.

"That was different."

"How so?"

"I was scared then…I was falling for you and I was afraid that…"

"I'd turn out to be like your douchebag date to prom?"

"Yeah, something like that." With her hands on his pecs, Ava tipped her head up and kissed him. "I'm not scared anymore. Your sexuality is a huge part of who you are, and I want to know all of you."

"Are you saying you want to watch me with a dude?"

"Yes."

"To see us fuck?"

"Yes."

The house lights went dark. A single bright spotlight illuminated a chaise of white satin on the platform. Brendan and Katie stepped onto it.

Ava's Bambi eyes got bigger. "What's happening?"

Matt turned toward her. "Showtime."

Katie, wearing only stockings, heels, and pearls, knelt on the chaise and unzipped Brendan's pants.

*That explains the white suit.*

"Showtime?"

Ava's friend freed her husband's monster cock. She covered her eyes. "I can't unsee that. Whatever this is, I can't watch. I'll never be able to look at either one of them again if I do."

Tapping Matt on the shoulder, he whispered in his ear.

"Yeah, okay."

Taking Ava by the hand, Bo took her to a private alcove. Matt followed them inside, pressed the signal on the wall, and closed the velvet drape. "You want to watch me fuck your man, Av?" Unbuckling his belt, he pointed to the bed. "Sit."

Bo reached inside the armoire, tossing condoms and lube next to where Ava sat. He was doing this for her. Matt only agreed to it for her. That, and he had enough whiskey running through his veins.

"Let's make it good, Bo-Bo." Matt dropped his pants. "Show her how you suck my cock."

Bo stripped out of all his clothes and pushed Matt onto the bed. "You can suck mine too, motherfucker."

They lay on the bed beside Ava, sixty-nine, deep-throating each other. Two men together are not the same as when they're with the opposite gender. Primal and raw. Rough and wild. There's no holding back. And if there was anything Matt was into, it was feeding that need.

Matt sat up, pulling on his hair. Bo glanced to Ava as he sucked his friend's dick. She was into it, judging by her hand going beneath her dress.

"We're all friends here, Av, and we all love each other." Matt pulled him up by his hair and kissed him. "I'd do anything for this guy and I know he'd do the same for me. Look at you working that pretty pussy. You like watching him suck my dick, don't you?"

"I do."

"We're friends, Ava." He crooked his finger at her. "You can suck me too, if you want."

Glancing to Bo, her hand ceased its movement.

"It's okay if you want to, baby." Her lips parted. "Take your pretty dress off."

Ava got out of her dress and came closer.

"Isn't she beautiful, brother?"

"Damn. They are real." Matt brushed his thumbs across her nipples. "There's enough cock for you both to share."

"C'mere, baby." Bo lifted his head from Matt to kiss her. "See? He tastes good. Suck him. I want to watch."

Ava lowered her head to Matt, his dick sliding down her throat.

"Fuck, Avie." He held her hair back. "I wish you could see how beautiful you are."

Bo joined her. They sucked Matt together, sliding their tongues up his length, meeting for a kiss at the head. Matt pulled on his hair. "I want you to give her my cum."

"Open your legs, baby."

Matt's dick in his mouth, he fingered her pussy. Sweetness dripped down his hand as he tasted precum on his tongue. Lovely whimpers. Deep groans. There was a melody to the sounds they made, a beautiful song.

Cum filled his mouth. Thick and salty, Bo held it there. Then he kissed her.

"Fuck, that's hot."

Ava moaned against his lips. This was one of the most erotic moments he'd ever shared with her. She didn't just accept his nature, she enjoyed it with him.

"My turn," Matt rasped, and they kissed her together. "Now, I want you to smother my face with that pretty pussy while you suck him off."

Bo knelt behind Matt's head. Holding onto his hands, Ava lowered herself. "Oh, fuck."

"Does it feel good?"

Biting her lip, she whimpered.

"I know it does." He held her head and she took him in her mouth. So turned on, Ava sucked on him with more fervor than she ever had before. "You deserve every pleasure. Enjoy him."

Bo reached for the lube and squirted some into Matt's palm. "Finger her ass, brother. My baby loves that and she'll come so hard for you." Squeezing his balls, Ava moaned, taking him deeper down her throat. "Fuck, Avie. Yeah, just like that."

Another verse to their wondrous song, the bridge building toward a climactic chorus. Bo memorized the sounds. The smells. Her beautiful face in rapture. One day he would write it all down. Musical notes on staves.

She sat there, mesmerized, watching Matt sheath and lube his dick. Bo eased her down on the bed, kissing her, groaning as he was entered from behind.

"I'm going to fuck you so hard, angel."

Together, the three of them discovered a glorious rhythm. Holding her chin, his fingers brushed her cheek. "You know all of me, Ava, like no one ever has. So, know this, his dick in my ass feels good, but there's nothing better than being inside your sweet cunt."

The three of them lay together, Bo in the middle, catching their breath.

"Don't get used to this, stud muffin." Matt exhaled, sniggering at the same time. "Not gonna be like the triple-layer cake upstairs. Poly ain't my thing." He smacked him on the behind. "Shit, man. You ain't my thing either, but your ass sure felt nice."

"What are you doing in here?"

Bo looked up. Kit stood there, just inside the velvet drape.

It was Matt who answered, "What's it look like, brother?"

Leaning toward Ava, Bo whispered in her ear, "You want Kit to play with us too, baby?"

She raised herself up onto her elbows. Kit sat down beside her on the bed. Reverently, he laid his hand on her breast. Turning her head, Ava went to kiss him.

"Don't."

And he left, purple velvet swishing in his wake.

# Twenty-Seven

Ava glanced up from the whiteboard, greeting each cherubic six-year-old by name as they entered the classroom. Every morning she wrote a message on the board with mistakes in spelling or grammar that her students needed to correct. It was a fun way to start the day. Not to mention, children love to learn, especially if they're having fun while they do.

Most days, filled with sight words, phonics, writing, and math, the hours she spent student-teaching flew by. Not today. After the club last night, Ava was already dragging. She hid a yawn behind her hand, and the tardy bell hadn't even rung yet.

*Note to self: No more parties on a school night.*

And it didn't matter whose birthday it was. She fingered the chain at her neck. It had been worth it. Ava felt so close and connected to Bo, even more so after last night. People would probably find that odd, considering what took place in that private alcove. Wasn't she ashamed? Didn't she feel dirty? Used?

Quite the contrary, actually.

That man loved her, and Ava knew it. Didn't matter that Bo had never really said it. Well, he did once. Kind of. But it was during sex, and she didn't think the words were meant for her to hear, so it didn't count. Nevertheless, he went out of his way to show her every chance he got. And that meant even more, didn't it?

It was well past time she had *'the talk'* with him. Ava was terrified. It was a huge risk. Bo could very well reject her, and she was trying to prepare herself for that, but their relationship couldn't go any further until he knew everything.

*If he truly loves you, it shouldn't matter.*

That's what Ava told herself, even though she knew it wasn't true. Because it did matter, and to Bo, it mattered quite a lot. He'd splayed himself open, showing her everything he was. And she loved him. It was only right she did the same.

Emery's third birthday was on Sunday.

She'd talk to him after that.

Ava was going to bake her a rainbow cake with pink frosting, donuts, and sprinkles. Because that's what her little cutie-pie wanted. After a birthday brunch with all the kids, she and Bo were going to take her downtown on the train to get a doll at American Girl Place and have dinner at the Sugar Factory. This was the first birthday he'd be celebrating with his daughter, and she didn't want to ruin it for him.

*You'll lose her too.*

Nope. She refused to even entertain that thought.

Seven hours and one skinned knee during recess later, three o'clock came at last. Bo and Emery waited for her at the curb just like they always did. A smile sprang to her face, and all of a sudden, Ava didn't feel quite so tired anymore.

She tossed her bag in the back, kissing Emery first. "How's my cutie-pie?"

"Daddy made zanna." *Lasagna?* Grinning, she patted Ava's cheeks with both hands. "I missed you, Mommy."

"I missed you too, baby."

Smirking, Bo licked his lip. "Did you miss Daddy?"

Leaning over the console, Ava took his face in her hands and kissed him.

His lips curved into that smile she loved. "I'm thinking you did."

"Then you'd be right."

And later, after dinner, a movie, and bedtime stories, Ava showed him just how much.

Basking in the afterglow, she rested her head on his chest, fingers tracing the ridges of his abs, while Bo played with her hair. "Are you okay after last night?"

"Yeah, why?"

"I just wanted to make sure, that's all." He kissed her crown. "No regrets then?"

"None." She raised herself onto her elbow. "You?"

Reaching for a lock of her hair, Bo twisted it around his finger. "Never."

"I'll admit I was a bit stunned."

Tilting his head, the corner of his mouth quirked up into a wicked, bad-boy grin. "Why's that?"

"I never would've guessed Matt's bi."

"That's because he isn't." Bo softly chuckled, her hair unraveling from his finger. "Not really."

"But…"

"I know what you're gonna say. Let me explain." He sat up, pulling her onto his lap, facing him. "First of all, he's not attracted to me, or men, generally speaking. Though, I've known him to top now and then—especially if he's a little sauced."

"I'm not following."

"It isn't who you've fucked that determines what you are, but rather who you're attracted to." Bo wrapped his arms around her waist. "Jesse's mom was happily married to his dad for more than twenty years, until he met another man. Did he turn gay all of a sudden, or was he bi? I'm sure you know someone at school who's experimented with another girl, and now she's engaged to the starting quarterback. Is she bi?"

"Not necessarily. Maybe. I don't know."

"See, this is why I don't do labels." Leaning forward, Bo kissed the tip of her nose and smiled. "I have a theory."

"What's that?"

"Human sexuality is a spectrum." He spread his arms wide. "Picture a half pie chart. On one extreme there's heterosexuals, and on the other homosexuals. Neither of those extremes would be even remotely attracted to, nor curious, about the same or opposite gender, as the case may be. A textbook bisexual is attracted to both genders equally. Fifty-fifty. They'd be right in the middle. Do you think every person in the world falls right on one of those three points?"

*Isn't that how the world sees it?*

"I don't know."

"I sincerely doubt it. There are few absolutes." Dropping his arms, they circled back around her. "My thought is we're all scattered across the spectrum. That guy who loves women could discover he's also attracted to one particular man. Men who identify as gay fuck women all the time. Bisexuality is rarely a fifty-fifty thing. Following me now?"

"Yeah, that makes sense."

"It's all up here..." He pointed to his head, and then his heart. "...and in here. We're all capable of loving anyone, but we're also very good at hiding what's inside if we believe the world won't accept it."

"What you see isn't always what actually is."

"Exactly." They lay back down, Bo pulling up the covers. He kissed her. "You get me. You're the only one who really does."

She heard it from inside the shower.

Boom. Bang. Smash. Crash.

Almost every day, Bo spent several hours down in the music room, pounding on his kit, of which he had several. He was always switching up the rig, as he called it, depending on his purpose at the time. There was the kit he beat the hell out of, like he was doing now, that he practiced on. Another in the studio he recorded with. And *'the beast'* he brought out on tour.

Giggling to herself, Ava put on a little makeup, and threw her hair up. She reached for her contacts, then changed her mind, opting to wear her glasses instead. Contacts were a hassle, and she was only running out to pick up a few things for Emery's birthday tomorrow. Besides that, her eyes could use a break. She leaned in closer to the mirror, inspecting the irritated sclera. Maybe she should consider getting Lasik, but the thought of a laser coming at her eyeball freaked her the hell out.

She pulled on her leggings, put on a comfy, oversized shirt, and made her way downstairs. Bo was behind his kit, sweat dripping down his chest, in his yummy gray sweats, with Emery, still in her pajamas, seated at a kiddie drum set across from him—a present they had planned to give her tomorrow.

"Couldn't wait, huh?" Ava chuckled, kissing her cutie-pie's blonde head.

He twirled his sticks. "I was too excited."

"Mommy, look." Emery stomped her little foot on the pedal, while whacking her stick on the snare. "I can do it."

"Did Daddy teach you that?"

She nodded, a proud grin lighting her face.

"I can teach you too." Wiping sweat from his chest, Bo winked from behind his kit. "C'mere."

"No way. I couldn't possibly learn how to do that." Ava shook her head. "I'm too uncoordinated."

"You said you couldn't dance either." He crooked his finger. "Now, come here."

Bo got up and sat her on his stool, draping his arms over her shoulders from behind. He chuckled. "This is how I got girls back in high school."

"And boys?"

Dipping his head, he kissed her neck. "Sometimes."

Why the thought of that turned her on, she couldn't say, but it did.

"Hold the sticks like this," he said, crossing her right arm over her left. "Now, I want you to count to four hitting that."

She did. "One, two, three, four."

"There you go. That's the hi-hat." Bo tapped on her thigh, pointing to the right. "Now, put your foot on that pedal over there. The kick drum pedal."

Tentatively, Ava pressed down on it.

"Yes, baby, I want you to give it a solid kick on one."

Feeling him smiling behind her, she began counting again. "One, two, three, four."

"You got it." His hand squeezed her shoulder. "Now, on the third beat, hit this guy right here. The snare drum."

And this is where it got tricky. Ava tried, but she really was uncoordinated. Bo was patient with her. He wouldn't let her give up.

"Start again with the hi-hat by itself. You're still counting to four."

"One, two, three, four." She counted slowly, and concentrated on adding in the kick and the snare.

"See? You did it." Clapping, he bent over to kiss her. "Good girl."

Emery waved her sticks. "Good job, Mommy."

Her little cutie-pie. She was so smart. That's how Ava praised her each time she completed a task.

"The piano teacher's coming on Monday to start her lessons." Bo beamed at his daughter.

"What if she doesn't like it?"

"Then she doesn't, and that's okay." He drew her to his side. "I want Emery exposed to everything…music, dance, art, sports… She'll know when her soul speaks to her."

This man. *He* spoke to her soul.

Ava got on her tiptoes and kissed him. "I'm running out to pick up a couple things."

"I can take you."

"Thanks, it'll be quicker if I just go." Then she whispered, so Emery wouldn't hear, "We're out of sprinkles and I've got a cake to bake, you know."

She slipped into a pair of boots, put on her coat, and a warm wool cap. The sun was shining, but the air outside was bitter. February sucked. With the exception of Valentine's Day and her cutie-pie's birthday, there was nothing to recommend it. Good thing it was a short month.

A car pulled up to the curb in front of Matt's house next door.

The driver got out, pizza box in hand. Her long, dark ponytail swished behind her as she bounced up his porch steps. Ava watched her ring the bell. Matt opened the door. Exchanging a few words, she handed him the box, and was gone.

Out on the sidewalk, Ava headed toward the gate to the park. She was punching in the code when a voice called her name.

"Kit?" He stood there, clutching an unzipped hoodie closed around his middle. "Are you nuts? It's freezing."

"I know." He scrunched his shoulders. "But I wanted to catch you."

"Why?"

"To apologize." He let go of the hoodie, exposing his bare chest to the frigid air, and skimmed his fingers along her jaw. "I need you to know it wasn't you. Being with you would have been…"

"It's okay, Kit. I understand."

"No. No, you don't." He touched his lips to her cheek. "Bo is so fortunate. Just know that I'm sorry."

Then he turned away, running back inside his house.

# Twenty-Eight

I t wasn't until Emery's little birthday party, and the train ride downtown, that Ava truly understood the depth of Bo's sadness over everything he'd missed during the first two years of her life. She could see it in his eyes, wistfully smiling at two-month-old, Charlotte, and one-year-old, Ireland. Robbed of her babyhood, he didn't know his daughter then. Hell, he didn't even know he had one. How fucking cruel was that? And he was such a loving, devoted father.

Outside of telling her how Emery came to be, and why he had her now, Bo didn't talk about it much. That was him. He held no grudges, preferring instead to focus on the present, to look forward to the future, instead of dwelling on a past he couldn't change anyway.

And so, Ava couldn't bring herself to have 'the talk' with him. Not then. She would, though. Soon. Maybe she'd try later tonight. After. That might be the perfect time, because right now she had other plans.

He was in the shower. Sloan wasn't kidding when he said Bo was a bathroom hog. It was certain he'd be in there a while, giving her all the time she needed to prepare.

Ava put some soft music on, lighting scented candles, turning down the bed. She arranged some fluffy pillows and warmed the essential oils. Bo always took care of everyone. Tonight she'd care for him.

He stood in the doorway of the en suite, naked and beautiful, long hair falling over his chest. Indigo eyes flicking left and right, candlelight reflected in them, his gaze settled on her. "What's all this?"

She took his hand and led him over to the bed. "My turn to surprise you."

Bo sat down on the edge of it. Wrapping his arms around her, he kissed her belly, then lower. Her hands on his shoulders, Ava stopped him. "You're here to just receive. Lie back."

"Avie…"

"Shh." She gently pushed him toward the nest of silk-covered pillows. "Go on."

Ava wanted to relieve her man of pressure, tension, and stress. This was his space, his time, his experience. Free to let go and just feel the sensations in his body.

He settled back against the silk, his hands resting on his stomach, fingers laced together. His gaze followed her to the bedside table, watching her intently as Ava poured a mixture of oils in her palm, its scent drifting into the air. Citrusy and woodsy, she used a blend of lemon and eucalyptus to activate his sense of smell, which is strongly connected to a man's primal sexuality.

Bo breathed in deep. "That's nice."

"Close your eyes."

She started at his inner thighs, pressing firmly and deeply into the muscle, her fingertips gliding over his skin. Ava took her time, feeling the smoothness of his flesh, massaging him with loving intent, from his groin, up the front of his pelvis. Mesmerized by the sight, she watched him fill, though she hadn't yet touched that part of him.

Ava longed to kiss him there. Not suck him. This wasn't a rush to his orgasm. She just wanted her soft lips to touch his hard flesh.

She listened to him breathe, watching his chest rise, then slowly fall. He softly groaned with each exhalation of air. And bit by bit, Bo relaxed, turning into butter in her hands as the tension evaporated from his body.

He reached for her hair, combing the ends of it with his fingers. "My angel."

With sensual strokes, Ava touched him then. Circling him with both hands, she slowly slid them up and down his rigid length. Using the flat surface of her palm, she languorously massaged the back side of it. She varied her movements, and their intensity, allowing him to fully experience every delicious sensation.

Attuned to the signals of his body, Ava knew when Bo was close. Several times, she brought him to the edge, without letting him go over it. Pulling him back, her fingertips fluttered up his arms, to rest one hand over his heart and the other over his weeping cock, until the beat inside his chest slowed.

He breathed in deeply through his nose, and exhaling on parted lips, Bo whispered so softly she almost didn't hear it, "Please."

Lifting her hand from his chest, she bent at the waist to kiss him there. And cupping his balls in one hand, tracing the rugae with her thumb, she brought him to climax with the other.

His groan was deep and guttural. Fully sensitized, she watched the orgasm ripple throughout his body. Limbs spasmed. His toes curled. Semen, hot and thick, spilled over her fingers, dripping onto his skin.

Then she held him. Ava wrapped him in her arms and just held him.

Bo opened his indigo eyes to look into her own. Moisture leaked from the corners, rolling past his temples, into his hair. Fingertips caressed her face, and he brought her lips to his, kissing her the way every woman dreams of being kissed.

"I love you, Ava." He held his lips to hers, squeezing her tight, repeating the words, "I love you."

Threading her fingers into his hair, Ava kissed him.

"Can you love me back?"

"I do love you." She held his face, gazing into indigo eyes. "I've been in love with you for a very long time."

"You just made me the happiest man alive, baby," he quietly said. Nestling her against him, his eyes drifted closed.

She took in the beautiful face of the man who loved her. *Tell him.* Her heart speeding up, Ava mustered every ounce of courage she possessed.

"There's something else I need to tell you," she whispered.

A soft snore was his only reply.

Three little words can change everything. *I love you.* Magical, how the world seemed so different now. Life had new meaning, took on a new direction, and Bo had a greater purpose than he ever did before. All because Ava had chosen him to love.

He glanced at her and Emery on the other end of the couch, Chester stretched out in between them, watching *Shrek*—the first one. Thankfully, Ava convinced her to watch something else besides *Frozen,* because if Bo had to listen to "Let It Go" one more time, he might lose it. She'd been obsessed with that movie, watching it on repeat, for weeks.

Ava tickled the arch of his foot with her toes. "What are you up to over there?"

"Looking at flights." He tried not to grin.

"For?"

The idea came to him as he lay in bed that night, after the mind-blowing massage Ava gave him and they made love. Bo wanted to take her back to the Hollywood Bowl, hike up those one hundred and sixty-eight steps to the top, and get down on his knee. It seemed fitting. Set against the backdrop of the Hollywood Hills. The place where he first kissed her. It was still his favorite picture.

"Thought we could take a trip to LA for your birthday. You're on spring break." He kept his eyes on his phone, attempting to appear casual. "Visit the fam." Looking up, Bo winked at her. "Get a burger at In-N-Out."

"And donuts at Randy's?"

"Absofuckinglutely."

"In that case, I'm in." Ava giggled. "I love you."

"I love you too." Leaning over, he ruffled Emery's hair. "Want to see Grandma?"

"I do. I do." Grinning, she scrambled from Ava's lap, returning with the iPad.

Months had passed since the tour, and LA, when she'd seen her last. Emery probably didn't have much memory of it, if any at all. She was used to seeing his mother on FaceTime.

"We can call her, baby." Chuckling, Bo pulled her onto his lap. "But how about we get on an airplane to go see her and Grandpa for real?"

She gasped, and her midnight eyes widening, a huge grin spread across her face. "Airplane."

Is that all she got out of that? But then Emery certainly didn't remember her first trip on an airplane either. The day he brought her home. Almost a year ago now.

Shelley. Cici. Florida. The beach. She didn't remember any of it, did she?

Glancing to the books her mother left him, Bo felt guilty she didn't.

He hugged his daughter extra tight, kissing her golden head. "Yes, darling, on an airplane."

Then he booked their flights.

"What kind of bullshit is this?" Glancing to Taylor and CJ, he tossed the paper onto the table.

"Christ, man." CJ snatched it back up. "It's nothing to get all worked up about."

"No?" He cocked his head and sneered, "Naked in a bubble bath, frying eggs in my underwear? Is that on your list, Tay?"

"Err, no."

Vanessa Parisi had sent over her list of requested photos for her article, and Bo was none too pleased. A freelance journalist—and after this, he used the term lightly—she was well known in the rock music scene, often contributing to publications such as *Revolver* and *Rolling Stone*, so he figured she was cool. Now? Not so much.

"Didn't think so." He slammed his hand on the table. "What the fuck, CJ?"

"You guys have an image. A rep," he said, flinching. "Sex sells. It's what the fans want to see."

With a snicker, Bo crossed his arms over his chest. "Right, so they want to see me in my underwear, but not Tay?"

"Guess not," Taylor muttered under his breath.

CJ threw his hands up. "Tay has a family. He's, um…unavailable. You know what I mean."

He understood what he meant, all right. Let the fangirls drool over Matt, Kit, and Sloan in their underwear.

"Yeah? Well, I have a daughter and Ava. I'm not available either." Adamant, Bo shook his head. "I'm not doing it."

"Your dick's been all over the internet for years. What difference does it make, man?" CJ swiped his tongue across his lip and grinned. "And you have to do it."

"That was then, this is now…" Bo poked him in the chest. "…and no, I don't."

"Enough." Grabbing him by the arm, Taylor separated them. He leaned into his ear. "Fuck her list. Just have Danielle take some photos. They'll have to be happy with whatever we give them."

Bo complied with Vanessa's requests. His way. Danielle got shots of him, Ava, and Emery in a bubble bath, but they weren't naked. Ava kissing his cheek, while he sautéed vegetables at the cooktop, fully clothed—which for him meant just a pair of jeans. In the music room, behind his practice kit. Teaching Emery how to play on hers. Sitting at the piano. Playing in the yard with Chester.

She might be pissed she didn't get quite the man-candy images she was hoping for. He was sure Vanessa would bitch about it during the interview tomorrow. She asked for a day in the life of Venery. And he gave it to her. Ava. Emery. The band. That was his life. And Bo wanted the world to know it.

He drew Ava closer, circling his arm around her middle. "Will you please change your address now?"

"Yeah." She lifted up to kiss his cheek. "I'll pack up the rest of my stuff at the house as soon as we get back."

"Finally." He held out his pinky. "You and me, Avie."

She hooked hers with his. "Together."

*Forever.*

# Twenty-Nine

Twenty fidgety six-year-olds stood in a single-file line at the door. Jackets on. Shoes tied. *And we're good.* Satisfied, Ava took the class outside for afternoon recess.

Her eyes were on the girls twirling a jump rope, but her mind was on all the things she still had to do. Get her nails done. Pack for their trip to Cali. Have *'the talk'* with Bo.

She couldn't do it now. Miss Perfect was visiting Park Place today to do the interviews with the band. Ava hoped she'd be gone by the time she got home, but she doubted she'd be that lucky. They had an evening flight to LA tomorrow. So, it would have to wait until they were back, and *before* she moved all her stuff in.

*You should've talked to him a long time ago.*

She should have.

But Ava had never imagined her ordinary life would turn into a romance novel. And now, the only thing she hoped for was a happy ending.

Reminded of Fourth of July at the lake house, laughing and clapping with Katie, Ava joined a game of Miss Mary Mack. She remembered Bo waving at her from the deck. The way he looked at her in the water. She should've known then, it could come to this.

The bell signaling recess was over put an end to her musing. Lining up her students, Ava led them back inside the classroom to wrap up their lessons for the day. They were working on distinguishing verbs from nouns. When three o'clock rolled around, the kids were still chanting, "A noun, a noun, a person, place, or thing. A verb, a verb, can run or fall or sing."

Bo wasn't waiting for her at the curb today. Ava knew he might not make it because, yeah, Vanessa was there. She didn't want to be in the way, or say something stupid like she did last time, so rather than go to the house, she opted to get her nails done instead. It was on her to-do list anyway, and Miss Perfect would surely be gone by then, right? Win-win.

Wrong.

Because she wasn't.

Close to dinnertime, when she opened the front door, Ava was surprised there weren't any delicious smells coming from the kitchen. There were voices, though. She stood there for a moment, unsure of what to do. Should she slink away upstairs or make her presence known?

Ava could see Miss Perfect's reflection in the hallway mirror. In a tight, short skirt and thigh-high boots, her hip popped out against the island, she appeared to be deep in conversation with Bo. He held Emery on his side, her little legs straddling his waist, fingers clutching onto his hair.

"She's so darling." Miss Perfect stroked Emery's cheek. "You need to find her a mommy."

*Grrr…don't you touch her.*

"Emmy has a mommy."

Ava closed her eyes and smiled. *That would be me.*

This was silly. She should probably just go on in there.

"You can't mean that girl." Vanessa sniggered, play-slapping his shoulder. "She's just the babysitter, right?"

*Not anymore, sweetie.*

Lifting his chin, that wicked smirk appeared. "That's right."

She felt the blood drain away from her face.

*What?*

Swallowing back tears, Ava choked on her own saliva. All this time he'd been playing her for a fool. And she let it happen. Why?

Turning around, she opened the door, and leaning back against it, closed it softly behind her. The wind blew, hair clinging to her wet cheeks. It was only then Ava realized she was crying. She tried to take in a gulp of air, but tears clogged her throat.

*You've got to go.*

*Can't let them find you like this.*

*Take a step. Go on.*

*Go, go, go.*

Ava forced her feet to move, and when she reached the sidewalk, bent over, with her hands on her knees, she finally took a breath and sobbed.

A hand rubbed her shoulder.

"Ava, is everything all right?"

*Fuck.*

CJ took her chin, raising it between his thumb and forefinger. "What did he do?"

She shook her head. "Nothing."

"C'mon now, Ava. You can talk to me." He put his arm around her, holding her to his chest. "Is Vanessa still in there? Were they fucking?"

They weren't, but just the thought of it made her cry harder.

"That's just Bo, baby. He fucks." CJ stroked her hair. "You were never going to be able to hold onto him, you know."

Ava shrugged out of his hold and headed toward the park gate.

"Hey, Ava…call me when you're feeling better."

She held up her right hand, extending her middle finger.

*Fuck you, CJ. Fuck. You.*

Adjusting Emery on his hip, Bo glanced at the clock on the wall. Almost six. Where was Ava? She should be here by now.

This was the lamest, most sorry-ass excuse for an interview ever. Her line of questioning was better suited to one of those teenybopper fan rags. *Do they even still have those?* It was dumb, and it certainly could have been handled over the phone.

And to think, at one time, he thought meet and greets were tedious. At least they gave him alcohol to get through those. This was fucking torture.

She stood too close, batting her false eyelashes, twirling a lock of hair around her finger. Dead giveaway. Bo wasn't the least bit interested.

"She's so darling." Leaning closer, Vanessa had the nerve to touch his kid. "You need to find her a mommy."

*Excuse me? Let me guess, you'd be perfect, right? I don't think so.*

"Emmy has a mommy."

"You can't mean that girl." With a shake of her head, she laughed, slapping him on the shoulder. "She's just the babysitter, right?"

*Playing that game now, are we?*

"That's right." Bo paused for a moment, then set Emery down. "Go ahead and watch Elsa, darling, while Daddy finishes talking, okay?"

"Okay."

He waited until she was out of earshot, then cocking his head, Bo folded his arms across his chest. "Let me make myself perfectly clear. I certainly do mean her. Ava. Is. Everything. My future wife, and Mommy to that little girl in every sense of the word. Put *that* in your fucking article."

Her mouth gaped and then shut like a fish out of water. "Oh, I see."

Bo didn't do angry often, but he was incensed. He could feel his jaw clenching, the veins popping in his neck, and he didn't like it. The audacity of this woman. She could walk her ass, in her skin-tight skirt, right on out the door.

"Who do you think you are to come here and disrespect my family like that?"

"I was given the impression you were…never mind," she stammered. "I'm so sorry."

"Whatever. The photos we sent should have made it obvious to you," he scoffed, unaffected by her bullshit apology.

Vanessa lowered her gaze to the floor. "Except I didn't get a chance to look at them yet."

"Seriously?" Bo snickered. "And you call yourself a journalist?"

She made no response, her eyes glued to her boots. The front door burst open, CJ sauntering into his kitchen like he owned the place. "How's it going?"

If looks could indeed kill, the guy should've dropped on the spot from the death glare Vanessa sent his way.

"I think we're done here. Aren't we, Ms. Parisi?" And he smirked. "Seen Matt yet?"

"I'm going there next," she answered in a low monotone.

"Try your luck with him, maybe. But a word of advice, don't make it too easy." Bo winked. "He likes to play with his dinner first."

He texted her. The messages went unread.

He called her. It went straight to voicemail.

He checked with Katie. Chloe. Neither one had heard from her.

Going on eight o'clock, Bo was starting to lose his mind. Ava sent him a text after school to let him know she was running a couple errands on her way home, but that was hours ago. Where the fuck could she be?

His mind was conjuring crazy things. Did she get hit by a car crossing the street? Mugged, or worse, in a dark alley? Fall off a bridge into the Chicago River? Maybe she just went shopping and lost track of time.

*Then why isn't she answering her phone?*

Something was wrong and Bo couldn't wait here another single minute. "Come on, darling." He helped Emery into her coat. "We're going for a ride."

Grateful she fell asleep in her car seat the moment they turned the block, Bo went by the school first. The nail salon. Akira. The campus library. He drove the likeliest route to the house, up and down First Avenue, scanning the sidewalks. Ava was nowhere in sight.

There was only one place left he could think of to look. Bo pulled up to the curb, parking in front of the row house near campus, that technically, was still her official address. He glanced up to her second-floor window. There was a light on.

Carrying a sleeping Emery with him to the door, Bo rang the bell. After a moment that seemed to go on forever, Ava opened it, head bent down, hair covering her face.

"Thank, God." Exhaling, he wound his free arm around her, yanking her to his chest. "I was so worried. I've been everywhere looking for you."

No response. Stiff as a board, her arms remained at her sides.

Bo let go of her to brush the hair from her eyes. Red. Swollen. She'd been crying. "Avie, what's wrong?"

And still she didn't answer.

Skimming her face with his fingers, he gently lifted it. She looked at him then, and blinked, fresh tears rolling down her cheeks. "C'mon, baby. Let's go home."

"I almost believed it," she said, her voice scarcely a whisper.

"What are you talking about?"

Ava closed her eyes, tears seeping past the lids. "But I was just the babysitter all along, wasn't I?"

"No, baby." Bo reached for her again, but she stepped back. "I love you."

She kissed Emery's forehead.

*Don't do this.*

"Ava…"

And without another word, she quietly closed the door.

# Thirty

**B**roken.

And not just her heart. Every part of Ava was broken. Her bones ached. Her chest hurt. She couldn't fucking breathe. She felt sick.

Heaving, she braced herself over the sink, but nothing came out. Not even bile. Ava wiped her mouth with the back of her hand, staring at herself in the mirror. Puffy eyes, splotchy skin, and unkissed lips stared back at her. She traced them with her finger. Was it really just yesterday she'd kissed him last? "You're fucking pathetic, Ava. Stop it."

At least no one was here to witness the pitiful state of her existence. Her roommates had all taken off for spring break. Why didn't she go with them? A week of getting drunk on a beach somewhere sounded pretty darn good. Maybe she could forget all this wretchedness for a little while, though she doubted it. She should have been on a flight to LA right about now.

She couldn't wrap her head around it. Bo had always been so wonderful. Ava truly believed he loved her, felt it deep in her soul. He'd gone to extraordinary lengths for someone who was just the babysitter to him. None of this made any sense.

*"What you see isn't always what actually is."*

Yeah. Didn't she learn that lesson back in high school? Guys will move heaven and Earth for pussy. Once they get what they want, or someone better comes along...poof. Bo was probably relieved she'd ended things for him, so he didn't have to be the one to do it.

With her back against the wall, Ava slumped down to the floor. She couldn't spend an entire week surrounded by these four drab walls. Already, they were closing in on her.

Her brother answered on the first ring. Baseball season was about to get underway. Perry's opening game was on her birthday, and she was going to be there for it.

*Stick that in your juice box and suck it, Bo Robertson.*

Twenty-four hours later, Ava sat on the balcony of her brother's fifth-floor condo, looking out at Clearwater Beach. She tipped back an ice-cold bottle of Corona, and swallowing the beer, she grimaced. It wasn't her drink of choice, but there was plenty of it in the fridge. And tequila.

Perry collected her from the airport, brought her here, and headed off to batting practice. They hadn't seen each other since Thanksgiving, and he rushed at her in the terminal, hugging her tight. Ava squeezed back, not wanting to let him go. He knew something was wrong, but he didn't ask. She could tell he wanted to, though.

Sipping her beer, Ava watched the westward migration of the sun over the Gulf of Mexico, listening to the silence that falls between the surf. A wondrous spectrum of colors, pink and orange. Reds and blues in a sky speckled with clouds of gray. Ava could have sworn she heard a sizzling hiss as the great ball of fire appeared to touch the water. It slowly dipped deeper, slipping bit by bit into the Gulf.

Going.

Going.

Going.

Just a crescent remained. And in a brief flash of color, the sun turned green. Then sinking into the water, it disappeared.

Gone.

Ava blinked tears from her eyes, sitting in the twilight. Perry stood behind her. His hand squeezing her shoulder, he plunked a bottle of tequila down on the table. "Want to talk about it?"

She shrugged.

"That's why you came here, isn't it?"

"I miss you." Ava reached for his hand. "And I wanted to see you play."

Draping his arm across her back, Perry took a seat beside her. "You hate baseball."

"*You don't have to love baseball.*"

"I'm still your biggest fan," she managed to say, smiling at him through her tears.

"Yeah, okay, but you're crying…" He gave her a noogie. "…so spill it."

Ava poured them both a shot of tequila, and let it all come out. "I just…"

"Assumed the worst."

"You think so?" Peeling the wet label off a beer bottle, Ava worried her lip.

"Yeah, you tend to do that." Perry took the bottle away, handing her a new one. "Look, you caught a snippet of a conversation. You don't know what was said before or after, the context of what you heard. Doesn't sound to me like you're just a babysitter he happens to be fucking." He downed his shot. "God, I cannot believe I just said that."

"So, you think I fucked up?"

"Maybe." But the look on his face told her that's exactly what he thought. "You won't know for sure until you talk to him."

"It's too late." Ava tipped her head back, and closing her eyes, she sighed. "Why would he even want to talk to me now?"

"Because he loves you." Perry yanked on the ends of her hair, prompting her to look at him. "And it's never too late."

"He's better off with someone like her. I'm not—"

"Stop it, Ava. Don't even start with that middle child syndrome bullshit." He rolled his eyes. "You're smart and I'll even admit you're pretty. You bake stuff all the time—better than Mom, but don't you ever tell her I said that. I'll deny it. You're incredible with kids, which is how I know you're an amazing teacher."

"Isn't it ironic," she scoffed.

"Okay, Alanis." Perry chuckled, clinking his beer bottle against hers.

"I never told him."

"Oh." He blew out a slow breath and poured her another shot. *Yeah, I know. I fucked up.*

A few days later—the day before her birthday, and Perry's season opener—he came home from the ball field, and after grabbing a Gatorade from the fridge, stretched his limbs in a chair across from hers. He downed the drink in one swallow, and handed her his phone with a smirk. "You might want to take a look at this."

An image of her and Bo, with Emery between them, and Chester at their feet, displayed on the screen. She was leaning into him, Bo kissing her temple. Ava recalled the precise moment Danielle had taken it. They'd been so happy that day.

The caption below the photo read, "*Bo Robertson, 34, drummer of the multi-platinum band, Venery, pictured here with daughter, Emery Sage, and Ava Liane Harris, 21, confirmed the two are a couple—and it's serious! Don't miss my exclusive interview with Venery in the next issue of Revolver.*"

"Oh, God." Squeezing her eyelids shut, she covered her mouth with her hand. "I really messed it all up."

"Yeah, looks like you did." Perry smirked, tapping away on his phone.

"What are you doing?"

"Sending it to Mom." Her brother chuckled. "She's gonna love this."

"Don't."

"Everything's going to be okay," he assured her. "Just talk to him."

"You don't know that."

"Yes, I do." Her phone pinged and the image appeared on her screen. Perry winked. "Because that's a family right there."

Hollow.

No, that word wasn't quite right. Devastated. Empty. Dejected. Numb. Bo could come up with a dozen adjectives if he could think straight, except he couldn't. His mind was still reeling. His chest ached. Used to having Ava beside him, he hadn't been able to sleep without her.

*Why the fuck is this happening?*

All night long, he wracked his brain, searching for an answer that eluded him. Glancing at her things on the vanity, Bo picked up Ava's perfume and held it to his nose. Blackcurrants, raspberries, jasmine, moss, and sandalwood. *Her.* Slamming the bottle against the marble, glass shattering, he squeezed his eyes shut.

He fucking loved her. And not like he loved chocolate cake or salted caramel ice cream. Not how he loved music, his drums and his boys. Not the way he loved Emery, his mom, or any other human on the planet. Bo loved Ava beyond definition. Utterly. Truly. Madly. Deeply.

She was his someone, dammit.

And he was hers.

*So then, why the fuck is this happening?*

The bathroom reeked of her. He cleaned up the mess he made, tossing shards of broken glass into the trash, though Ava's scent would never leave him. Scrubbing his face with his hands, Bo stared at himself in the mirror. He looked like shit. Dark circles. Weary, bloodshot eyes.

"Daddy?" Bo glanced down. His daughter stood there, holding her pink hairbrush. "I need Mommy."

*I need her too.*

"Mommy's at school, baby. I told you that." He picked Emery up, and sitting her on the bathroom vanity, facing the mirror, began to brush her hair. "And we have a plane to catch, don't we?"

"Uh-huh." She exuberantly nodded.

He plastered on the smile he used for the fans, sectioning her silky blonde hair to braid it. "Are you excited to see Grandma?"

"Yes, and Pop-Pop!" She grinned, looking back at him, over her shoulder.

Keeping her distracted, he continued, "What about Auntie Allie and Uncle Ryan?" Bo tickled her.

Emery giggled. "Ry-Ry."

"Don't forget Logan." He tied off the braid, kissing the top of her head. "He'd be awful sad if you did." Bo set her back down on her feet. "Let's get you dressed, sunshine. It's almost time to go."

This wasn't going to be the trip he'd originally planned, but he was determined to make it a pleasant one for his daughter. Emery sat next to the window. Bo buckled her in, then glanced to the empty seat on the other side of him. He scanned the aisle, half expecting to see Ava board, yet knowing she wouldn't. His hopes were dashed when the plane taxied from the gate.

Emery squealed a little as they took off into the sky. Her eyes flicked back and forth between him and the city shrinking below them out the window, excitedly clutching her Blabla doll of pink alpaca fleece. Funny, how at the very last minute, she pulled it off her bed to bring with her. Her mother died a year ago today.

*"Do you have someone special in your life, Bo?"*

*I did, but I think I might have lost her.*

He could have sworn he heard the sound of Shelley's laugh.

Allie was waiting for them at LAX. Bo tossed their bags in her trunk, while she buckled Emery into her car seat. Wordlessly, he got in on the passenger side. She turned her head to look at him. "I thought Ava was coming."

Glancing at his daughter behind him, he shushed her. "Not now."

"Okay." Allie nodded, and leaving the airport, headed north on the 405 to Santa Monica. "Want to stop at In-N-Out?"

"I'm not hungry," he absently replied, gazing out the window. "Emmy would like that, though."

She got off the freeway. "I have a better idea."

Sitting at a table outside, as the sun set over the Pacific Ocean, they ate double cheeseburgers at the Pier. His sister made him eat. And while Emery was preoccupied watching the lights on the giant Ferris wheel, their voices lost in the rattling of the steel roller coaster and the cacophony of arcade games, she made him talk.

"What's going on, Bo?"

"I wish I knew." Pressing his lips together, he shrugged. "I really thought she loved me, you know?"

"She does."

"Ava made a choice, Allie, and it wasn't me." Bo turned his head, looking out at the water.

"What frequency are you vibrating at, little brother? Love or fear?"

"She's not here." His gaze swung back to his sister. "We should get to the house. Mom must be wondering where we are."

"She knows. I texted her." Allie stood up. "I promised Emmy we'd get ice cream."

And with that, she left him sitting there. Pondering. Love or fear? His love wasn't in question, and he had nothing left to fear.

His sister returned with the ice cream, placing a cup of vanilla, with sprinkles of course, in front of Emery. She resumed the conversation right where she'd left off. "You're so easy to love, babe, and *everybody* loves you."

He lifted his brow.

Allie reached across the table, taking his hand in hers. "It's the bullshit that comes with loving you that's hard."

Cocking his head, he asked her, "What do you mean?"

"I saw it, Bo. We all did. That girl is so in love with you." She squeezed his hand hard. "But it's easy to understand how a young woman, unaccustomed to that world, could be made to feel inadequate next to someone like Vanessa Parisi. I saw that too."

"I don't give two shits about that woman. I love Ava."

"I know that," Allie said, wiping ice cream from Emery's chin. "I overheard Vanessa on the phone that night, backstage. She told whoever it was, '*I'll get him*' and to thank CJ for hooking her up. Then she called the photographer over to get that picture of you and Ava."

"And he sold the shot, but why?"

"Greed? Who knows? The why doesn't matter." She flapped her hand in the air. "My point is, you've always got people on the outside looking to get in. Riding your coattails to get ahead and make a name for themselves. And CJ's always got his nose up everybody's ass. Those people don't care about any of you, or who the other casualties are. Tay was lucky. But look at Sloan. Get me?"

"Yeah."

"Sit her down and talk to her. Don't let Ava become another casualty." Glancing at Emery spooning ice cream into her mouth, Allie smiled. She leaned across the table and kissed him on the cheek. "Choose love, little brother."

# Thirty-One

April. Her birthday month.

When she was a kid, it might have been her favorite month of the year. She'd get to have a party. Presents. Spring arrived, bringing rain showers and warm weather with it. Windows would open, the breeze smelling earthy and new.

But Ava wasn't a kid anymore.

While today was particularly mild, especially this early in the season, April no longer held its appeal. Holding onto the plackets of her sweater, Ava walked First Avenue at a brisk pace. She hadn't even unpacked from her trip to Florida, having returned only last night, when Linnea called her. She was in a bind and needed a babysitter to look after Charlotte.

Only two houses separated Linnea's from Bo's. She'd have to walk right past it. And Ava wasn't quite ready to face him yet. *Tomorrow.* She needed today to gather her thoughts, her courage, and prepare herself for the inevitable goodbye.

It was no surprise to find Beanie's hopping this early on a Monday morning. The shops weren't open yet, but commuters lined up to grab a hot cup of joe on their way to catch the train downtown. Usually, the place would be packed with students, dosing themselves with caffeine before class too. And stay-at-home moms with strollers, taking their older kids to school. None of them were here. They'd be back in full force come Wednesday.

Kelly, Katie, and Leo got customers through the line, while Kevin sprinted between tables. Probably not how he wanted to spend what was left of his spring break. She heard he had a girlfriend now.

Luckily, the line was moving quickly. "*Bébé.*" Leaning over the counter, Leo kissed her on the lips. "*Si charmont.*" He didn't have to ask her, scribbling Ava's order on a cup. "You look like you could use a muffin. Where's that pretty smile I love, *ma belle?*"

And of course, because it was Leo, and that was his gift, her lips quirked up. Just a little. Enough to make him happy.

"There it is."

"*Girl,*" Katie exclaimed, looking up from the milk she was frothing. "Nice tan! That California sun sure looks good on you."

"Florida." Ava bit her lip, her voice warbling, "I didn't go."

She couldn't help it. Her eyes filled. She tried so hard to keep them from coming, but the tears escaped to trickle down her face.

"Kell, take over for me here, will you?"

Katie's aunt spun around from whatever it was she was doing, ready to protest, Ava was sure. But one glimpse of her and Kelly changed her mind. She nodded. "Yeah, sure."

Grabbing her by the hand, Katie whisked her away from the counter, and sat her down on a stool in the back. "What do you mean, you didn't go?"

Maybe they were the kind of friends that told each other things now. Confidantes. Because Ava told her everything. Well, almost. Miss Perfect and what she overheard. CJ. Closing the door on Bo. Going to Florida to see her brother.

"Look at this." She pulled up the image on her phone, a new crop of tears falling. "I'm so stupid."

"Sh, sh, sh." Katie hugged her, patting the mop of hair piled on top of her head. "Bo loves you, babe. The two of you just need to talk it out."

"He's never going to forgive me," Ava sniveled. "I wouldn't forgive me."

"*Now* you are being stupid. Of course, he will. It's a

misunderstanding, that's all." Holding her at arm's length, she let her shoulders down, and smiled. "This is Bo we're talking about, remember?"

Ava took a stuttering breath. "I've been keeping a secret from him. A big one. And that's the same as lying." She cast her gaze down to the floor, pulling on the cuffs of her sweater. "A lie is the one thing Bo will not tolerate. He told me so."

"Let me tell you a little story." Katie gently tipped Ava's chin up with her finger. "I kept a secret from Brendan once too. It was before we were married, and it was a big one. I was almost five months pregnant before he found out he was going to be a father, and it wasn't me who told him."

"Who did?"

"Cam."

Ava gasped. "Oh, shit."

"Yeah." Nodding, Katie raised her brow. "Trust me when I tell you, that did not go over well. I was going to tell him. Thought my reason for keeping it from him was valid at the time. It wasn't. I should've never listened to that silly voice in my head. Sometimes, we're our own worst enemy, you know?"

*Truth.*

"But it all worked out."

"Yeah, because he loves me," she said, squeezing Ava's shoulders. "So I know it's going to work out for you and Bo."

Ava wasn't so sure about that, but she hoped so.

"Maybe."

"It will." Katie took a step back. She folded her arms, a smirk appearing on her face. "Okay, girl, you don't have to tell me, but you've got me really curious. Are you having a baby? Is that the big secret?"

And for the first time in ten days, Ava laughed. "No, Bo would probably love that."

"Yeah, I know he would."

"Yeah." Her chin quivering, she managed to put on a tremulous smile. "Look, I've got to go. I'm watching Charlotte today." Ava hugged her friend tight. "Thank you."

Bo glanced at the photo on the wall.

He missed Ava. His world didn't feel right without her in it.

There'd been no reason to hike up those steps to the top of the Bowl. In fact, he hadn't gone anywhere near the place. Yet somehow, in spite of how wretched he felt on the inside, Bo made sure Emery had a nice visit with his family in California. He and Allie took the kids to Knott's Berry Farm. The beach. He even got her a little surfboard to paddle on with her cousins.

Emery sat at the island with jumbo crayons and a coloring book, trying her best to stay inside the lines, while he fixed them some lunch. Bo was straining alphabet pasta when Katie breezed into his kitchen. She peeked over his daughter's shoulder, watching her color, and kissed the top of her head. "Looking good, Em."

She glanced up from the paper, waving a purple crayon with a grin.

"Hey, Katie-Kate," he acknowledged her, transferring the hot pasta to a bowl. "How goes it?"

"It goes." She sidled up beside him. "How was LA?"

"All right, I guess." Bo continued with his task, mixing in butter and grated cheese.

"You didn't ask me."

"Ask what?" He looked up at her.

Sticking out her bottom lip, Katie feigned a pout. "Where's my kiss?"

"Oh, yeah. What's wrong with me?" Bo chuckled, tapping a finger to his cheek. "Give it to me, baby."

Sliding her arm around his waist, Katie planted a kiss on the side of his face. "Is everything okay?"

"No, but I'm guessing you already know that." He resumed his stirring. "And that's why you're here."

Biting her lip, she nodded. "I saw Ava this morning."

"Oh, yeah?" Pressing his lips together, Bo pushed the bowl aside. "How is she?"

"She's a mess." Katie squeezed his bicep. "You need to talk to her."

*I tried. She closed a door in my face.*

"If Ava wants to talk, she knows where I am."

"Bo…"

"She did this, Katie, and I have no idea why." Bo threw his hands up, bringing them down to slam a fist on the counter. "I love her, but I'm just so damn mad at her right now."

And Bo didn't like that he was. It's not that he didn't want to talk to Ava, he did. But he needed to work out his anger first. He was afraid of what the outcome could be if he didn't.

"Ava overheard you and the reporter chick," Katie murmured, pursing her lips. "And she jumped to conclusions, I guess. Then CJ got ahold of her outside."

"CJ? That mother—"

"Little ears, Bo."

"Right." He gathered his daughter, her coloring book, and crayons. Settling her at the play table in the family room, Bo ruffled her hair. "Finish your pretty picture, baby. I'll get you when it's time to eat."

"Okay, Daddy."

"I should have known," he announced, returning to the kitchen.

CJ, that meddlesome, conniving sonofabitch. At least some of it was beginning to make sense. He was the one who'd been pushing Vanessa at them, insisting they had to do that ridiculous interview. And he did seem to have a thing for Ava.

"So you're not mad anymore?"

"No, I'm disappointed." Pausing, Bo chuffed out a breath. "And mad."

"Disappointed? Why?"

"How could she doubt me?" He cocked his head. "I would never…"

"I know that." Katie grasped him by the arms, aqua eyes boring into his. "So does Ava. I think it was her own worth she was doubting, you know?"

Bo shrugged. He still didn't know what to think.

"That's why you have to talk to her." She angled her head, petting his shoulders like he was a puppy that needed soothing. "Put it all out there. It's okay to let Ava know what you're feeling. And then listen—you're good at that part."

He sniggered.

"That's how it works, babe." Squeezing his biceps, Katie nodded. "Then you get to kiss and make up. That's the best part, yeah?"

Bo imagined it, his teeth pressing into his lip. "I'll spank her ass raw."

"Exactly." She winked. "Sometimes, I make Brendan mad on purpose," she admitted, biting her lip.

"You're bad."

Katie giggled. "I know. So are you."

He couldn't argue with that, now could he? "Yeah, well…"

"Ava's at Linn's watching the baby." A sly grin rose on her face. "You should bring Emmy over to play with Declan after she has her lunch."

Bo glanced to the photo on the wall. It was still his favorite.

"I want another kiss." He smacked one to Katie's lips. "Thank you."

# Thirty-Two

He leaned against the railing of his front porch, Chester sniffing at a big empty flowerpot by his feet. Bo chuckled to himself. No doubt, Ava would want to start planting a garden soon, never mind it was still too early. It might be warm today, but they could still see some more snow before April was over.

Running his fingers over his bare chest, he surveyed the block, waiting for the moment Ava stepped outside Linnea's front door. With the exception of music softly wafting from Kit's open window across the street, Park Place was quiet. He paced the length of the porch, the pup dutifully trailing along behind him.

Bo got down on his haunches, giving Chester's chin a scratch. "You miss her too, don't you, boy?"

The dog replied with sloppy, wet kisses.

"Okay, Chester. That's enough." Wiping slobber from his face, he opened the door. "Go on. She'll be here soon." And he returned to the railing alone.

Keeping up his vigil, Bo tapped out a beat to the song in his head, playing it on the top rail with his fingers. *My beautiful Ava.* He thought he had the words now.

There was movement to his left. Bo stopped his tapping and turned toward it. Dillon stood at Linnea's door, waving, as Ava went down the steps. Barefoot, heart hammering in his chest, he blew out a breath, and stepped out onto the sidewalk.

Head down, gaze glued to her purple Chucks, Ava didn't see him standing there at first. She must have sensed him, though. Halfway in front of Matt's, she stopped in her tracks, and then she looked up.

He walked toward her. She just stood there, nervously pulling on the sleeves of her sweater, big blue eyes swimming. Bo didn't say a word. He took her hand, and placing it on his bare chest, her tears began to spill.

"Feel that?" He pressed his hand on top of hers. *Boom-boom.* "That's the beat. Now listen to the fill. I choose *you*, Ava. Out of however many billions of people there are on this planet, I choose you."

"Eight." She sniffled.

"What?"

"There's eight billion people—"

And he kissed her. Right there on the sidewalk, in front of Matt's house, to the song in his head and the music from Kit's window, Bo claimed his woman. Pushing the backpack off her shoulders, he wrapped her in his arms, his tongue delving, desperate to taste the sweetness he'd been missing.

Fingers tugging through his hair, Ava clasped her hands around his neck, and pulling him closer, she kissed him back. Just as needy. Just as desperate, she slung her legs around his waist.

His hands dropping to her ass, he held her there a moment. "We need to talk." Bo let her down, picked up the backpack, and taking her by the hand, led her inside the house.

Chester was waiting to greet her, tail wagging a mile a minute, the moment she came through the door. Ava bent over to stroke his fur. "Hi, baby. How's my boy?"

He wasn't about to share her affection with the dog. Not now. "Go on, Chester. Go lay down."

Grabbing her by the nape, Bo kissed her again, and there was nothing gentle about it. Or tender. Or sweet. It was possessive and primal. Hungry and raw. Backing her into the room, he pulled the clip from her hair.

"Where's Emmy?"

He bent her over the sofa, so she was facing the mirror. "Katie's."

"You said we needed to talk."

He yanked her pants down and popped the button on his jeans. "We are."

Ava took off her glasses, tossing them to the sofa.

Bo picked them up and put them back on her. He held her face up. "Leave them on. I want you to see what I see. I want you to know how beautiful you are. I want you to feel how much I love you while I fuck you."

He sank into her from behind. Bracing her in his arm, a hand at her throat, Bo made her watch them together. "Look at us, baby."

Nuzzling her neck, he nipped at her tender skin, breathing in her scent. He didn't hold back, thrusting as hard, and as deep, as he could go. He'd make slow, sweet love to her later. That base, animal part of him was in control here. Fight or flight, and Bo was fighting. For her. For them. This was fucking for survival, because he couldn't do it without her.

"Bo." She whimpered with every plunge of his dick.

That fucking delicious sound that made him insane. Faster. Harder. Deeper. He pushed inside her, sweat dripping from his face, the burn building at the base of his spine. "You. Are. Mine."

Teeth on her flesh, fingers squeezing at her throat, he roared, exploding inside her.

"I love you," she warbled, as he lifted her up. Ava pawed at his chest. "I'm sorry."

"Don't you ever doubt my love for you again." Bo carried her around to the other side of the sofa, placing her upon it. Then he lay down beside her. "I'm sorry I didn't do a better job of making sure you believed it."

"I did. I do. It wasn't you." She shook her head, combing her fingers through his hair. "It was me. You're everything. I'm a stupid idiot."

"Don't say things like that, Avie." He kissed her forehead with a chuckle. "You're a very smart girl. You know things, like there's eight billion people on the planet and grass cries. Seriously, though…"

And he kissed her on the lips. "...I don't like to hear you say negative things about yourself. Don't you know I see you as perfect?"

"But I'm not."

Nobody is perfect. God knows, he sure wasn't. But Ava was perfectly made for him, and if it took Bo the rest of his life to convince her of that, he would.

"You are to me, angel," he whispered, sliding his hand beneath her shirt to feel her skin. "Because I love you and you're mine."

"I love you so much." She pulled his mouth to hers and kissed him.

Bo couldn't put his finger on it, but this kiss felt different somehow. It almost felt like goodbye.

Reaching inside his open zipper, Ava took a gasping breath. "Please..."

Then again, maybe it was a very enthusiastic hello, or I missed you...or I just fucking need you. He'd be more than happy with any of those.

"...I want you."

"Did you think we were done?" He squeezed her breast. "Baby, we're just getting started."

Bo stood up, pushing his jeans to the floor. The moment he removed her sweater, shirt, and bra, Ava's fingers flew to her nipples. He gripped her wrists, holding them above her head. "Oh, no, you don't." And proceeded to pull her pants off the rest of the way.

He gazed down at her, naked and beautiful, needy and wanting. *Perfect.* Strumming his fingers through her pussy, swollen from fucking, dripping with their cum, Bo licked his lips. "Look at this delicious cunt."

Straddling her waist, he dove right in, devouring salty and sweet. Bo loved the way they tasted together. He craved it.

Fingers sliding between his cheeks, a wet tongue probed at his hole. *Jesus, fuck.* He didn't deserve this girl, but hell if he wasn't keeping her anyway.

"I can do this for you, Bo," she crooned, a finger following her tongue.

*Yes, you can.*

She pushed through the resistance and adding a second finger, Ava delved for his sweet spot.

"Fuckkk," he groaned when she found it.

And once she did, Ava didn't let up.

Kissing his flesh, she stoked him inside, like she'd done this a million times, though she never had before. Holding onto her thighs, he kissed her clit, engulfed by the sensations in his body. Wave after wave of pleasure jolted through him, his cum spurting onto her belly.

Bo didn't even wait to catch a breath. His cock still hard, he turned around and buried himself inside her. Loving her slow. Kissing her skin. Whispering in her ear.

She was crying when she came.

"There's something I've been wanting to tell you for a while now." Ava sat up, chewing on her lip, her gaze cast down at the floor. "In the beginning, I didn't think it would matter, and then when I realized it did, I made excuses not to in my head."

Bo sat up beside her.

"Keeping it from you is the same as lying," her voice cracked. "And I'm sorry."

"Look at me." Gently, he tipped her chin up and held her face in his hands. "What is it, baby?"

Ava squeezed her eyes closed, with tears saturating her lashes, she inhaled a stuttering breath. The anguish on her face reminded him of Shelley, crying at having to say goodbye to her little girl. His heart seized with fear. *Please, don't let it be that.* He could take almost anything the universe wanted to throw at him, but he couldn't lose her. And Emery couldn't lose another mother.

"That just it, you see." Ava opened her big blue eyes. "I'll probably never have one."

Bo was confused. "Have what?"

"A baby."

"Of course, you will." Breathing a sigh of relief, he kissed her lips. "I was afraid you were going to tell me you were dying. We'll have lots of babies. As many as you want."

"No, we won't." She shook her head, tears rolling down her face. "Because I probably can't. When I was seventeen, the doctors informed me my chances of getting pregnant were slim to none."

He was just thankful she wasn't sick or dying, but he realized she was mourning for the child that never was, and might not ever be.

Bo pulled her onto his lap, and holding her tight, he smoothed the hair down her back while she cried. "I love you, Ava, and there isn't anything in this world that could ever change that."

"But you want another baby. I know you do." She hiccupped.

"Yeah, and so what?" He lifted her face so she had to look at him. "It doesn't matter, because what I want, more than anything, is *you*. If we can't have kids, then so be it. Don't you know you're everything I wished for?"

"I was holding Charlotte today..." She took a breath, her chin trembling. "...and I wished so hard..."

To see her like this was killing him. He wanted to be the one to make all her wishes come true.

"If you ever decide you want to, we can explore our options, okay?" Bo gently dried her tears. "We can see Linn's doctor."

Lifting her gaze to the ceiling, Ava blinked. "What good would that do?"

"I don't know, but they helped her, so that's a good place to start." Combing his fingers through tangled tresses, he offered her a reassuring smile. "They did say *probably*, didn't they? Absolutes are rare." He winked. "If there's a chance, we'll find it."

"And if we don't?"

"Then we'll look into something else." Tilting his head, Bo skimmed her cheek with his fingertips. "A surrogate or adoption."

"Okay." Nodding, Ava released a breath. She relaxed against his chest. "Okay."

He held her. Lying together, naked on the sofa, Bo stroked her hair and gazed into those big blue eyes he'd love for the rest of his life. No matter what the universe had planned for them, he knew they'd be all right. As long as they had each other. And they did.

*"The beginning is always today."*

He smiled.

"I love you, Ava." He held out his pinky.

She hooked hers with his. "I love you, Bo."

*We got this.*

And he kissed her.

# Thirty-Three

A whisper-soft giggle woke him.

Yawning, Bo rubbed the sleep from his eyes and stretched. Light had just begun to creep in through the stained-glass window above the bed, veiling the room in shadows. Her fingertips softly brushed the inside of his thigh to cup his balls. Gentle squeezes. A thumb tracing along the rugae.

*God, I love when she does that.*

His bottom lip caught between his teeth. He reached for her, grasping long, luxurious hair in his fingers. Bo opened his eyes.

Locks of flaxen silk.

His dream come true. Ava held him in her palm.

"Mmm…my angel."

"I'm gonna make you feel so good, baby." She smiled, taking his cock inside her mouth.

Fisting her hair, he sucked in a breath.

*You always do.*

Heaven.

Every day with her was like heaven.

Bo had been right. Ava started the garden, putting in flowers, well before April was through. They got snow the first week of May. Luckily, the next day it was already gone. No harm done.

She graduated from college—*summa cum laude*, of course—earning her degree in elementary education. Bo threw a big party to celebrate. He was so damn proud of her. Ava's family came to the city for the occasion. Perry even took a day off from baseball and flew in. It was his first time meeting them. They were pretty cool. Good people. And before the day was over, Emery had them wrapped around her little finger, claiming a new aunt, an uncle, and another set of grandparents.

Now that college was behind her—for now anyway, since she was already talking about grad school—he and Emery had Ava all to themselves. All day. Every day. Bo loved having her at home, and he was going to take advantage of it while he could.

She'd be teaching come fall.

He'd be working on Venery's next album.

And Emery, she was going to start preschool, at the same school where Ava would teach first grade.

Elliott and Chandan were going too, of course—those three were inseparable. Declan wasn't too happy about it, but he'd get to tag along with them next year.

So, yeah, Bo planned on making every day count. And today was going to be a fanfuckingtastic day. Tomorrow would be even better.

He was outside on the terrace, off the main floor living area, watering the plants and tidying up, while Chester did his business. In actuality, the plants didn't need any water. It rained last night. Bo was just trying to keep himself occupied. Working off his nervous energy.

He loved outdoor spaces, and Kyan had incorporated plenty of them into the design for this house. A huge balcony off their third-floor bedroom, the ground level patio below the terrace, and a rooftop oasis. He'd already tended to those.

The glass door opened. Hand in hand, Ava and Emery stepped outside. "We're going. We should be back before dinner."

"Where are my pretty girlies off to?" Bo asked, as if he didn't already know. Which, of course, he did.

"Girls' day. Katie has a certificate for some spa, and it's going to expire." Leaning in to kiss him, Ava shrugged. "She insisted."

"Just roll with it, baby." He brushed his fingers through Emery's hair. It was getting so long. "Enjoy yourself."

"Yeah, okay." She pecked him on the cheek. "They're having a movie in the park tonight. Want to go?"

"Maybe."

But Bo had other plans.

Smiling to himself, he stared up at the sky. Clouds still lingered. He hoped it didn't rain.

"Hey, brother." Kodiak appeared out of nowhere. Hooking an arm around his neck, he hugged him to his side.

Bo hadn't even heard him come in. Stealthy motherfucker.

"I was just at Linnea's. I wanted to see you…"

"I know. You miss my dick," Bo quipped. He waited for the wisecrack that would typically follow, but none came. Kodiak vacantly looked out over the railing. "Hey, what's wrong? Did something happen between you and—"

"Yeah, but I can't talk about that right now." Kodiak's arm dropped to circle his waist.

He knew better than to push him. Bo reciprocated in kind, and arm in arm, the two men stood there in silence.

After a few minutes, his voice soft and deep, Kodiak spoke again. "I'm leaving for Crossfield in the morning. Linnea's coming with me."

*The fuck?*

That godforsaken shithole of a town he and his sister came from. The place was Stephen King creepy. Real *Children of the Corn* vibes.

Bo shuddered. "Why the hell would you do that?"

"Our father is dying."

*The crazy preacher.*

"So?" Good riddance. Evil, sadistic fucker.

"I'm his son." Kodiak turned his head toward him then. "I've got to do this."

Maybe he did.

"And Linnea?"

"She's his daughter, isn't she?" He sniggered. "Linnea's not doing this for him. She's doing it for me."

"But…"

"It's fucked up. I know." Kodiak pressed his fingers into his side. "Don't worry."

"Can't tell me not to, man." He squeezed back. "I love the shit out of you both."

"I love you too." Half turning, Kodiak held onto the ends of his hair, their foreheads touching. "You know that, right?"

Pain laced his light green eyes, swimming in the soul-deep torment Bo knew he wrestled with. "I know." And he kissed him.

"I should go." With a squeeze of his shoulders, Kodiak took a step back. "Linnea tells me you've got big plans going on here."

"Yeah." Bo couldn't contain his grin. "She helped me. Got a crew up on the roof right now."

He winked, that trademark smirk appearing on his face. "See you when we get back."

With the work crew finished, Bo showered and pulled on his favorite pair of jeans—the ones his mother got him when he was sixteen—because they felt good. He put a shirt on too, even though it didn't. Then he went up to the roof. Everything was perfect. All he had to do now was wait.

Stretched out in the family room, Bo pretended he was engrossed in a book when Ava came in the door. She leaned over the back of the sofa to kiss him hello. "I'm home."

"Where's Emmy?"

"Katie's," she answered, pursing her lips with a shrug. "She wanted to stay. All the kids are there. Brendan set up a Slip N Slide in the backyard."

Yeah, he already knew that too.

"C'mere." Bo pulled her over the back of the sofa, on top of him. He kissed her, soft and slow. "Let's have dinner up on the roof, and afterward, we can get naked and fuck 'til the sun goes down."

"Why stop then?" Biting her lip, Ava smiled. "Maybe I want to stay up there all night and fuck 'til the sun comes back up."

"Baby, I love the way you think." Caressing her nipples through her shirt, he kissed her again. "Why don't you go get changed and I'll meet you up there?"

The table was set for two. Candles flickered in the breeze. A lattice archway, covered in summer blooms, had been erected in the corner. And not a single cloud remained in the sky.

Ava came onto the rooftop in a little white sundress. Beautiful and glowing, her big blue eyes got even bigger as she took in the transformation of their favorite spot. They gazed up at the sky together here. Made love under the stars here. And right here is where they'd begin their forever too.

He'd waited long enough. The ring was in his pocket.

She walked over and kissed him. "Always full of surprises, aren't you?"

"Told you I'm good for that, didn't I?" Bo threaded his fingers into her long, blonde hair, his thumbs at her temples. "I will never be done falling in love with you."

Tears swam in her eyes.

Bo dropped to his knee. "Will you marry me?"

"I love you." She nodded. "I will."

He slipped the emerald-cut diamond onto her finger. Then standing beneath an archway of flowers, Bo kissed his future wife. His lover. His partner. His friend. The person he'd chosen to share all of his life with. And she'd chosen him right back.

"You just made me the happiest man alive, Avie." Bo swooped her into his arms, carrying her over to the table.

"I think July *is* my favorite month after all."

"Oh, yeah?" He sat her on his lap. "Why is that?"

"Umm, let's see…Fourth of July, movies in the park, your birthday, tour buses, epic adventures…"

"Want another one?" Bo asked, brushing his lips over hers. "It took you way too long to change your address, and I don't want to wait for you to change your last name. Let's get married tomorrow."

"We can do that?"

"We can." Thanks to Linnea, he already had everything arranged. "Tomorrow, downtown at noon—you, me, and Emmy. Unless you want a big wedding."

He'd be good with that too, if Ava decided that's what she wanted.

"No, the three of us sounds perfect to me."

Bo kissed her. "God, I love you so…"

And he kissed her again. And again. And again. They made love on the rooftop, until the sun sank in the sky, and the moon rose to bathe them in its glow.

Bo was someone's everything.

He was Ava's.

And Ava, she was his.

# *Epilogue*

Bo stood at the window, peering through the glass at the most glorious September morning there ever was. Everything looked different. The sun, reflecting off the cityscape in its spectrum of colors, seemed brighter. The blue of the cloudless sky, more vivid. Life was just so fucking beautiful.

Sipping weak, lukewarm coffee from a Styrofoam cup, Bo wondered how he was so wide awake. He'd been up for what, forty-eight hours now? He glanced behind him at Ava, sweetly slumbering on the bed. God, he loved his wife. He didn't think he could love her any more than he already did, then she became the mother of his children—a whole new, incredible, wonderful feeling.

The distinct sound of heels clicking on tile could be heard coming down the hall, from the other side of the door. All of the nurses wore sneakers or funny-looking rubber shoes that sometimes squeaked, but otherwise were silent. It had to be them. Their hushed giggles approaching the doorway confirmed it.

Katie poked her head in first, her smile as wide as her face. She glanced down at Emery, who excitedly clutched her hand, and holding her index finger to her lips, signaled her to be quiet.

As they tiptoed into the room, Bo gently nudged his wife awake. Rubbing her shoulder, he leaned over the bed and kissed her forehead. "Emmy's here, baby."

Her Bambi eyes fluttered open, and she sat up in the bed, extending her arms out to their daughter. "It's okay, cutie-pie." She tapped the space beside her. "Come here."

"I missed you, Mommy." With a book in her hand, Emery climbed onto the bed, and snuggled up with Ava.

"I've missed you too." Hugging the six-year-old, she kissed the top of her head. "Sooo much. Have you been having fun with Auntie Katie and Uncle B?"

"Oh, yes." She exuberantly nodded. "We went to the zoo yesterday and saw the lions. I can throw a French fry and catch it in my teeth too. Uncle B showed me how. Wanna see?"

Giggling, Katie, Chloe, and Linnea exchanged glances. Turning to him, Linnea held up her hands with a shrug. "It wasn't mashed potatoes, right?"

"Next time we have French fries, I absolutely do." Bo combed his fingers through Emery's long blonde locks. Like his and Ava's, it reached her waist now. Their family trademark. The Byrnes had their baby-blue eyes, and they had their hair. "I love you, sunshine."

"I love you, Daddy." She smiled up at him. "Can I see baby brother now?"

He bent over and kissed her. "Yes, you can."

Bo turned around and reached inside the bassinet. He lifted the tiny, blue-wrapped bundle, gazing into the face of the beautiful boy Ava never thought she'd be able to have. Absolutes are rare. They'd found their chance.

Hair so pale it was almost translucent covered his little head. A cute button nose. Cupid's bow lips. Bo kissed his son and carefully laid him in his sister's waiting arms.

"Hello, baby." Emery tentatively touched his tiny fist. The baby opened his hand, reflexively grasping her finger. She squealed.

"He's so sweet," Chloe gushed, patting her very round, pregnant belly. "Have you picked out a name for Ashton's future partner in crime yet?"

Shaking her head, Linnea laughed.

"What? They're only going to be a few months apart, you know…"

Chloe was right. They were creating the next generation here. Their legacy to the world. And growing up together as they were, like their parents, the kids were all super close. There were ten houses on Park Place, but one big, crazy, happy family.

"…and, God help us, these two are the babies of the bunch."

"What's his name?" Katie asked.

"Well, we were going to name him Forrest," Ava began to explain.

Bo fondly remembered that night in the park. The smell of crying grass, his best girls by his side, and his favorite movie on the screen.

He glanced to Linnea. His beautiful seraph and kindred spirit. She was his person too, not in the same way as Ava, but his life would always be entwined with hers and her brother's. Not only was his son born on this spectacular day in September. It was four years ago, on this very day, that Kyan left them.

*"You got this…Love you."*

*Love you too, brother. I fucking miss you.*

Seemed only fitting.

"If it's okay with you, we'd like to name him Kai." Bo grabbed Linnea's hand and squeezed it. "Kai Forrest Robertson."

"He would've loved that." Nodding, she swiped at her eye and hugged him. "And I love you."

"Mommy, Cici told me I have to read to my brother every day." Ava lifted Kai from Emery's arms. "So, I brought the book you always read to me."

"*Frankenstein?*" Bo chortled.

"No, Daddy. That's the book *you* read to me." She rolled her eyes with a giggle. "This one."

*Mama, Do You Love Me?*

Ava glanced over at him and winked. She smiled at Emery. "Shall we read it to him now?"

Bo gazed at his family, sitting together on the bed. He wasn't the same man he'd been four years ago. Because of them, he was a better one. Not only did he find his someone, when he found Ava, he found his dimension. True happiness. A life worth living.

Holding their son, as Emery read Kai his first story, Ava looked up at him standing beside the bed. She stretched her arm over their daughter's head, and stuck out her pinky.

He hooked his with hers. "I love you, angel."

"And I love you, drummer boy."

Life was good.

Life was beautiful.

And now his life was full.

# *Epilogue*

*Christopher "Kit" King*

K it sat on a stool in the corner of the studio, plucking at the strings of his bass. He pretended to tune it, while one by one, the boys packed it up and went home.

As usual, Taylor left first. But then he had Chloe, Jesse, and two kids waiting for him, so he couldn't say he blamed him.

Sloan went next. And he didn't have shit waiting on him. Just a big-ass house across the street.

Kit sniggered to himself. Like he had it any different? His life was just as pathetic. Sad part was, the fact that he remained alone was of his own choosing. He had plenty of women, fucked them all the time, and usually two or three at once. He preferred it that way. One on one was too personal.

Bo got up from his kit, wiping sweat from his chest with a T-shirt. Dude rarely wore the damn thing, only using it as a towel. He glanced over at him and Matt, who was hanging up his guitar. "You guys doing anything? Want to come over? Ava has to stay at school—parent-teacher conferences. We can order pizza. Drink some beers."

"Thanks, man." Matt grinned. "I've got plans. I'll take a raincheck, though."

He always had plans now. With *her*.

Raising his brow, Bo looked at him.

"Another time, maybe. I've got plans too."

He didn't. Unless another night by himself at the club counted.

After Bo left, Matt turned to him. "You're not doing shit."

"So?"

"What the fuck is wrong with you lately?"

Ignoring his question, Kit set his bass in its stand.

When he straightened, Matt was standing in front of him.

Kit shrugged. "I'm just…it feels like I don't have my brother anymore."

"You're wrong." Matt grabbed him by the arms, fingers pressing into his biceps. "I love you, man."

"Yeah? Well, it doesn't feel like it." Cocking his head, Kit snickered. "You even fucked Bo, but never me."

*Shit. Why'd I say that?*

"Do you want me to?"

*I think I do.*

"Maybe."

*I'm not gay. I just love you.*

The End

…until *Son of a Preacher Man*

# Acknowledgments

I love Bo Robertson.

If you follow me on social media, you've seen me say that a lot, because I do. I've had a soft spot for him since his character first appeared in *Serenity*. Like Jesse, his heart is pure gold and he's good down to his soul. I only hope I was able to do him justice. *The Other Brother* was such a tough act to follow.

Taylor Hawkins, legendary drummer of the Foo Fighters, and to whom I dedicated this book, sadly passed away while I was writing it. In many ways, he was an inspiration for Bo. He had an infectious personality, a contagious smile, and a brilliant gift he shared with the world. His loss is tremendous, and he will be greatly missed. We were lucky to have him for the time that we did.

The Pinterest board and the playlist for *Drummer Boy* on Spotify and YouTube are open. Kodiak's story, *Son of a Preacher Man*, is next in the *Red Door Series*. Another twisty standalone, *The Third Son*, is also in the works for 2023. Like always, I've included sneak peeks following these acknowledgments.

Just as I predicted I would, I'm going to say it again—this is so surreal. Book 5. We're a little more than halfway through the series now. And even though I planned it this way from the beginning, it was just a dream when I was writing the first book in the series (and my first book ever) three years ago. I've learned a lot along the way. You make some friends, you lose some, and other people? They become your family. Your tribe. Your heart.

I say this every time too—I'll try not to be so wordy. I will more than likely fail.

Thank you to my babies. **Michael** & **Raj, Charlie, Christian, Josie Lynn** & **Josh, Zach** & **Sam, Jaide, Julian, Olivia,** and baby **Jocelyn.** Even if you weren't already mine, I'd still choose you—I love you!!!

My editor extraordinaire, **Michelle Morgan.** What can I say that I haven't already said? I love you, beautiful, and I'm always going to need you!!! xoxo

**Linda Russell** and the fabulous team at **Foreword PR.** I would not be here without my Linda, and I couldn't do this without her. I've been sitting here, trying to find a word that describes all that she is and does. There isn't one, except everything, and I love her lots!!! Forever a Foreword girl!!! xoxo

**Michelle Lancaster,** my gorgeous, talented friend, my Cover Queen of Hearts—could that cover image be any more perfect? She nails it every damn time!!! I've been sitting on this image for a couple years now, and keeping it to myself has been killing me. I couldn't wait for you to see our beautiful Bo, and **Dylan Hocking** *is* beautiful—inside and out. My thanks to you both—I love you to infinity!!! xoxo

**Lori Jackson** created some cover magic again, but then she always does. I love how her designs showcase Michelle's art. I love how easily we work together. I just love *her*. And there's more magic coming!!! xoxo

**Ashlee O'Brien,** my girly, my alpha reader, book daughter, and the design goddess that is *Ashes & Vellichor*. She makes *all* the pretties—graphics, sheet music, and those phenomenal book trailers!!! We have some insane conversations, as you can probably imagine. During one of them, we were talking about our favorite smells. She's the one who informed me, the lovely smell of fresh-cut grass is actually the grass dying. Told her I was going to use that in a book. I did. Inspo is everywhere. And…I finally did it, didn't I, Ashlee? Not saying what, but she knows. I love you!!! xoxo

**Stacey Blake**, of *Champagne Book Design*, for making the pages so pretty each and every time. Love you bunches!!! xoxo

**Hilary Robinson**, my proofreader, and more so, my friend. She even got herself a Red Door tattoo, y'all!!! I love you, beautiful!!! xoxo

My beta team—**Charbee Balderson, Jennifer Bishop, Kim DiPeiro, Heather Hahn, Marjorie Lord, Anastasia Meimeteas, Melinda Parker, Hilary Robinson, Sabrena Simpson, Rebecca Vazquez**, and **Staci Way**, together with my **ARC team**—I hope you didn't go through an entire box of tissues this time. Thank you for taking the time out of your busy lives to read Bo's story, but most of all for being my ride or dies. I love this crew—who has more fun than we do, girls? xoxo

**Bloggers, Bookstagrammers**, and **Booktokkers**. I can never say it enough—thank you, thank you, thank you!!! For supporting me and the books I write. Sharing posts. Creating so many wonderful edits, reels, and TikToks. Selflessly giving your time and talent to the book community. You make it a better place. I appreciate everything you do so much. xoxo

My beautiful **Redlings**—these humans are some of the most incredible beings on the planet!!! Love you the mostest!!! They, and I, would love to welcome you *Behind the Red Door* on Facebook. xoxo

And as always, my lovely **readers**. Thank you for sticking around and loving the *Red Door* world. Your messages and emails make my day—I appreciate each and every one of them. Thank you for wanting more Kyan, Dillon and Linnea, Chloe, Jesse, and Taylor,

Brendan and Katie, Bo and Ava, Kodiak, Matt, Kit, and Sloan. We're not done yet.

Until *Son of a Preacher Man...*

Much love,
Dyan xoxo

*Seth, ten years old.*

He sat buckled in the passenger seat of his father's old Chevy. Spice Girls playing on the radio. It reeked of cigarette smoke, whiskey, and cheap aftershave. Jarrid Black never smoked in the house. His congregation was blind to his fondness for the demon drink. Seth was more than well-acquainted with it, though.

They were on the way to Miss Catherine's. He hated going there and he didn't like her very much. She was surly to everyone, with the exception of his father. That didn't surprise him at all. Folks from church worshipped the preacher as if he were God himself. Sometimes Seth thought he actually believed he was.

His father lit up a Marlboro. Choking, Seth cracked the window open, letting the cold, damp March air rush in, and turned his face toward the glass.

"Seth." Jarrid glared sideways, taking a drag off his cancer stick. "Close it."

"But I can't breathe and it stinks."

Turning his head toward him, he exhaled. "Must I tell you again?"

"No, sir." He cranked the window back up.

Seth knew better than to disobey him. He was in a halfway decent mood this morning, and if he wanted permission to ride his bike with Jonathan to the arcade this afternoon, it had to stay that way. He'd deal with the stench.

The Dairy Queen rolled by. Closed for the winter, it wouldn't open again until the end of April. *Dumb.* Did they really think no one wanted ice cream when it snowed?

Then the car took an all-too-familiar turn at the next corner. Lowering the window all the way down, his father flicked the cigarette out onto the street. It bounced a couple times, the embers creating a cascade of sparks before rolling into a puddle at the curb.

He left it down, in spite of the cold, waving his hand in the air around him. Then he spritzed on more of that nasty cologne. As if that smelled any better than his disgusting smoke.

It didn't.

At least with the window open, Seth could breathe.

They parked at the curb in front of the small two-story clapboard house. Catherine must have been waiting for them at the door. She opened it the moment they arrived.

Seth was sent to sit in the parlor, with the promise of a Coca-Cola that he knew would never come. Same as always. Glancing around the room he'd sat in a million times before, he twiddled his thumbs. A photo of Grace, when she was around his age, stood in a frame on the mantel. He liked her. She was nice. His father said she was his angel. When he was younger, she'd come to his house and stay with him while the preacher took care of church business. But he was too old for a babysitter now.

After what felt like an eternity, Jarrid and Catherine returned to the parlor. She carried a bundle wrapped in a fluffy white blanket. Grace stood by herself behind them. Hands balled into fists at her sides. Head hanging low, her pale-blonde hair covered her face.

"Son." His father stepped forward. "God has fulfilled his promise."

Miss Catherine put the baby in his arms. "She's for you, Seth Thomas."

He gazed in awe at her beautiful, precious face.

"Now, you must keep your promise to God, and everyone here, that you will love, cherish, and protect the gift that has been bestowed upon you..." Jarrid bent over and kissed the baby's head. "...every day of your life."

"I will. I promise."

She was given to him the day she was born.

*God's promised gift.*

He fell in love with her the moment she was placed in his arms.

And he'd loved her ever since.

Linnea. Was. His.

Coming out of the bathroom, Arien stubbed her toe, close to taking a tumble over a stack of forgotten boxes in the hallway. "Ouch. Motherfu…"

She held onto her foot, hopping the rest of the way to her bedroom in the small townhouse apartment she shared with her mom. It was all packed up, cartons neatly labeled, identifying the contents inside. Bed stripped. Closet and drawers emptied.

It wasn't like she had a choice.

A moving van was parked outside.

Holding her towel closed, her back against the wall, Arien sat cross-legged on the bare mattress. She had exactly thirty minutes to put on some makeup and get dressed. It would only take her ten.

*This is so not fucking fair.*

She blew out a breath. A week ago, her room was pretty and her life wasn't packed away in cardboard boxes. That all changed when her mother and her boyfriend—if that's what you call a man in his forties—took her out with them to dinner.

And that alone should have told her something was up.

Jennifer Brogan had been dating Matthew Brooks for about six months now, but Arien didn't know him all that well. A real cowboy, her mother said. He had two sons and lived on some ranch up in Wyoming, an eight-hour drive from Denver. He'd come into town for business, and to see her mom, a few times a month.

He was the one to break the news to her. "Arien," he said with a smile, taking her mother's hand in his. "First off, I need you to know I love your mama very much. So much, I've asked her to marry me."

She about choked on her green-chili cheeseburger.

Her mom held up her left hand, waving the huge diamond glittering on her finger. "I said yes."

*Okay.*

Arien was seventeen, soon-to-be eighteen. She'd be going away to college at the end of summer anyway. Her mom deserved some happiness, right?

Swallowing down the cheeseburger, she put on a smile. "At least you won't have to change your monogram. When's the wedding?"

"Next week," her mother announced, biting her lip. "I'm pregnant."

"Three months already," Matthew said proudly, patting his new fiancée on the shoulder. "I'm coming back with the boys. We'll get married and have you all moved in before Thanksgiving."

*What? To Wyoming? Nope. Not happening.*

"Wait. You want me to move, to change schools during my senior year?"

"I'm sorry, sweetie."

"You're going to love Brookside." Her soon-to-be stepfather patted her on the hand. "We have a superior private school there. The ranch. The mountains. You can take lots of pictures."

"There's mountains right here."

Isn't thirty-six too old to have a baby anyway? Apparently not. And what happened to all those lectures her mother gave her about having sex, taking precautions, and all that stuff? She should've listened to her own advice. If she had, Arien wouldn't be going to a courthouse wedding to leave Denver, and the only life she'd ever known, behind.

*Only for a little while.*

True. She had her acceptance letter to UC. She'd be back.

"Sweetie, are you ready yet?" her mother asked from downstairs. "Matt and the boys are here."

*Dammit.*

"Almost," she answered, plucking through her makeup bag.

Clearly a lie. She hadn't even begun.

Holding a compact mirror in one hand, Arien applied mascara with the other, the towel slipping away from her.

She couldn't say for sure what made her look up. A feeling she was being watched, maybe.

Two boys—no, these weren't boys, they were hot-as-fuck men—stood smirking in her doorway.

"Who the hell are you?"

"I'm Tanner." The man smiled, and taking a step inside her room, he hitched a thumb behind him. "That's Kellan."

"And I'm naked." She snatched up the towel, covering herself.

Kellan snickered.

Tanner came closer. "Well now, that's a mighty fine hello, little sister."

# Books by

# DYAN LAYNE

**Red Door Series**

*Serenity*

*Affinity*

*Maelstrom*

*The Other Brother*

*Drummer Boy*

*Son of a Preacher Man (coming soon)*

**Standalones**

*Don't Speak*

*The Third Son (coming soon)*

# About the Author

Dyan Layne is a nurse boss by day and the writer of edgy sensual tales by night—and on weekends. She's never without her Kindle, and can usually be found tapping away at her keyboard with a hot latte *and* a cold Dasani Lime—and sometimes champagne. She can't sing a note, but often answers in song because isn't there a song for just about everything? Born and raised a Chicago girl, she currently lives in Tampa, Florida, and is the mother of four handsome sons and a beautiful daughter, who are all grown up now, but can still make her crazy—and she loves it that way! Because normal is just so boring.

# One

*'m going to fuck you. You may not know it yet, but I do. It's only a matter of time. I've been watching you. I swear that you've been watching me too, but maybe it's all in my head. No matter. Because I've seen you, I've talked to you and I've come to a conclusion: You are fucking beautiful. And I will make you lust me.*

The words danced on crisp white paper. Her fingers trembled and her feet became unsteady, so she leaned against the wall of exposed brick to right herself, clutching the typewritten note in her hand. She read it again. A powerful longing surged through her body and her thighs clenched.

Who could have written it? She couldn't fathom a single soul who might be inspired to write such things to her. Maybe those words weren't meant for her? Maybe whoever had written the note slid it beneath the wrong doormat in his haste to deliver it undetected?

Linnea Martin, beautiful? Someone had to be pulling a prank. *Yeah. That's more likely.*

She sighed as she turned and closed the solid wood front door. She glanced up at the mirror that hung in the entry hall and eyes the color of moss blinked back at her. Long straight hair, the color of which she had never been able to put into a category—a dirty-blonde maybe—hung past her shoulders, resting close to where her nipples protruded against the fitted cotton shirt she wore. Her skin was fair, but not overly pale. She supposed some people might describe her as pretty, in an average sort of way, but not beautiful.

Not anything but ordinary.

Linnea slowly crumpled up the note in her hand. She clenched it tight and held it to her breast before tossing it into the wastebasket.

Deflated, she threw her tote bag on the coffee table and plopped down on the pale-turquoise-colored sofa that she'd purchased at that quaint secondhand store on First Avenue. She often stopped in there on her way home from the restaurant, carefully eyeing the eclectic array of items artfully displayed throughout the shop. Sometimes, on a good day when tips had been plentiful, she bought herself something nice. Something pretty. Like the pale-turquoise sofa.

Linnea grabbed the current novel she was engrossed in from the coffee table and adjusted herself into a comfortable position, attempting to read. But after she read the same page three times she knew she couldn't concentrate, one sentence blurred into the next, so she set it back down. She clicked on the television and scrolled through the channels, but there was nothing on that could hold her interest. The words replayed in her head.

*I'm going to fuck you.*

Damn him! Damn that fucker to hell for being so cruel to leave that note at her door, for making her feel…things. The words had thrilled her for a fleeting moment, but then the excitement quickly faded, replaced by a loneliness deep in her chest. Love may never be in the cards for her, or lust for that matter, as much as she might want it to be.

Once upon a time she had believed in fairy tales and dreamt of knights on white stallions and handsome princes, of castle turrets shrouded in mist, of strong yet gentle hands weaving wildflowers in her long honeyed locks—just like the alpha heroes in the tattered paperbacks she had kept hidden under her bed as a teenager. She thought if she was patient long enough, her happily-ever-after would come. She thought that one day, when she was all grown up, that a brave knight, a handsome prince, would rescue her from her grandmother's prison and make all her dreams come true.

*Stupid girl.*

Her dreams turned into nightmares, and 'one day' never came. She doubted it ever would now. It was her own fault anyway. She closed her eyelids tight, trying to stop the tears that threatened to escape, to keep the memories from flooding back. Linnea had spent years pushing them into an unused corner, a vacant place where they could be hidden away and never be thought of again.

It was dark. She must have been sitting there for quite a while, transfixed in her thoughts. The small living room was void of illumination, except for the blue luminescence that radiated from the unwatched television. Linnea dragged herself over to it and clicked it off. She stood there for a moment waiting for her eyes to adjust to the absence of light and went upstairs.

Steaming water flowed in a torrent from the brushed-nickel faucet, filling the old clawfoot tub. She poured a splash of almond oil into the swirling liquid. As the fragrance released, she bent over the tub to breathe in the sweet vapor that rose from the water and wafted through the room. Slipping the sleeves from her shoulders, the silky robe gave way and fell to a puddle on the floor.

Timorously, she tested the water with her toes, and finding it comfortably hot, she eased her body all the way in. For a time serenity could be found in the soothing water that enveloped her.

*You may not know it yet, but I do. It's only a matter of time.*

At once her pulse quickened, and without conscious thought her slick fingertips skimmed across her rosy nipples. They hardened at her touch. And a yearning flourished between the folds of flesh down below. Linnea clenched her thighs together, trying to make it go away, but with her attempt to squelch the pulsing there, she only exacerbated her budding desire. And she ached.

Ever so slowly, her hands eased across her flat belly to rest at the junction between her quivering thighs. She wanted so badly to touch herself there and alleviate the agony she found herself in. But as badly as she wanted to, needed to, Linnea would not allow herself the pleasure of her own touch. She sat up instead, the now-tepid water sloshing forward with the sudden movement, and reaching out in front of her she turned the water back on.

She knew it was wicked. Lying there with her legs spread wide and her feet propped on the edge of the tub, she allowed the violent stream of water to pound upon her swollen bud. It throbbed under the assault and her muscles quaked. She'd be tempted to pull on her nipples if she wasn't forced to brace her hands against the porcelain walls of the clawfoot tub for leverage.

Any second now. She was so close.

*I'm going to fuck you.*

And he did. With just his words, he did.

Her head tipped back as the sensations jolted through her body. The sounds of her own keening cries were muffled by the downpour from the faucet. Spent, she let the water drain from the tub and rested her cheek upon the cold porcelain.

# Prologue

"**A**idan, baby."

His mother took him by the hand and pulled him along behind her as she hurried out of the kitchen. He'd only eaten half of his grilled cheese sandwich and some grapes when the banging started. It startled him and he knocked over his juice. By the time she went to the front door to see who it was, the banging noise was coming from the other side of the house.

"You can't keep me out, bitch."

It was a man. He was yelling. He sounded angry. Aidan didn't recognize his voice.

His mother seemed to, though. Her eyes got real big and she covered her mouth with her hand. It was shaking.

There was a hutch in the living room that the television sat on. It had doors on the bottom. He hid in there sometimes. His mother opened one of the doors, and tossing the toys that were inside it to the floor, she kissed him on his head and urged him to crawl inside.

"We're going to play a game of hide and seek from the loud man outside, okay, baby?" his mother whispered.

Aidan nodded.

The banging got louder.

"You have to be very, very quiet so he doesn't know you're here."

It sounded like she was choking and tears leaked out of her eyes, but she smiled at him.

"Like at story time?"

Aidan's mother took him to story time at the library every Saturday, and afterwards if he'd been a good boy, she would let him get an ice cream.

"Yes, baby. Just like that." She nodded with tears running down her face. "Now stay very still and don't speak a word until I tell you to—no matter what, okay?"

He nodded again. "Okay, Mommy."

"I love you, Aidan."

"I love you, Mommy."

Everyone said the place was haunted. The kids at school. The people in town. It didn't look scary, but nobody ever went anywhere near the two-story white clapboard house that was set off by itself on the cove.

It was to be her home now.

Molly stood at the wrought-iron gate with her mother, holding onto her hand. She clutched her *Bear in the Big Blue House* backpack, that she'd had since she was four, with the other. A boy with sandy-blond hair sat on the porch steps. Aidan Fischer. He didn't pay them, or his father unloading their belongings from the U-Haul, any mind. He had a notebook in his lap and a pencil between his fingers. It looked like he was drawing.

The boy chewed on his lip as he moved the pencil over the paper. Even though he was in the fifth grade, and three years older than her, Molly knew who he was. Everybody did. He was the boy who didn't talk. And six days from today, when her mother married his father, that boy was going to be her brother.

# Cast of Characters

*In alphabetical order by first name*

Aggie—owner of gift shop on Maple Street

Alicia "Allie" Robertson—older sister to Bo

Angelica—vamp (blood fetish) girl at masquerade ball (also referenced in *Don't Speak*)

Ashton Michael Thomas Kerrigan Nolan—youngest child and son of Chloe, Jesse, and Taylor

Ava Liane Harris—Katie's college classmate and friend, babysitter

Axel—head of security for the Red Door

Bea—hospice social worker

Becky Brinderman—Taylor's date to senior prom

Bethany—former high school sweetheart to Jesse

Elizabeth "Betsy" Bennett—mother to Michael, grandmother to Chloe

Billings—Kyan's friend from high school, now with the state attorney's office

Robert "Bo" Robertson Jr.—drummer of Venery, father to Emery (also appears in *Don't Speak*)

Brendan James Murray—eldest of the Byrne cousins, runs the Red Door/CPA, husband to Katie

Brigitta Thurner—wife/submissive to Hans, hostess at the Red Door

Brittany McCall—high school classmate of Chloe, former fiancée to Danny

Cameron Mayhew—Katie's college classmate/former boyfriend

Catherine Lucille Martin (*deceased*)—grandmother to Linnea

Chandan William Arthur Kerrigan Nolan—eldest child and son of Chloe, Jesse, and Taylor

Charles Alexander "Xander" Byrne—son of Dillon and Linnea, twin to Madison, brother to Charlotte

Charles Dillon Byrne—brother to Kyan, cousin to Brendan and Jesse, second husband to Linnea

Charles Patrick Byrne (*deceased*)—father to Dillon and Kyan, uncle to Brendan and Jesse

Charlotte Kyann Byrne—daughter of Kyan (*deceased*) and Linnea

Chester—Bo's Australian Shepherd

Chloe Elizabeth Bennett Kerrigan Nolan—wife to Jesse and Taylor

Colleen Byrne Nolan O'Malley—mother to Jesse, sister to Charley and Mo, aunt to Brendan, Dillon, and Kyan, second wife to Tadhg

Connie "Cici"—Shelley's next-door neighbor

Courtney—Kit's ex-wife

Curtis "CJ" James—Venery's manager

Cynthia Robertson—mother to Bo

Danielle Peters—photographer, wife to Monica

Danny Damiani—Chloe's high school classmate and former boyfriend

Declan Byrne (*deceased*)—father to Charley, Mo, and Colleen, grandfather to Brendan, Dillon, Jesse, and Kyan

Declan James Murray—son of Brendan and Katie

Andrew "Drew" Copeland—Katie's dad

Ed—Bo's driver on tour

Elliott Peters—son of Danielle and Monica

Emery Sage Robertson—daughter of Shelley Tompkins (*deceased*) and Bo

Eric Brantley (*deceased*)—son to Hugh Brantley

Gillian—bartender at the Red Door (resigned)

Gina Rossi—labor and delivery nurse, family owns Rossi's Pizza and Italian Bakery

Grace Martin (*deceased*)—mother to Linnea

Hailey—girl at warehouse accident

Hans Thurner—husband/Dominant to Brigitta, host/manager at the Red Door

Hazel—Tommy's mother, waitress at diner in Crossfield

Hugh Brantley—real estate investor

Ireland Aislinn Kerrigan Nolan—second-eldest child and daughter of Chloe, Jesse, and Taylor

James Murray (*deceased*)—father to Brendan, uncle to Dillon, Jesse, and Kyan

Pastor Jarrid Black (*deceased*)—father to Seth and Linnea

Jason—kitchen boy at Charley's

Jenkins—construction/warehouse project manager

Jesse Thomas Nolan—cousin to Brendan, Dillon, and Kyan, husband to Chloe and Taylor

Jimmy Tascadero—friend of Bo's at age 14

Jonathan Reynolds (*deceased*)—childhood best friend to Seth

Kai Forrest Robertson—son of Bo and Ava

Kara Matthews—aunt to Katie and Kevin

Katelyn "Katie" Copeland Murray—wife to Brendan, barista at Beanie's/college student

Kelly Matthews—aunt to Katie and Kevin, owner of Beanie's

Kelsey Miller—girlfriend (former) to Dillon

Kevin Copeland—younger brother to Katie

Kim Matthews—aunt to Katie and Kevin

Christopher "Kit" King—bassist of Venery

Seth "Kodiak" Black—half-brother to Linnea

Kristie Matthews Copeland—Katie's mother

Kyan Patrick Byrne (*deceased*)—brother to Dillon, first husband to Linnea, father to Charlotte, cousin to Brendan and Jesse

Leah Brianne Murray—daughter of Brendan and Katie

Leena Patel Kerrigan—mother to Taylor

Leonardo "Leo" Hill—baker/Kelly's assistant at Beanie's

Linnea Grace Martin Byrne—half-sister to Kodiak Black, widow to Kyan, wife to Dillon

Logan—nephew to Bo

Lon—Venery's driver on tour

London Elizabeth Kerrigan Nolan—third child and daughter of Chloe, Jesse, and Taylor

Lucifer—friend of Brendan's, devil-masked member at the Red Door

Madison Margaret Grace Byrne—daughter of Dillon and Linnea, twin to Xander, sister to Charlotte

Marcus—manager at Charley's

Matthew "Matt" McCready—rhythm guitarist of Venery

Michael Bennett—father to Chloe

Milo Veronin—Angelica's partner (also appears in *Don't Speak*)

Mitch Rollins—State Senator, member of the Red Door

Monica Peters—clinical psychologist, wife to Danielle

Margaret "Peggy" Byrne (*deceased*)—mother to Dillon and Kyan, aunt to Brendan and Jesse

Maureen "Mo" Byrne Murray (*deceased*)—mother to Brendan, sister to Charley and Colleen, aunt to Dillon, Jesse, and Kyan

Meaghan O'Malley (*deceased*)—first wife to Tadhg O'Malley

Murphy—Brendan's childhood friend, detective with the police department

Nick Rossi—second-eldest Rossi brother, same class as Jesse, family owns Rossi's Pizza and Italian Bakery

Paul—rigger on Venery's tour

Payton Brantley—son to Eric and grandson to Hugh Brantley

Perry Harris—older brother to Ava, Minor League baseball player

Phil Beecham—Brendan's attorney

Robert Robertson Sr.—father to Bo

Roberta Torres—obstetrician

Roman—Jesse's Bernese mountain dog

Rourke—alias of arrested priest and former Red Door member

Roy Francis Martin (*deceased*)—grandfather to Linnea

Ryan Sr.—husband to Allie, brother-in-law to Bo

Ryan Jr.—nephew to Bo

Salena Dara (*deceased*)—former hostess at the Red Door

Shelley Tompkins (*deceased*)—mother to Emery, groupie who instigated "baby-mama drama"

Siona Dawson (pronounced *Show-na*)—receptionist at O'Malley Ink Emporium, step-niece to Tadhg O'Malley

Sloan Michaels—lead vocalist/lyricist of Venery

Stacy—former girlfriend to Kelly Matthews

Tadhg O'Malley (pronounced *Tige*)—Colleen's second husband

Tammy—hospice nurse

Taylor Chandan Kerrigan—husband to Chloe and Jesse, lead guitarist of Venery

Thomas Nolan *(deceased)*—father to Jesse

Timo—Chloe's Bernese mountain dog (Roman's son)

Tommy—classmate of Linnea's, cook at diner in Crossfield

Anthony "Tony" Rossi—eldest Rossi Brother, same class as Brendan/Venery, family owns Rossi's Pizza and Italian Bakery

Vanessa Parisi—music journalist for *Revolver*